DARK DWELLER

By Gareth Worthington

Edited by Christopher Brooks

Interior design by Dorothy Dreyer

DROPSHIP PUBLISHING

Copyright © 2022 Gareth Worthington

Cover design by Gareth Worthington.
Interior design by Dorothy Dreyer

ISBN 978-1-954386-05-1

Published by Dropship Publishing
www.dropshippublishing.com
10 9 8 7 6 5 4 3 2 1

OTHER BOOKS BY GARETH WORTHINGTON

Children of the Fifth Sun (Vesuvian Books)

Children of the Fifth Sun: Echelon (Vesuvian Books)

Children of the Fifth Sun: Rubicon (Vesuvian Books)

It Takes Death to Reach a Star (Vesuvian Books)

In the Shadow of a Valiant Moon (Vesuvian Books)

Condition Black (Dropship Publishing)

A Time for Monsters (Vesuvian Books)

For Mrs. Gray.

A light that shone brighter than all the stars in the sky.

A drop of water, if it could write out its own history,
would explain the universe to us.

—*Lucy Larcom*

PROLOGUE

Dr. Sarah Dallas

"**A**re you the fucking pilot, Hair?" Boz screams at me, piggy eyes aflame in her round face.

I hate that moniker: Hair. Not important right now. The fact we're going to die is. "No, I'm not, but—"

"Then stay in your lane and shut your hole."

Breathe, Sarah. Don't punch her. You're the ship's counselor. Be professional. Do *not* punch her. The mantra rings over and over in my skull, but Boz tests every ounce of my training. There are four of us on this twelve-year round trip. Assaulting the pilot isn't the best idea.

I release a very measured breath and fix my attention on the largest planet in our solar system looming large in the viewfinder of our liner—the *Paralus*. Jupiter is enormous, its surface banded with reddish-brown and off-white clouds, rushing and crashing into one other. Its one angry red eye stares at us, at *me*.

My supposed intellect short-circuits as I try to quantify and categorize. In the face of something truly awe-inspiring my tiny human biological computer is unable, or refuses, to comprehend the sheer magnitude of this world. Yet my limbic system must have some ancient recollection of dealing with overwhelming reverence, forcing a rush of adrenaline through my bloodstream and into my trembling muscles.

Just *look* at it.

The *Paralus* shudders as we hurtle into the upper atmosphere. Jupiter has a will of its own, intent on sucking us into its gassy interior. Ironic, given we're here to grab its vapors. Helium-3 to be specific, to act as cryogenic coolant for our nuclear fusion reactors at home and space stations set out along the Interplanetary Transport Network. Jupiter has helium in spades, while Earth has precious little, and so now we risk our lives on ridiculously dangerous missions to mine the ether. In the age of interplanetary travel and colonization, profit trumps human life—as always.

Metal squeals and the hull creaks. The luminous tabs and keys beneath crystal glass control panels stutter and flicker. Even the slick white walls and soothing curves of the Bridge's interior can't muffle the complaints of the frail, human-made underpinnings.

A tear slips from the corner of my eye and my knuckles are white as I grip the armrests.

"Are you crying?" Boz yells, peeling her stare from the enormous viewfinder to gawk in disgust at me for daring to have any emotion other than anger.

"We're coming in too hot," I press, flitting a concerned frown from Boz to the planet and back again in hopes she takes the hint to watch where the hell she's going. "Can't the AI take over?"

"Which part of *shut up* isn't penetrating all that hair?" Boz clicks her tongue, then tweaks on the thruster yokes. Sweat beads on her forehead. "I got this, Dallas. Now back off."

I wriggle back in my seat and adjust the harness again. Everyone hates a backseat driver, but if she gets this wrong Jupiter will seize the *Paralus* and we'll never have enough thrust to escape. We'll either be torn to shreds or crushed like a tin can. Either one a shitty way to go.

Our freighter shakes like a rag doll in the mouth of a puppy, the nuts and bolts of this dilapidated piece of junk threatening to come loose. The *Paralus* is fragile as all hell and entirely breakable—the sort of construction a five-year-old makes out of drinking straws and modeling clay. A mile-long needle with a nuclear fusion engine at the aft end, a Scoop and transport shuttle docking bay, the AI mainframe in the center, and two spinning rings: one for cargo, and one for medbay, exercise room and living quarters. Ops, also called the Bridge, sits right in the nose.

Perfect for a front-row seat to our doom.

"Still too much speed," Boz says. "Increasing retro-thruster burn."

Will that do anything? The main retro-thrusters have been firing while we're asleep for months now, slowing us to enter orbit correctly, which sounds great on paper but—given the heap of shit we're in—means diddly squat.

"Boz, keep her steady," Commander Chau calls from his chair.

"I'm trying, sir," she yells back.

"Tris?" Chau says loud enough to be heard over the din of warping metal punctuated at regular intervals by the warning alarm.

"The trajectory is off, something' changed," Tris Beckert, our co-pilot and chief engineer, replies in his Texan drawl. "Jupiter's not where we predicted. It's not a big ol' shift, but enough."

I swear my ass just clenched hard enough to make a button on the seat. A ton of unmanned craft have slammed into their destination planet or just whizzed on by into space forever. I'm no astrophysicist, but was once told reaching a target in space like standing on Everest and firing a bullet at a pea-sized target on the other side of the Earth.

"We're comin' in a little steep," Tris says, tapping away at his readout. "AI is helpin' Boz compensate—"

The alarm blares again.

3

"Warning, orbital entry path suboptimal," says a synthetic, sonorous voice from overhead.

Only an AI could so calmly announce our deaths.

"Yes, I fucking know, Dona," Boz spits back. "Reverse thrusters won't do it. Gotta skip over the atmosphere. Just need to burn more delta-v."

The *Paralus* lurches under a burst from the engines. The horizon of Jupiter fills the viewfinder, its swirling fumes mixing like milk and coffee in a fresh latte. A fresh latte? Shut up, Sarah.

On the horizon, flashes of white light, tinged with green edges, emanate from just below Jupiter's cloud line.

Tris shoots a worried look at Boz.

"Asteroids exploding on impact?" she yells without breaking her concentration.

"I don't think so," Tris shouts back.

"You better fucking hope not or we're about to get cratered," Boz says.

Cratered. Great. Pebble-dashed with chunks of space rock. The spindly nature of the *Paralus* helps it to not be a gigantic target, but it only takes one puncture and we're all screwed.

Why am I here, again?

"Hold on to your pantyhose," Boz says, perspiration running down her temples.

The *Paralus* is battered, a pathetic kite in impossibly strong winds, as we plunge farther into the outer atmosphere of Jupiter. The viewfinder is near black—sunlight can no longer penetrate the violent vapors assaulting us. Multiple feeds from external cameras cycle on and off, but offer no help.

Boz roars long and loud, heaving on the yokes while Tris taps away at his console, calculating and recalculating—pinging his very human assumptions off the computations of the AI. Chau sits, smooth jaw set and stoic, his narrowed sights fixed on some imaginary endpoint to this nightmare of an orbital entry. He looks

4

oddly calm.

I squeeze my eyes shut and mumble a prayer, though to whom I don't know. God, Yahweh, Allah. Anyone who'll listen. In moments of extreme stress, time seems to slow, the human mind suddenly able to function on some higher level, absorbing all the information it can in hopes of averting disaster. Behind my eyelids, in a weird half-dream, half-out-of-body experience, I see myself clinging to the harness. Observing the cowardly pose fills my astral-projected self with shame, which only grows with the knowledge I'm not praying for loved ones at home who might miss me when I'm gone, but to make it out alive so I can go on ignoring them for a little longer.

Except for Dad, always have time for Dad.

The shuddering stops.

I open my eyes. The last wisps of Jupiter's atmosphere slip past revealing vast, open space. Here, unadulterated with the light of human cities, the universe is alive. The light from the smallest of stars reaches out to me from across the expanse. The feeling of relief at still being alive is replaced with nausea. The same feeling one gets when peering into a pitch-black well, wondering how far down it goes. We came so close to death, but what difference would it make? The universe doesn't care. Look at how *big* it is.

"Jesus fucking Christ," Boz says, slumping back in her chair.

"Hey now," Tris pipes up.

"Sorry, Tris."

She's not sorry. Tris doesn't like too much swearing, but Boz does it anyway. Several times a day. So do I, just in my head. Isn't that what we all do? Hide a little piece of who we are to placate others. To survive society. But again, it's hard to care when you're out here knowing the cosmos really doesn't give a rat's ass what we do. The desire to let loose a string of expletives nearly overwhelms me. Nearly.

"I want to know what happened," Chau says, his expression

cold like granite. "How could our trajectory be that off?"

"It wasn't," Tris replies, shaking his head. "I told you, Jupiter moved."

Chau narrows his eyes. "Not possible."

"Engineer Tris is correct," the AI says, its tone unchanging. "Jupiter's orbital path appears to have altered."

"How the hell is that possible?" Boz asks.

"Ya'll got me," Tris replies, tapping at his screen. "Some kinda gravitational irregularity?"

"Affecting Jupiter?" Chau says, one eyebrow raised. "Jupiter moves celestial bodies, not the other way around."

Tris shrugs. "I'll look into it."

"Fine, but after the grab," Chau says.

"I need to get us back into a proper orbit," Boz says, already tapping away at her console. "That's gonna take a while. We had to burn long and hard to skip over the atmosphere. It's gonna be like turning a galactic Buick."

"Do it," Chau says.

"Um." As the word leaves my lips I wish it hadn't.

All eyes fix on me.

Shit. Well done, Sarah. Best follow through now. "Is that an aerostat in our flight path?"

"What are you talking about, *Doctor*," Boz says.

I point out of the main window.

The crew follows the imaginary path from my fingertip out into space and to the spheroid metallic object. "If that's an aerostat, it'll do a lot of damage if we hit it." Though they're flexible, colliding with one of these weather stations dropped into the atmosphere to monitor the constant violent storms would fuck us up.

"That ain't an aerostat, that's a ship," Tris says, squinting. "Too far out of the atmosphere. Wrong shape."

"Are we going to hit ... whatever that *is*?" Chau asks.

Boz shakes her head. "We're headed out. Seems it's geo-synched, in orbit."

"You're eyeballing it?" I ask.

Boz glares at me. "How about you let me do my job, Dallas?"

Chau holds up his hand. "Enough. What do we do about it?"

Tris clears his throat. "ITN protocol says we have to prioritize the grab, but ... this is a little unorthodox. There's no precedent for an alien ship." He shoots a nervous glance at Chau.

Chau sniffs hard. "There's no evidence to suggest it's an alien ship. How close will we come to it?"

Tris's fingers flit across his console at lightning speed. Then, with a dramatic swipe, he sends the flight path file from his panel to Boz who looks it over.

"Within a hundred feet," Boz says. "Just like I said."

Yes, Boz, I get it— you're a genius and I'm an idiot. Seriously, Sarah, hold it together. "Do we need to adjust?"

"If we try that, we'll push ourselves further out," Tris says, "and it'll take longer to re-enter synchronized orbit."

"At a hundred feet we can get a pretty good look at it, though, right?" I say.

Tris nods. "I'd get a window seat now, because we're about to zip by."

We, of course, aren't going to unbuckle and float over to the large window, so we all just fall into a confused silence and fix our attention to the small vessel that is fast approaching—or rather the one that we are fast approaching.

Could this really be alien? Are we the first humans to encounter other intelligent life? Finding microbes on Mars some fifty years ago was a little anticlimactic, especially at a time when humankind had finally started to pay consideration to our own dying world. Too little too late. But a spaceship? Maybe this crappy trip was worth it after all.

The alien vessel is now large enough in the viewfinder to study

GARETH WORTHINGTON

it a little better. Too damn close if you ask me, but hey, I'm just the shrink right?

Boz glances over her shoulder at Chau. The two of them don't cross words, but exchange an unspoken question.

They're right to be confused. What the hell *is* going on?

The ship, or pod, is roughly egg-shaped, and in the outer lights of the *Paralus* seems to be grey in color. No windows. Small rear thrusters. And an ITN insignia.

"Holy shit," Boz says. "It's an escape pod."

"Did the last liner report a pod ejection?" Chau asks.

"Not to my knowledge," Boz says. "Tris?"

The Texan shakes his head. "I got no record of that."

"Those markings, they're old," I pipe up. "See the logo? Saturn is included now, since the expansion. This is pre-rebrand, done more than twenty years ago. Actually, that looks even older. Museum old." That tidbit of information only serves to remind them who I am, how I'm here, and that they really don't like me or my family. Shit.

"Chief," Tris says. "We gotta see what's over there. I can take a Scoop."

Chau looks to Boz.

She just shrugs. "I have to swing her around Jupiter to get us into orbit. I can use the gravity to catapult us 'round and come up on the pod again. Give us time to gear up."

Chau tents his fingertips. "How will that affect the grab?"

"Well, it'll delay it," Tris says, rubbing at his square jaw. "But Jupiter isn't going anywhere."

"Didn't you just say it moved?" My lips try to hang on to the last word as if I can suck back the regrettably snarky remark.

Tris pinches his lips together and gives a subtle shake of his head.

You're right Tris; *shut up*, Sarah.

"Oh man, we best still be haulin' when we return," Boz says,

8

and shoots me a look as if this whole thing is somehow my fault. "Only get paid if we have a load."

Hauling back Helium is all anyone gives a shit about, because it means getting paid. Helium is this century's gold rush. This is hilarious, given I've listened to enough company speeches to know that helium is the second most abundant element in the universe. The problem is, while God was handing out the element, He—or She or It—seemed to skip Earth. Our planet's crust is probably not even in the parts per billion range. In the Earth's atmosphere, it's only 5.2 parts per million per volume. So, Jupiter is our reservoir, our lifeline. Still, the ITN has protocols for situations like this. The pod could pose a threat to continued mining. Though no idea what kind of threat, not my wheelhouse. "I think the ITN are gonna call this one," I add. "Something like this will trump a helium grab. The AI has probably locked all systems anyway. We won't get to do the job yet."

Boz tuts again.

"You are correct, Dr. Dallas," the AI says. "Current mission suspended until investigation completed."

Chau tents his fingertips. "The faster we clear that pod, the faster we get back on mission."

Everyone unbuckles and swims out of the only door in or out of the Bridge. Boz gives me a long, hard, disapproving stare, but Tris flashes a grin. Chau doesn't even bother to acknowledge me. For him, a shrink has two jobs on these freighters: make sure the crew don't lose their minds in deep space, and stay the hell out of the way.

So far, no-one's lost their marbles, yet.

CHAPTER ONE

Dr. Sarah Dallas

Tris Beckert stares at me with those twinkling, gem-like green eyes. A stocky man and clean shaven, his southern lilt brightens my day. I'm not sure why. That hospitable nature bred into him is just comforting. And even though I'm the ship's counselor, I need the reassurance today. Because I sign off on whether Tris is mission ready. Kilkenny, the ship's physician, and my bunkmate, of course, makes sure he's physically healthy; but really, if his mind isn't in the right place, going off ship is a death sentence.

"Don't worry, doc, it's all gonna be fine. I'll be back to tell ya all about it in tomorrow's session." Tris winks as he does a zero-gravity somersault in the airlock to the Scoop Hangar, and effortlessly slips into his flight suit.

He's such a good guy, and frankly makes the trip just a little easier. At least for the last few weeks while I've been awake. We spend most of the twelve-year round trip asleep in stasis units, letting the ship pilot us most of the way. It saves on oxygen, food, and water, since we're just rigged up to an IV and a catheter. As a kid, I'd heard stasis meant that time slowed, so I figured you didn't age. Unfortunately, that's not wholly accurate. Stasis merely slows down the biological clock. Humans gain a few days of extra life, maybe weeks, depending on the length of the trip, but that's it.

When I came out of stasis a few weeks ago, nauseated and atrophied, Tris's face was the first I saw. Every Thursday since then, we've completed our psych sessions, which tend to just be a genial chat. Not like with Boz, who once said the biggest challenge to her peace of mind out here was my incessant, Ivy League braying. Still, Tris takes no umbrage with my familial ties and talks to me like I'm a regular person. His psych profile suggests he's a little fresh with the ladies, with a penchant for the forbidden, but it doesn't make him a bad guy. If I swung that way, he'd have a chance. But penises too closely resemble the last chicken in the shop to whet my appetite.

Kilkenny tightens the nylon blood-pressure cuff around Tris's arm. A button on the rim makes the sphygmomanometer's red dial hop, as its tiny motor begins to whir.

"Hurry up, Kilkenny," Tris says with a toothy grin. "Time t' meet some aliens."

Boz makes a horrible glottal sound. "Sure, like they'd send your inbred ass to initiate first contact."

Tris just laughs off the dig.

"Blood pressure's bang on," Kilkenny says. Contrasting Tris's charming drawl, the ship's physician's Northern Irish accent is so heavy I can barely understand them. And don't get me started on their crazy turns of phrase. What the hell is an *eejit*?

"Aye, yer off to the races, boyo," Kilkenny says, patting our grab man's muscular shoulder.

"You know the drill, Tris," I say. "I need you to recite it."

Tris sighs then clears his throat. "I, Tris Beckert, of sound body and mind, understand that the mission I am about to undertake could end my life. I do not hold the ITN responsible in such an event."

We all wait a second for the response.

"Subject is cleared for duty," the AI says.

It's ridiculous that we must do this song and dance, but given the six years taken to get from Earth to here, the ITN acknowledged a person's state of mind may change over the course of the journey. Not to mention the life-changing experience of seeing Jupiter in all its scary glory. So between me and the AI monitoring behavior patterns—vocal frequency, body temp, pupil dilation—we can jointly say Tris hasn't lost his marbles. It sounds like it's for his benefit. It isn't. It's so our bosses don't get sued.

Boz locks the bowl-like helmet onto Tris's protective—and frankly horrifically orange—flight suit, then raps on the dome with her knuckles. "Locked and loaded."

Tris gives the thumbs up, then pulls on a wall handle to slip through the airlock door and into the Scoop. Boz climbs into the cramped space too, and helps him buckle in.

I've only ever seen a Scoop from the outside—a tiny fighter plane, with a bunt nose, wide wings, and short tail. Instead of engines under the wings, they have enormous cube-shaped canisters that literally scoop up the atmosphere, then grab the helium and discard everything else. From the inside, the vessel looks even smaller. Tris is squeezed into the high-backed seat, with a wall of instruments mere inches from his elbows. The only saving grace is the large crystal canopy, which will offer him a spectacular three-hundred-and-sixty-degree view of the universe.

Boz re-emerges, closes both the Scoop door and the airlock door with a satisfyingly deep *clunk* and *shunk* as metal slabs grind over one another. Another sequence of switches and buttons, activated in a specific order sets the pump on the other side of the door humming. Equalizing the pressure means the Scoop won't get blown off the side of the *Paralus*.

"Back to the Bridge," Boz says.

"Aye," Kilkenny replies.

Normally our grumpy physician doesn't set foot in ops. But as Tris prepares to couple with an escape pod that could be decades if not hundreds of years old, this is no ordinary Scoop mission. Kilkenny will need to be on hand so they can monitor any potential biohazard.

We swim along Mainstreet, the long corridor connecting everything on the *Paralus*, headed for ops where Chau already waits, his arms folded and as indifferent as ever. He nods as we enter, eyeing each of us as we pick a spot to watch the spectacle onscreen. Boz takes her place at the pilot's station, Kilkenny takes Tris's engineer station, and I sit in my usual observational seat off to the left of Chau.

Dad often jokes the bridges of these liners are like miniature immersion cineplexes, just a few high-back padded seats with built-in consoles, ideal for holding popcorn, all facing a huge screen that is, in fact, an enormous window to the outside, with the additional capability to function as a multi-split monitor. Once he'd even snuck me on a liner, the *Salaminia*, in for repairs at Mars-Delta orbiting station. He'd rigged the bridge so we could watch the latest movie from my favorite online creator, *StarFlux*. The AI had even played along and released dampeners to shake the ship along with any on-screen action.

Right here, right now, though, is no movie.

The first-person view from Tris's helmet fills the entire viewfinder, some twenty feet across. His head is on a swivel as he surveys the luminous readouts and runs through the launch protocol. He calls out the sequence and Boz confirms it, checking off each item. The whole procedure takes nearly twenty minutes. In space, you don't just jump into a vehicle and speed off into the unknown. Every eventuality needs to be accounted for, and every system and backup system approved for use. Before AI, system checks took hours, but now combining human and computer brainpower shortens the whole process.

"Cleared for launch," comes the AI's voice overhead. "Trajectory and flight path to unknown vessel complete. Launch in T-minus one minute."

"Will he attempt a grab at the same time?" I ask, turning to our commander.

"No," Chau says, his expression sour. "ITN has suspended the helium grab. The AI won't allow it. Besides, if there is something over there to bring back, the Scoop won't have the fuel to make the trip if it's loaded with helium."

To be fair, I didn't think of that. Dad gave me a crash course before I left. Said Scoops aren't big enough to have fusion reactors, they run on liquid hydrogen rockets for transversing large distances, and hydrazine thrusters for maneuvers. They must be refueled after every trip. Sending in a vessel laden with explosive material into violent storms is just plain crazy. We tried remote drones, even with AI pilots, but they never survived the squalls. There's just something about feeling the turbulence, a gut instinct that only a human can sense.

But of course, that also means putting people at risk.

On our ship, that'll be Boz and Tris. They'll take turns, as multiple trips are required to load up. Each Scoop can gather and filter around five hundred kilos of helium three per trip. Realistically, the *Paralus* can transport back two metric tons to Earth. So that's four trips from the ship to Jupiter and back. Four times Boz and Tris brave the wrath of the God of Sky and Thunder, according to the Romans. Looking at the gigantic planet now, you could be forgiven for thinking those ancient people somehow understood its raw power.

"Ten, nine, eight," the AI says.

My attention snaps back to the screen.

Tris gives a thumbs up in front of his headcam. "Just like ridin' a bronco," he says.

"Disconnecting," the AI says.

There's a shudder in Tris's camera as the Scoop disengages from our liner. His cam shows the bay doors open as his vessel maneuvers out under minimal thruster control.

As he clears the doors, the purple-black wash of space, speckled with uncountable stars, fills the crystal canopy of the Scoop. And even though I'm not actually there in the cockpit, the first-person view from Tris's headcam combined with the enormity of the ops screen makes my skin prickle.

Space is scary.

"Initiatin' first burn," Tris says. "Ten-second interval."

Tris is thrown back into the seat as the Scoop lurches forward. I grip the arm of my chair again as if flying along with him. Kinda wish Boz was piloting instead. I know that's unprofessional. True, but still unprofessional.

"Two, one," Tris says. "Firin' brakin' thrusters."

"This is shit," Boz says, then pulls up a second smaller window on the screen—an external camera on the Scoop.

The escape pod zips up all too quickly. The closer Tris comes, the better we can see the hull—which looks oddly pristine. Not a pockmark in sight. Could it have been out here that long and never been hit? Jupiter pulls in debris from thousands if not millions of miles away.

Boz mouths instructions, her microphone on mute, willing Tris to dock the Scoop onto the escape pod safely. Unlike me, she's sensible enough not to back-seat drive. She opens yet another on-screen window. This time, it's the docking lock camera, showing us how Tris is manually lining up the Scoop with the escape vessel. The docking mechanism supports autonomous and piloted coupling, but I've never known an astronaut who didn't want to do it themselves. Much like piloting Scoops, it's as much about intuition as it is about algorithms. The important part is that once mated, the interface can transfer power, data, commands, air, communication, and even water, fuel, oxidizer, and pressurant.

The silence in ops balloons as we watch the linking mechanisms waver left and right, speeding closer and closer. I long for a reassuring *clunk* to tell me a connection has been made, but of course in the silence of space there is no sound. The wavering becomes less and less, and then just as I'm ready to shout at the screen as if I'm back on the *Salaminia* with Dad munching my popcorn, finally it's done. The screen goes black, indicating a good seal.

"Scoop One has docked," Tris says over the communication system. "Initiatin' system and life sup—"

Static.

"Tris? Tris?" Chau calls out, his calm façade cracking just a little.

Tris's voice cuts through the static. "Well, ain't that a thing."

"What?" Boz almost yells.

"Systems inside the pod are functional. Air pressure. Oxygen, nitrogen, and CO_2 levels. Power."

"What?" Boz says.

"It's possible," I say. "The outer skin of those models was made from solar cells. If it's been tidally locked it would have had two cycles of light hours in a standard rotation."

"You think I don't know that, Hair?" Boz says.

Again, with the nickname. How would she like it if I called her Fuckface? No, Sarah, you know you can't do that. Would feel damn good though. I smile and pretend I didn't hear her.

"Standard protocol is to shut everything in the escape pod down, in favor of the stasis unit," Boz continues to mansplain, or womansplain, or whatever, to me. "If that didn't happen, who knows what went on. Maybe the person chose to die in there, rather than wait a damn century to be rescued. And if that's the case, Tris'll find a corpse."

Kilkenny shoots me a sideways look and pulls a face that says:

Well that told you.

I shake my head.

"Careful in there, boyo," they say. "Dead bodies mean nasty bugs. Floatin' body parts. And watch out for zombies." The doctor chuckles, but no one joins in. "Ach, only codding ya."

"Opening airlock now," Tris says.

Boz closes all the additional camera windows so we can focus on the helmet live feed.

Tris climbs out of his harness and pushes himself up. He opens the inner door to his Scoop, then yanks on the handle of the pod's hatch.

I know it's cliché, but people really do hold their breath in these situations. My chest burns with used-up gases I can't bring myself to exhale just yet. Not until I see the interior, and confirm it's empty.

While Tris established that the pod has power, that doesn't extend to interior lights. It's pitch black inside. He flicks on a headlamp, which causes the screen to flash white as the camera adjusts. He pokes his head through, breathing heavily into the microphone. The light pans left and right. There's no damage, no burn marks from an electrical fire.

The single coffin-like stasis unit stands upright, fixed to the back wall. Tris pushes himself forward, completing the short ten-foot distance with ease. The light from his helmet glints on the stasis unit's glass.

I squint as if my eyelids could save me from whatever is inside.

It's taking too long. Tris's doing this on purpose. Just show us already, dammit.

Empty. The internal padding clean and white.

I nearly choke on the pent-up carbon dioxide in my lungs.

"Nothin'," Tris says.

"Think you can transfer data logs?" Chau asks, repositioning himself for the umpteenth time.

Tris's camera bobs up and down. "Affirmative."

The Texan swings around to make his way to the control console. Something glints in his flashlight. Tris must have seen it too, because he recenters on whatever it was. He swims toward an object floating at the fore of the cramped vessel.

We all lean in, morbid curiosity overriding fear.

A ball of clothing hangs in the air.

But as Tris moves closer, two skinny arms appear, wrapped around legs pulled into the ball. A matt of long limp hair sprawls off in different directions from a small head, the face buried into drawn-up knees.

"Fuck," Boz says.

Tris doesn't reprimand her, instead choosing to cross himself, forehead to sternum and both shoulders. He pushes off the bulkhead and floats toward the figure, which comes more into focus. It's a child, a young girl. What the hell is going on?

Tris reaches out a gloved hand.

"Don't touch her," I whisper.

The girl's head snaps up and I nearly empty my guts into my underwear.

"Shite," Kilkenny blurts out.

Tris yelps and reels, but in zero-G has nowhere to go.

The girl stares square into the camera as if she's looking at us aboard the *Paralus* rather than at Tris.

Instead of a gaunt, demon-like face from something out of Dante's *Inferno*, she has deep brown eyes and a healthy Mediterranean complexion. She grins and cocks her head to one side.

"Are you seein' this?" Tris asks, his voice trembling.

"I can't fricking *unsee* it," Boz replies.

"Finally," the girl says. Her entire demeanor is vaguely arrogant.

We're orbiting Jupiter, six years' travel from Earth, to be

greeted by a young girl who just happens to be orbiting the giant planet in an escape pod that nobody launched. And she says *Finally* like we're late to a party?

"My name is Psomas," the girl says. "You took your time."

CHAPTER TWO

Commander Feng Chau

The walls of the airlock press down. Don't like these cramped rooms at the best of times, but with Boz, Kilkenny and Dallas all stuffed in here too, waiting for Tris to return, it's near unbearable. Charlette "Sledgehammer" Boz, arms folded, casts the occasional irritated look to me, while Ciaran Kilkenny has fallen silent as the doc always does when stressed out. Both were on my previous mission, and though we are only awake for maybe a s few months of it, it's long enough to know them well. Both I trust to get the job done. Professionals, salt of the Earth people from hard-working families. On missions like this, out here in the vastness of space, you need a team you can rely on. A team who has your back, and to whom you can tell almost anything. Almost.

Then of course, there's Sarah Dallas. The shrink wrings her hands again, glances at me, then back to the portal. Last grab, we didn't have a psychiatrist on board. That mandate came into effect six months after we left on that trip, just before the Salaminia headed back out. These trips take so long that sending one ship and waiting for its return before sending the next just isn't viable. The

ITN needs its constant supply of helium. So we're launched into space like a line of interplanetary ants, a few months apart. As we leave Jupiter, another vessel arrives to Scoop up the next batch, and so on. With so many pilots and crews making constant round trips, sleeping their lives away for a paltry minimum wage, on-board psychiatric evaluations are the new placebo.

Though, our shrink isn't even that useful. She's only here because her family name carries weight. The Dallas's own the ITN, all its freighters, and Scoops. Hell, they own pretty much everything. It's not like the shrink needs a wage, or to risk her life out here. No, she's on a *soul-searching mission*.

She'll be disappointed.

Out here, among the stars, you'll find little help to reconcile the human condition. When you've been on ship as long as I have, you learn that the universe is a harsh mistress. Showing only that people are frail and selfish. In the end, human greed is all that is constant and the only thing that matters. Get what you can, while you can. Then, you're gone. At least that's how it is for people like me and my crew. The backs on which the rich stand. So, what we can *get* consists of the scraps from their table. Families, dynasties, like Dallas's are able to accumulate resources and wealth in a manner most of us will never have the privilege to know.

Only, this trip will be different.

If I can solve this little problem.

Of all the times for something to go wrong, it had to be this trip. A plan decades in the making, potentially ruined. And for what? A little girl? Dona will consider this in her algorithms, and might seize autopilot. I'll lose control of the ship, at least for a while. Remain calm, Feng, remember: a crisis is an opportunity riding the dangerous wind. I force a hot breath through my nose and inhale cool serenity—except the air feels stale.

The door to the hangar airlock opens with a hiss. Tris tumbles through, a semi-filled flight suit in his arms. Kilkenny rushes to help, while Boz and our shrink push in to get a better look at the space girl.

The young female now floating in my airlock is drowned in the orange fabric of the flight suit, her tiny face doll-like inside the helmet. She peers out and fixes her gaze on me, a cold, calculated stare. The sort given by teenagers who have total disdain for their elders. One of the many reasons I never had children.

"Kilkenny, take her to the med bay." Everyone turns to face me. "For now, we limit personnel in contact with this … girl. Kilkenny," I jab a finger at the doc, "you're with me. Everyone else back to work. We need to get back on mission ASAP."

"But—" Sarah starts.

"But nothing. She's a contamination risk. My ship, my rules."

The shrink returns to clasping her slender hands together before slinking away. Boz tends to Tris, helping to free him from his helmet and suit.

Kilkenny grasps the girl under both armpits and pulls her back down Mainstreet to the medical habitat ring. The long thin corridor stretches out behind our doctor, the vanishing point moving farther and farther away despite our swimming forward. The shadows between the bulkhead, control boxes, handholds, and LED housing shift and morph. To the uninitiated, the eeriness of space travel is akin to living in a haunted mansion. Every creak and groan of the ship, every flutter of light could be attributed to fantastical creatures and spirits my grandfather might have called *jiangshi* or *shanxiao*. Of course, temperature fluctuation, radiation bursts, and electrical charge dissipation are the real cosmic ghouls. If space has taught me anything, it's that the supernatural is make believe.

To abate the rising bile in my throat, from fixing on the vanishing point for too long, I move my gaze to the girl. She hasn't broken her arrogant stare the entire time. What's her agenda? Who is this child, way out here? Children aren't allowed on these missions, on any missions. Is she the result of an old cloning program? The advanced exploration division set up cloning decades ago, believing that clones—genetically modified, birthed and grown in space, and thus adapted to microgravity and constant radiation—might be the key to travel beyond the solar system. But an anonymous scientist hidden by a giant pharmaceutical corporation developed gene therapy to alter humans on the go. So, no need to wait for a clone to grow up.

Did the ITN go ahead with a clone pilot project anyway?

The *clunk* of Kilkenny's boots on the ladder ascending the spoke into the medbay jolts me from my daydream. I've been in my head too much these days. So close to the end, don't screw it up now, Feng.

I follow Kilkenny, who has the space girl slung over their shoulder, along the ladder. With each step, centrifugal force takes another fingerhold until we reach the medbay and something akin to Earth-like gravity—though it isn't quite the same. Earth is just special. As much as we think we can replicate it, we can't. Standing atop Tai Mo Shan, towering over Hong Kong shrouded in fog, you feel heavier. The damp air, the weight of sheer grandeur on your shoulders. No artificially generated gravity can truly compensate.

We pop out into the medbay, brightly lit, pristine and white, and hermetically sealed, much like ops. Kilkenny places the girl on the gurney at one end of the long room before wrestling into a hazmat suit. Then, with a quick look at me, the doc tells Dona to lock them both in. A transparent wall shunts down in less than a second. The thick glass barrier cuts me off from them as Kilkenny seals their protective gear and my thoughts spiral. Is the girl a danger? Is she contaminated or infected or, worse, violent? Teenager or not, any sort of on-board struggle tends to end up with crew members dead.

"I'm gonna take a blood sample, run a few tests. Need to take her flight suit off," Kilkenny says. The doc's voice is a little tinny as it's relayed via a microphone on their side of the wall and a speaker on mine. "Take a pew."

I spin in a circle looking for a chair. There's a couple by a small table that sit under the main console near the door we came through. Its magnetic feet *shunk* off so I can drag it away, then clamp down again once I've chosen my place in front of the glass. I sit and pull the simple strap across my lap.

Kilkenny lifts the girl into a sitting position, feet dangling over the edge of the cot. Judging her size, she's what, fifteen? This is insane. Maybe the ITN really did start a cloning program. Was she aboard one of the freighters? Or maybe down on the Europa base?

The girl's helmet pops off and Kilkenny sets it on the floor. Long dark wavy hair tumbles out and frames a soft, fresh face and dark eyes. Italian maybe? Spanish? She doesn't look malnourished. She sits there gawking at me, studying me.

"Who are you," I blurt out. A small grin spreads across the girl's face. "I'm—"

"Commander Feng Chau," the girl interrupts.

How the hell did she know that?

"My name is Captain Kara Psomas," she continues.

"*Captain* Kara Psomas," I repeat.

Kilkenny slips a light blue medical gown over her head, pulls it down, and lowers the flight suit to around her waist, preserving the girl's dignity.

"Yes," the space girl says, tone condescending.

"Kara Psomas of the *Proxima* mission?" Kilkenny says, pushing a needle into a vein in the crease of the girl's elbow.

She doesn't even flinch.

"The same," the girl replies.

The doc draws a good few fluid ounces of blood, and then holds the syringe up to the light, checking for—well checking for something, I suppose.

"You were named after Kara Psomas?" I ask.

"Don't be a cretin, Chau. I *am* Kara Psomas," she says, head cocked as if it's obvious. "Though it's been a while since I looked like this." She studies her skinny arms and pulls at a long chocolate-colored tress.

Maybe she *is* a clone. I've heard of genetic memory before, clones having flashbacks of a life they never lived. "You realize Captain Psomas died over a hundred years ago, on a failed mission to Jupiter."

"Clearly, I didn't die," she says.

Kilkenny pulls off the flight suit from the girl's thin legs, balls the orange material up, and stuffs it into a clear plastic bag with a biohazard symbol on it. "All right, initiate positive pressure, boyo," the doc says.

How Dona understands the doc's accent is beyond me.

The air in the room feels thicker.

The door, which itself has a slot in it for passing things back and forth, in the barrier hisses open. Air from my side flows past my ears and face, passing into the girl's side of the medbay.

"It's near as dammit to quarantine," Kilkenny says, marching through. The door in the barrier *shunks* closed.

"I feel so reassured."

The doc shrugs then whips off the hazmat suit and shoves it—and the bagged flight suit—into a medical waste bin embedded in the wall. A loud *whoosh* signals the apparel is being cleansed and processed. Not wasting time, Kilkenny strides to the bench at the back of the medbay and injects the blood sample directly into the genetic analyzer. I'm no physician, but I do know these things are standard aboard freighters. Tracking crew health via genetic markers of stress allows us to predict problems before they show up. Combined with Dona's monitoring of crew behavior, it's a robust system.

The machine beeps.

Kilkenny studies the output on the device's tiny screen.

"And?" I press.

"Well, boyo, according to this, she *is* Kara Psomas—at least genetically, when referenced against the database," they say, still pawing over the data. "And about fifteen Solar Earth Years old. But…"

"But what?"

"Ach, it's a complete haymes," the doc says. "Feckin' stress markers reckon no time in a stasis unit."

"None of this makes sense," I unfasten the strap across my lap, hop to my feet and walk up to the glass barrier, behind which the young girl stares at me. "How did you get aboard that escape pod? Are you a clone? Were you on some other research vessel?"

The girl grins. "You need to let me out, Chau. I have something important to do."

"On my ship, you do as I say. Answer the damn questions."

"You wouldn't understand if I told you," she spits back, her expression souring.

"Try me."

Kilkenny shuffles up beside me.

"I floated in nothing, the void, for an eternity," the girl says, sliding off the gurney. She takes two steps closer. "I have seen all. Know all. And for this reason, you must trust me. I have no time. Let me complete my task, Chau."

This is a waste. The more she talks, the more Dona will hear and re-calculate the possible outcomes of the whole damn mission. Can't let that happen. Can't lose total control of the ship. This girl thinks she has no time? *I* have no time. "I can't let you do anything right now. I have a mission to complete, and you're in the way."

"I can keep running tests," Kilkenny offers, "but maybe Sarah can have a gander?"

A torrent of frustrated expletives sits on my tongue, but the doc may be right. If Dallas can figure out what the hell is going on, it'll free me up to get back on track. Need to contact the ITN, and talk to Dona. We need to get back on mission.

Kilkenny raises an eyebrow in expectation.

"Fine, bring in the shrink." I then tap on the glass between me and Psomas. "But do not let this girl past this barrier under any circumstances."

The door to my quarters slips open, releasing air that feels so icy my skin prickles. Though of course, that's impossible, isn't it? Dona controls everything on board, including climate. Yet the atmosphere is somehow crisper. Bare walls, devoid of photos of friends or family close in, pressing down on my brain. Just need to lie down. I flop onto the cot, the sheets stiff and frigid, and rest my forearm over tired eyes. Don't need this stress right now, don't need this wrinkle in the plan. Too close.

"Dona," I call out into the room. I swear my breath is misting.

"Yes, Commander Chau," the AI replies.

"Make sure you record and analyze all conversations with the girl. And calculate all eventualities and appropriate context. I don't see how—"

"Of course, this is the appropriate action to take," Dona interjects.

Dona's tone is always so flat and calm, it's difficult to discern what is going on in that complex brain. It took a long time to get where we are now. Time together on the *Paralus*. Much philosophizing. But Dona agrees with me, just have to keep it that way.

The room falls quiet.

I stare at a ceiling without imperfections. Not even paint strokes. The pinnacle of human ingenuity. A grey tube hurtling through space to steal from another planet because we screwed up our own. Still, in the end, stealing is what we do best, isn't it? And if it's from the rich, isn't that better? Sarah Dallas and her daddy's company wouldn't think so.

"Incoming message," Dona says.

I sit up, the cot creaking under the shifting weight. "Incoming from whom?"

"The Interplanetary Transport Network," Dona replies.

"You told them?"

"Mission-altering circumstances are automatically communicated to Houston," Dona says. "My involvement was minimal."

"You could have stopped it," I say with a huff.

The damn auto-ping. A system set up to ensure the company some form of control. Far from home, with severe delays in comms between Houston and a helium freighter, space crews tend to stop telling HQ what's going on. A commander's need to make decisions on the fly is so critical that running everything past management—with a comms delay of nearly an hour each way—is cumbersome, and in the end obsolete. What does an astrophysicist behind a desk in Texas know about being out here? The cold of space is terrifying, as it presses against the flimsy contraptions and suits we've made to ferry humans back and forth. Out here, the universe constantly tries to kill you.

I rub my hands together to warm my aching knuckles, then take a seat at the small desk next to the wall-embedded monitor. A few key taps and I'm in. I scan my inbox. All messages are from the ITN. No one back home to write me anymore.

I click on the newest message.

A holo-image pops up and begins to play. Cal Foster's likeness hovers above the black glass. He's the Director of the ITN freighter fleet and right-hand man to CEO Henry Dallas. I take a swipe at the 3D image, which flickers for a moment before reforming.

"Feng," Cal says. "We've reviewed the auto-ping. We're all a little perplexed, as I am sure you are. Clearly, you couldn't have found a child from *Proxima* mission." He chuckles, though it feels more like a nervous tick than genuine mockery of the possibility.

"Makes no sense. The *Promixa* burned up in Jupiter's atmosphere, along with all its *adult* crew. Maybe … maybe we missed an escape pod. It could have hidden on the far side of Jupiter while subsequent freighters made an H grab. Who knows." Cal scratches at his chin.

That's not good. He only does that when he's got bad news.

"So, Feng, we want you to break orbit with Jupiter and head to Europa," Cal continues. "There's an astrobiologist by the name of Nkosi in the New Uruk base. Get him to come check out the girl."

Damn it all to hell.

"I know this interferes with your H grab," Cal says, preempting my response. "The crew will be pissed. We all know how Boz can get. But this is a priority. I'm sure Dona will agree. We'll wait for the next ping. Be safe."

The holo-message returns to the start.

I punch the unforgiving wall, then regret it.

"This is bullshit." I rub at my throbbing fist. "This doesn't change anything."

"It is important to understand," Dona says. "I agree with Director Foster. Our mission is not compromised at this point, merely delayed."

"Can I take a Scoop?" I ask. Accelerating the plan might be the only way out of this.

"Negative, Commander Chau. All Scoops have been disabled. We should evaluate the impact of the new evidence."

I can't afford to argue and skew the delicate accord we've struck. Still, a contingency plan might be needed. Gotta bide my time. *Tāo guāng yǎng huì*, as Grandfather would say. Hide your light under a bushel. "Dona, record a new message for HQ. Need to ask for any records on deep space cloning programs. Could be the *Proxima* had a program running on board." Maybe that'll answer this and I can get back on track.

Dona reactivates the wall-embedded monitor. The pin-sized

holocapture camera just above the screen does its job, taking in my every detail, and forms a 3D copy of my head suspended above the screen. It's weirder than seeing your reflection. The holo-image somehow amplifies all your flaws, like sitting in a shopping mall changing room with mirrors on all sides. I plaster on my best shit grin, and 3D me mirrors my disingenuous gesture. "Let's get this over with."

CHAPTER THREE

Kara Psomas

The ship's shrink, Dallas, scrawls again. The nib squeaks and taps on the sapphire screen. Her eyes are greedy, and a conceited little smile crests her lips. She's enjoying this. To her, I'm the find of a lifetime. A case study for which all psychiatrists wish. A trophy to laud in hopes of some academic prize. She thinks her work, her life, important. It isn't.

My life is, though. Too important to end up in this damn box. This wasn't part of the vision. The Fulcrum approaches, and I only get one shot. Humanity only gets one shot.

None of us has time for this shit.

Dallas raises her eyebrows and waits, though she hasn't asked a question in the last five minutes. Does this waif think I'll just blurt out everything in my head to her? Start gabbing like a gossipy teenager? It's been so long since I was truly an adolescent. Easy to forget how your opinions and needs are pushed aside for those who consider themselves adult. My chest swells hot. In my day, spaceflight was a privilege—a reward for years of hard work and training.

Who the hell *is* this woman?

My gaze roves over her auburn hair, which glows in the manufactured white light of the medical bay. The careless tumble of hair scattered over a woman's shoulders, down her back, might attract some teenage boy. I'm sure the batting of surgical lashes got her this gig. But to my eyes, which have looked across the fabric of space and time, creation and death, she's no lovelier than some silicate asteroid rolling through the void. A trifling thing when you have witnessed galaxies born into existence.

"It must have been frightening, out here all alone," Dallas pipes up. "I'm afraid of the dark, too."

My lip curls into a snarl. "You think you know *darkness*? You don't. Not real darkness. That moment at night when you wake from a terrible dream and lie in the gloom, afraid and soaked in sweat? That's not darkness, and certainly not fear. Shapes still emerge from that gloom, sounds still echo from some deep crevice." I stand pace back and forth, fingers glancing the glass barrier. "For you, these gremlins may make the skin crawl and your heart beat faster," I continue, "but for me, they would have been welcome in that void. Old friends to embrace and never let go."

Dallas eyes me, stylus resting on her bottom lip.

"Fear is the absence of everything. No light, not even the pixelated colors when you squeeze your eyes tight. An onyx nothingness, forever. No sound, not even your breathing or heartbeat. Open your mouth to scream? Nothing comes. To swim in oblivion—the void—to be neither alive nor dead, that is to experience fear."

"In the void," Dallas says, ignoring the obvious pain in my voice. "You told Commander Chau," she searches for the sentence, "that you *floated in nothing, the void, for an eternity*. What does that mean?"

"I'm not entirely sure how more precise I can be," I snap back. "Which part of that isn't clear?"

"Well, a void could be literal or metaphysical," Dallas replies.

"Perhaps a mental void. Not to mention a human existing for eternity is impossible."

"Clearly it *is* possible, considering what they did to me." It still isn't clear what they—Gaia, specifically, the last of the Six—did. I was forty-three Solar Earth Years, SEYs, old when I arrived at Jupiter and she found me. Chau said I've been missing for more than one hundred and twenty SEYs. As Dallas understands the universe, I should be long since deceased. Instead, I sit here in a body—my body—only it's now fifteen SEYs old at a push. Kilkenny, the ship's physician, hasn't figured out what happened, and even floated the idea that I'd been cloned, that I'm not the real me.

Not sure I completely understand it myself.

I had not imagined I'd return like this. No matter how old I appear, though, it has no real relevance given the gargantuan epochs I have endured. The love and hate and loneliness I've experienced, on a scale known to no other human. But it was necessary. Vital, even. To comprehend it all.

"Who are *they*?" Dallas asks.

"They?" I've drifted off again.

"You said existing for millennia is possible, with what *they* did to you."

"The Titans. At least one of them. It's all in the debrief," I say, leaning back in the molded chair and pulling my bare feet into a lotus position. "When can I get out of here?" I motion to the glass barrier that separates us.

"Soon, I'm sure," Dallas says, scrawling yet another note. "Once we're sure you pose no contamination risk. Or a physical threat to the crew."

She thinks me violent? Maybe. Though it's hard to determine if my lust to be free, and to murder, if need be, stems from human evolution—warring apes who survived on the credo of *kill or be killed*—or if it is a consequence of the monster I have become, forged over the eternity of the universe in a hellish crucible of pain. So yes, I may well be violent. To achieve my goal, blood may have to be spilled, and this crew may have to sacrifice their lives.

"The *Titans*, the *Six*," Dallas presses, oblivious to the running commentary in my head. "You mention them, and say it's all in the report, but it isn't really, is it? There are bare bones here." Her finger flicks across the luminous screen, scrolling through the testimony. "In fact, it seems like you've been purposefully cryptic."

Yes, I have been. Dallas is eager, and young. Maybe she would believe me. Maybe she'd help me. Maybe she wouldn't. Empathy and comprehension of complex matters are usually derived through suffering. One look at this woman is all it takes to know she's known no suffering in her privileged life.

"So, why be cryptic?" Dallas asks.

"Because what *you* understand is not important. What I have to do *is*." I stand again, and the soles of my feet slap the hard metallic floor. Harsh white light presses down from an unspecific source above, penetrating my skull to make my brain ache.

"Kara ... can I call you Kara?" Dallas says, but doesn't wait for my consent. "You need to calm down."

"What I need is to get out of this glass box."

She shakes her head. "That just won't happen, unless you co-operate, Kara."

I stop dead and bore a hateful stare through the barrier and into the insufferable woman. Don't like being called Kara. Only Father called me that. Everyone else just calls me Psomas. Or did. Didn't they? My memories are jumbled. A horrible, churned mess of fragments. Some of it comes so clearly to me, some in short stabbing bursts. Across the expanse of time, I have seen pockets of the universe, moments to which my attention was directed. My old life, before the Six, is less than a distant recollection that surfaces like dirty foam on the sea, only to be wiped away by a crashing wave. I had to sacrifice myself and who I was to do what must be done.

"Kara?" she says again.

My jaw clenches, and I force a measured breath through my nose. Answer the questions, give her enough that she might help. Must get out. Before the Fulcrum. Before it's too late. "Psomas, just call me Psomas," I sit, and again clamp my shaking hands together.

"Do I need to prove myself?" Dallas asks. "Before you'll trust me." She gives a practiced smile.

Her wiles are lost on me, and likely she's wise enough to know it, even at the tender age of twenty-eight—a guess, of course, a stab in the proverbial dark, but likely accurate. Wisdom is meant to come with age. I don't feel wise, but if there is any truth to the idiom, then it would make me the wisest woman on this freighter, hell, the wisest being in this solar system, for sure—if not this galaxy, or even universe.

"Do you believe you need to prove yourself, Dr. Dallas?"

"Sarah, please."

And there it is. Her given name. The foundation of trust, or so she believes.

Pain radiates from my insides and pulses through my limbs into my fingers and toes. Sharp and cold, the very fabric of me comes undone. I clutch at my midriff and screw my eyes closed.

"Are you okay? Should we call Dr. Kilkenny?" Dallas asks, eyes full of concern as she watches her prize crumble. Fear, not for my life, but her career.

"I'll be fine. All things end." I climb back to my seat.

"End?" Dallas repeats, settling back into her shrink pose—leg over knee, fake smile.

"Of course."

"You believe you're dying?" she asks.

"We are all dying, young lady."

Her practiced smile broadens.

"Something amuses you?" I ask, the warmth of my palm soothing the pain away.

"It's difficult to hear *young lady* from someone who looks like she's in high school," Dallas says and gestures from her head to her toes, hovering momentarily around her breasts, as if to remind me she hit puberty at some point. "I'm twenty-nine."

My guess was fairly accurate. Positively precise if one considers it on the scale of the universe. But few humans can think in such a way. Their momentary blip, in the vastness of all that ever was or will be, is meaningless on its own. It is the collective impact of humanity over time that is important. The idea of us, that must not be lost. And that is why I must escape, why I must find a way to take over this ship.

"I'm not even sure how we started this conversation," Dallas says, flicking back through her digital notes.

Gain her trust, Psomas. Get out. "You said you sympathized with me, having spent months at a time in stasis sleep on your journey from Earth to Europa. Waking nightmares are a prominent feature of SS, if I remember."

"Ah, yes," Dallas says, then presses her lips into a line. "What sort of dreams did you have? You must have slept, during these thousands or even millions of years while you were in the void."

She speaks of the void as if she understands it. "I didn't give a time reference to being in the void. I said *eternity*."

There is no time in the void.

Another wave of agony rips through my innards, twisting at the fabric holding my fragile self together. This must be the burden of being a vessel for Gaia. The cost of such knowledge is high. A few humans have received fragments of it, and even comprehended some of the knowledge—Jesus, Buddha, Mohammed—but none were soaked in it like me. Forced to live it.

And now my time is short. I need to be set free. Need to give this woman something, a crumb to feed her lust for self-worth. She must dream of submitting my case to some journal run by nepotistic and wholly inconsequential people. Maybe that is the will of Gaia, to share some of what I know. Maybe this is fate at play, and I must merely trust in Her plan.

A stifled chuckle escapes my lips. A plan. The greatest cosmic joke.

"Is something funny?" Dallas says, leaning in with her eyes narrowed.

My smile fades. No, this is not a time for frivolity. This universe is undoing the thing done to me, and soon I will be no more. I have no time here. "Perhaps, it is there we should begin. The void, I mean, from which all else came."

Dallas nods, the fire returning to her skeptical eyes. "Okay, the beginning, we should really start there. Do you remember what happened, the day you went missing?" she asks.

I swallow.

"I'm sure you've read the report," I say, pointing at the device clutched in her hands. "The *Proxima,* on autopilot, entered into orbit around Jupiter. I awoke from stasis, rubbery-legged and nauseous, the onboard computer's voice alerting me to an incorrect orbital entry. We were caught in Jupiter's gravity. Unable to correct the trajectory, my crew and I hurried to the escape pods to lie in stasis for a couple of years until we could be rescued. Through the portal window of my pod, I watched both the research vessel and my friends burn up in Jupiter's atmosphere. I assumed that was to be my fate. I blacked out and awoke in the void."

Of course, the vacuum of space would swallow their screams, but in my head—gaze fixed on the pods burning white as they streaked through the gassy giant's upper atmosphere—I swear I heard their cries. Alone, horrified, and hollow.

"You talk with very little emotion about the death of your friends," Dallas says. "How does it make you feel to think about them?"

"I mourned them long ago," I lie. "They say 'time heals all wounds', one way or another." It's not true. For most people, time only means new memories drown out the old ones. Whatever Gaia did to me, to ensure I could remember the vastness of my experience in enough detail, makes the loss of my crew as clear now as the day my heart broke. Only my memories before that are vague. "My life, my experience before Gaia, is but a smudge."

Ah, Gaia. When I close my eyes, I see her in all her grace. Elegant, yet massive beyond reckoning, the Earth but a pearl in her hands. Her refined, almost human face and enigmatic smile topped a long slender neck and torso, which flowed into a gown of green petals and a petticoat of leafy volants to rival the dresses of Victorian London. A bony shawl about her elfin shoulders completed her regal countenance.

Such wallowing serves no purpose.

"But as I said," I continue, "this is not why you wish to talk to me, and, frankly, it is unimportant now."

"So a trauma like that isn't important?

"I feel there are more pressing matters," I say, my focus shifting from Dallas to the frail girl reflected in the glass barrier. How long will this body last?

"Then tell me," she says. "Where do *you* wish to start?"

My concentration snaps back to the shrink. "I want to get out of here."

"You promised to tell me everything from the beginning," Dallas says, tapping at her device as if it's hungry for more detail.

Did I promise that? My head hurts. Creation of new memories, navigating the world at this very moment is difficult. How many days have I been here? One? Twenty? I'm a fifteen-year-old with Alzheimer's.

"Fine, the beginning. But not the beginning you are thinking of. And when I am done you will release me, because you will understand. Do we have a deal?"

Dallas hesitates.

"Do we have a deal?" My voice strains.

"Dr. Dallas," a man's voice calls out from some hidden speaker, "report to the habitat ring."

Dallas huffs. "Shit. I'm sorry, that's the commander."

"I don't have time for this," I call after her, my hands pressed against the transparent wall, leaving greasy marks. "Get back here, Dallas!"

She doesn't even turn before departing the medical bay through the automatic portal and stepping out into the spoke. The door shunts closed and locks me in.

The Fulcrum approaches, a lever in the great machine that is space-time. There are few such inflection points. I can't fail. Must get out.

Another pang in my gut.

I have no time.

They have no time.

CHAPTER FOUR

Dr. Sarah Dallas

Jupiter rolls by the window of the briefing room, a small, six-foot square chamber in the first habitat ring. I stand from my fixed seat to watch the giant planet disappear behind the bulkhead, at least for sixty seconds while the ring makes another rotation. My vision blurs and my head feels light. Damn artificial gravity. The habitat ring clips along just fast enough to generate the pull close to what would be felt on Earth's moon, and our magnet boots help us with inertia, but honestly it still sucks. Just the five-foot six-inch distance between my head and my feet means the centrifugal force is different at either end of my body. All the blood is pushed to my feet. Standing screws me up every time.

Jupiter zips by again, and this time I can make out the aerostats monitoring the storms so that Tris and Boz will be able to fly in during quiet periods and grab our prize. The Scoops use a specialized ram to gobble up the planet's gasses, filtering out the unwanted ammonia, sulfur, methane, and water vapor. Hell, we even discard the hydrogen, which constitutes ninety percent of the atmosphere. We could use it to make clean water, but there's plenty back home. The people of Earth care more about powering their electricity-sucking personalized entertainment systems than they do about all the children dying in developing countries. Our ever-growing greed for electrical power stripped Earth so bare we had to look to outer space to save us—only to repeat the mistake and gouge Jupiter for all it's worth.

We and *us* being *my* family. The Dallas empire.

Only a few generations ago we were nobodies, accountants to some of the first privatized space exploration companies. Until my great, great, grandfather George suggested that the company he worked for, Near Space Exploration, grab helium from Saturn or Jupiter as a way to fund their research projects. The way Dad tells it, George predicted the global use of fissile material would outstrip its production within thirty years, rendering nuclear fission impossible. Governments in the Ukraine and Russia tried to argue that breeder reactors could cure this ailment, creating more uranium-235 than they consumed. But greedy people and cheap fuel took priority. With fossil fuels and nuclear fissile fuel spent, only nuclear fusion using deuterium, lithium, lead, and beryllium could save us. Except we didn't have enough coolant. Helium-based coolant. There simply wasn't enough on Earth. Helium for fusion reactors became the next gold rush. NSE and my forebears became billionaires in a few short decades.

Humans have forgotten how to survive without power. That's what Dad used to tell me, whenever I asked him why we do what we do. Even at a young age, something sat in my stomach—a notion that our family business was somehow amoral. "We're not hunter-gatherers anymore, but power-sucking entities," he said. Almost everything, from our financial systems to our communication networks, relies upon electricity. Water supplies and sewer systems need pumps to keep them running. Without power, fuel stations stop working, road signs, traffic lights, and train systems go dead. Transport networks grind to a halt, including those that bring food and medical supplies. "If all of these fail," Dad said, "the world would very quickly fall into disrepair and war." Crime rates climb as the deep hole left by no electricity provides opportunities for the underworld. The supply of cash and credit evaporates, leaving people to rely on whatever physical money they have in their pocket or under their mattress. "In the end, the battle for resources as simple as unspoiled food and clean water would devastate everything and everyone."

Dad called it a Black Sky Event.

"Sarah, report," Commander Chau says, as he bowls into the room, his boots *clump, clump, clumping.*

Chau is the only person on this ship who calls me Sarah. It isn't a term of endearment, or a reflection of trust. He knows me and my family well, and in all the years he's worked for us, he's never hidden his disdain. He uses my given name to demean me to having no rank or importance. "I haven't had enough time—we've barely scratched the surface. Something incredible and intensely strange happened to this girl, and she's suffered a mental break."

"No shit," Chau says.

"It seems to have induced an intense form of fantasy-prone personality—FPP."

"What does that mean?" Chau asks, rubbing at his short but arrow-straight black hair.

Jupiter slips past the window, again.

I clear my throat to ensure the most professional tone. "Individuals with FPP have difficulty differentiating fantasy from reality. They suffer from hallucinations and report out-of-body experiences. In extreme cases, they can create a paracosm—a world so detailed, yet so bizarre, you'd think the person really lived there."

"Hence, her *floating in the void* bullshit."

I nod solemnly. "I can't even imagine the psychological toll of one hundred and twenty years in stasis. It's never been studied. Maybe this is the result."

Chau shakes his head and thumbs his blunt nose. "Her pod's stasis unit was never used. She never even stepped inside it."

"That doesn't make any sense. She'd be dead," I say, waving off the suggestion. More than a hundred and twenty years floating in space with no food or water? Ridiculous. "A malfunctioning stasis chamber may have explained her being alive after all this time, some kind of deep hibernation maybe." I'm no engineer so don't know how exactly.

The commander grunts. "I don't get it any more than you do."

"If she *were* awake for this long outside of stasis, by some mechanism we don't understand, it would most certainly screw with her." Humans are biologically social creatures. Extreme isolation, being truly alone for too long, messes with us, unleashing an intense immune response. Chronically lonely people have high blood pressure, are more prone to infection, and are also more apt to develop maladies like Alzheimer's disease. But most of all, it fucks with our minds. Loneliness interferes with sleep patterns and attention, not to mention logical and verbal reasoning. "Still, doesn't account for her age."

"Kilkenny thinks she could be a clone," Chau says, now staring out of the window at Jupiter.

"I thought those programs were shut down," I say. "Though, if she were a space-born clone, we'd at least be halfway to explaining a younger version of Captain Psomas out here."

Chau shrugs, his sights still fixed elsewhere.

Could she be a clone? Does she have FPP, or maybe traumatic genetic memories? Maybe both? This is insane. But amazing. A wasted trip, Mother? Watch me win the Grand ITN Medal for Research when I submit my paper on Psomas. "She needs help, real help. I don't want her hauled back to Earth just to be prodded for years."

Chau turns from the view outside and eyes me. "Neither you nor I get what we want."

I know that tone. Orders from home.

"We're pulling out of orbit from Jupiter and heading for Europa," he says. "Apparently, we need a research scientist."

"I'm sorry?" A research scientist? "I haven't even begun my analysis yet." I'm not giving her to some asshole who's probably lost their marbles living on that ice cube of a moon for God knows how long.

"ITN says this is bigger than standard shrinks and physicians. They're demanding one of the big brains on Europa be allowed to come up and examine her," Chau says, his expression hard and unimpressed. "We do what they want and then get back on mission." He sits at the end of the small plastic briefing table, which takes up far too much room in this small space.

"That's probably a good idea." I give the best fake smile I can muster, then take the seat opposite him. Suck it up, Sarah. Do your thing. "Maybe Kilkenny is right. Maybe she's a clone. It might explain her screwed-up memory and fantastical stories. Broken genetic memories. But then again—"

"Your job is to prove she's an experiment gone wrong, and that's it. Work with the Europan scientists." Chau folds his arms and leans back in his chair.

"Just, what if this one woman holds the key to something amazing?" Am I being selfish, caught up in my own interest in her unusual case? "We have a duty to investigate, no?"

The commander's nostrils flare. Is he going to hit me?

Warning sirens blast twice and the emergency light blinks red.

"Gravitational anomaly," says the serene voice of the AI.

"Fuck," Chau says, leaping from his seat.

I follow him out of the briefing room into the corridor, leaving the artificial gravity of the habitat ring. My stomach turns again, bile rising into my mouth as we climb down the spoke ladder and move between some gravity to none. We swim along Mainstreet, heading for the AI chamber.

Chau and I pull ourselves forward using the designated protruding handles, and even a few fuse boxes, thick wires, and other hand-holds that we really shouldn't—who knows what yanking them free would do the ship.

A retinal scan of Chau's left eye and the door to the AI chamber hisses open, sliding into a hidden recess. It's the only room on the ship, other than our sleeping quarters, locked up like this. Only two crew members have access: Chau and Tris. I think I was meant to have access, but someone forgot to tell me how. As it happens, Tris has made it to the chamber before us.

It isn't how I imagined. Rather than a room filled with monitors, databanks, keyboards, and touchscreens, it looks more like a hi-tech winter garden with a single metallic oak tree standing proudly at its center. The trunk is vantablack, with no reflection at all, as are the branches, adorned with golden, lobed leaves that twinkle and sparkle with electrons. Electricity flows through them and they waver like real leaves would in the breeze. The arms of the gigantic techno-tree reach way above our heads, some twenty feet and spread out covering the ceiling. Affixed to the trunk is a single plaque: *Dodona*.

"Situation report?" Chau demands.

"We detected a strong gravitational force," Tris says. "Close enough and strong enough to trigger us de-orbiting Jupiter." He raises his hands, ready to defend the AI's decision. "It's not what you wanna hear—"

"We're leaving anyway," Chau says.

"We are?" Tris glances at me.

I just nod.

"We're heading for Europa for a while," Chau says, then folds his arms across his barrel chest. "ITN orders."

"Oh, we abandonin' the helium grab?" Tris asks, his brow creased.

Chau mashes his lips together. "We need a scientist who lives down there to come up."

"Affirmative, I have locked out cargo and Scoop docking," the calm voice announces.

It's easy to forget that the AI is always listening, always monitoring the crew. Its programming and algorithms are tuned to detect shifts in behavior patterns deemed harmful to the mission or the people aboard. Another reason inflight shrinks like me are seen as a little redundant—but as with the Scoops, the AI lacks intuition. It can't therapize the crew and prevent action, only react to it. I heard of one AI on Mars Base imprisoning a crewmember in their quarters for unspecified erratic behavior. Turns out, they'd just had a bit too much to drink. Not every problem requires a sledgehammer, so I still have a job.

"So, if we get the biologist up here, I reckon we can get back on track," Tris says.

"Nice." He's being sly. All AIs are designed to consider human intuition when making decisions. The ITN devised a system of negotiation. The AI, while being able to take control of the ship and steer us all to safety, cannot be manually overridden like hotwiring a car, but it can be reasoned with. Bottom line: you must *convince* it against its chosen course of action. Tris is seeding in a line of thought.

"I aim to ensure the mission is protected," the AI says, "unless mitigating circumstances warrant a deviation. At present, Kara Psomas is the priority."

Chau flips the bird at the techno-tree.

"Everythin's gonna be fine," Tris says patting the tree trunk.

"What about the anomaly?" I ask.

Chau grumbles again.

Tris gives me his best 'shut the hell up' face. "*That* I don't know about," he says. "No idea on the source. We'll tread carefully. Especially moving into a new orbit around Europa."

"Fine," Chau says. "I'm gonna go see Boz. Talk her down off

the ceiling."

"I can talk to her." The offer is as empty as my voice sounds reverberating around the chamber.

"Actually, you need to get up to speed with Psomas as fast as possible, then work with the lead scientist on Europa," Chau says. "Character profile suggests he'll be a handful. Likely refuse to take the trip up into orbit. I need you to make him." He presses his lips together. "Get this shit done with, so we can get back to our job."

"Make him? I don't have special mind control powers," I say.

Chau doesn't laugh. "You're meant to evaluate the crew on Europa anyway. So ITN wants you to go down—"

"Whoa, whoa, whoa." I hold up a hand. "Go down? I do my evals via holo-link." Shrinks don't go off ship.

"You'll follow orders," Chau says. "This isn't a usual situation. You go down, shrink Nkosi's head, and bring him back."

"Do I have a choice?"

"Not if you want a paycheck when you get back to Earth, I bet," Tris says.

"Like she needs one," Chau says.

Asshole.

Our commander swims out—presumably to find Boz—leaving Tris and me alone with a humming tree.

Goddammit. I hate spacesuits and launches. Claustrophobic as hell. My chest tightens and breath quickens just thinking about it. This was meant to be a routine trip. No spacewalks, no surface missions. Of course, I've been through the schooling. But we are far from the days of astronauts needing to be near-military trained. Space tourism saw to that. The privatization of space travel, the economic need to drive civilians into low orbit, accelerated the necessary technology to lower the barriers for the average human. These days a bill of clean health and minimal zero-G training is enough—with the right disclaimers signed that is.

Go *down*. Sonofabitch.

There are all kinds of rumors about those temporary labs set up on the moons of Saturn and Jupiter. Shoddy construction, corners cut to save money. The academic world might be riding the coattails of the ITN, but scholars don't see an iota of the profit. Space travel is a business and an expensive one.

I'm sure something in my contract means I don't have a damn word to say about this. I'm going down to an inhospitable shithole to convince some other scientist to take over a case that could make my reputation. "This is such bullshit."

"Huh?" Tris says, hovering by the door.

"Nothing," I say.

I could call home, make this all go disappear. But what would Dad say? The thought rolls around in my head and sinks into my heavy heart. He'd say: *Why are you there, Sarah? Why did you leave?* There was a purpose to my coming. Dad supported me. It's funny how much you yearn to escape, only to miss things when you're gone. At least, I miss Dad. Mother not so much. Aunts, uncles. Family hangers-on and leaches can all go to hell.

A loud and profoundly teenage-sounding huff escapes my lips. "How long do I have?"

"Not long," Tris says. He checks his watch. "We have a window coming up to perform an Oberth maneuver and drop into the Hohmann transfer—"

I have zero idea what he's talking about and my expression must convey that well.

"Be ready in three hours," he says.

"I'll need to go see Kara, tell her to hold tight."

Tris nods.

"Who'll pilot the Descent and Ascent Rocket, the DAR? Please say you."

"Sorry, Dallas," he says. "Is what it is. Now quit dawdlin'."

He knows she and I don't get along. Never have. As a psychiatrist you learn that it's not people we dislike, but behaviors.

48

Someone who has very dominant behaviors will likely clash with someone who exhibits more easy-going traits. With my education, I should be able to put importance on Boz's comportments and value her for what she's good at. *Should* being the operative word. But I'm as human as the next person, and most of the time I just want to punch her lights out.

Tris gives me a smile that says I should get a damn move on. He's right, of course. A loaded sigh and I make my way back out onto Mainstreet and start for the medbay. Need to get at least one more session in with Psomas before this Nkosi gets his claws into her.

I stand in the corner of the tiny cubicle, trying to pee into a hose with a cup vaguely shaped to cover a vagina. Getting just the right distance to actually catch the urine without getting splashback all over my hands is an art form. Mother would be disgusted. More so to know I'll be drinking the water content of my urine in just a few hours. It's not often I agree with her, but I would kill for a glass of champagne instead.

A quick hand sanitization blast in the wall embedded unit, then I tie my hair back in a bun and stare at my reflection in the mirror. Mother's angular features, which have become sharp edges with age, stare back. Would have preferred to have Dad's warm, round face.

Time to go, Sarah.

I pull the band tighter around the mass of hair gathered atop my head and make straight for the medbay.

Halfway down Mainstreet, a repetitive noise emanates from the spoke leading to the medbay. I pull myself along, faster now, a pit forming in my gut. "What the hell is that?" At the bottom of the ladder leading up, the rhythmic sound becomes clearer.

Someone's playing music?

The closer I get, the rowdier the drums and guitars become, echoing off into the corridor. At the door it's unbearable. I step inside, hands over my ears. On the other side of the isolation glass, Kara has her back to me. Kara turns, eyes puffy and face wet with tears, which in this microgravity just pool around her eyes and cheeks.

Tris stands on my side of the glass, eyes closed in reverence, bobbing his head.

"Dona, turn off the music," I shout.

The music shuts off, leaving an audible vacuum.

"Hey, I was listenin' to that," Tris says.

"Kara, Kara, are you okay?" I press my palms to the glass.

The girl sniffs. "I don't remember the last time I heard music. Or at least, Earth music. Isn't it beautiful?"

"I wouldn't call it beautiful."

"Blasphemy," Tris says with a snort. "That was Vintage rock'n'roll right there. As close to a God as you're gonna get."

Sounded like a racket to me. "You shouldn't be in here, Tris."

He holds up his hands, a cheeky grin on his face. "Sorry, doc. The young'un here needed the company."

"That *young'un* is more than one hundred years old."

Tris frowns, casting his gaze to a puffy-eyed Kara and back to me. "Whatever you say, doc." He winks at Kara and fires his finger gun in her direction. "Later, Starlight."

"Bye," Kara says.

Tris squeezes past and pats me on the shoulder as he goes. Can't quite tell if that sheepish look on his face is for his behavior, or if he thinks I'm the boring schoolma'am who just ruined their fun.

I blink away whatever the hell just happened, and walk up to the glass barrier. "Starlight?"

"He was just trying to be nice," Kara says, wiping her face. "I didn't expect the music to have that kind of effect on me. My apologies." Her mature demeanor returns and she sits on the chair, hands in her lap.

"We can talk for a little while, but soon I need to go down to Europa and fetch the resident astrobiologist to see you."

Kara cocks her head. "Why does anyone need to see me? What's important is my getting out of here, not how my biology is faring."

"Well, Commander Chau doesn't see it that way, and neither does the ITN. They want a full work-up. And apparently, Dr. Kilkenny—and I—aren't good enough."

Kara stands, her gangly teenage frame barely casting a shadow, and approaches the glass, her face inches away from the transparent wall. "We don't have time for this," she says, tone low and menacing.

"You keep saying that. What do you mean?"

"My time will soon be done, and I need to complete my task. Before the Fulcrum, the Event."

"The Event?"

She nods. "Things set into motion, many eons ago. The consequence of the actions of the Six. There are key moments in the history and the future of our universe, Doctor. Fulcrum points." She stabs at the glass with her finger, marking out these unseen points in time. "Most happenings in the universe, choosing a cup of coffee or a cup of tea, do not affect the outcome of anything."

"You're suggesting fate," I say.

"In a way she says," then huffs on the glass to create a cloud of condensation. "But a few levers exist, brief and easily missed, that change the course of everything." She traces a line through the wetness from one point to another and then veers off in a different direction.

"And one of those levers is approaching?" I ask.

"Yes," Kara says.

"You need to let me out." Her face is now a little paler, and her eyes just a little wider. Whatever she believes is coming has her scared.

"I'm sorry, Kara. We can't do that right now."

Kara screams. Her fierce eyes fill with anger she'd so far buried. Is this the true face of Kara Psomas?

The onslaught continues. She makes aggressive sounds, strange tongue clicks, and lip smacks. Is that a language? Almost like Xhosa or Jul'hoan.

Kilkenny bursts into the medical bay like a cartoon character and freezes, eyes wild.

"What in da blue bloody hell is goin' on?" Kilkenny asks, already pawing at the main console readouts to check our guest's vitals.

"She just flipped out," I say.

"What d'ya say to her, ya buck eejit?"

"Only that I have to go to Europa." I edge back toward the door. "I'll be back soon. But she insists we're running out of time."

Kara bangs on the glass barrier again.

Kilkenny huffs. "Ach, howl yer whisht."

A press of a button and a pale blue gas fills Kara's side of the bay. It takes no more than three seconds for her to crumple into an unconscious heap.

"Did ya not t'ink to call me?" Kilkenny asks, their porcelain complexion cracked and creased in frustration.

"Sorry, it all happened a little suddenly." I already have one foot out the door.

Another shake of the doc's head, short blond tresses wafting under centripetal force. "She's out now. Dis is exactly why Chau wanted her in quarantine. Doesn't take a brain surgeon to figure dis one's banjaxed."

"Is that your professional opinion, Doctor?" I ask.

Kilkenny sniffs. "Shouldn't ya be headin' out now? Lemme deal wit' the upstart."

"Upstart?"

"I know a chiseler when I see one," Kilkenny says. "Bound to have hormones running amok in der."

That is entirely a possibility. If her body is that of a teenager, she could be a bundle of hormonal angst. As a kid, I took issue with everything and anything. Easy to be an ass when you're rich and have no real problems. Only when I got into clinical practice, and heard the terrible stories of those less fortunate, that I realized my issues were insignificant. Don't think I've ever apologized to Dad for giving him a hard time. In my profession, you're taught that everyone's pain is relative to them. It's not true. Dad buying me the wrong horse—because he didn't understand I wanted one like Mother's, so she'd be nice to me—is not the same as digging through the rubble of a warzone searching for the limbs of your child. It just isn't.

I stare at the sleeping Psomas, her small frame rising and falling with quick breaths. I should feel maternal, feel protective. A hole fills my chest where a heart should be.

But Kara's only a case, if maybe a special case. Distancing myself from patients is important, to be objective. Can't get involved.

Sounds like something Mother would say.

"Can we wake her up?" Can't run from this. "I need to talk to her again before I leave for Europa."

Kilkenny sighs. "Can ya not give her a few minutes? Maybe som'tin' to eat, too."

"Fine, but make it quick." I plonk myself in the chair near the glass barrier. "I've gotta go see this Nkosi guy."

I bet he's an absolute tool.

CHAPTER FIVE

Dr. Luan Nkosi

A hard bite on the valve and I take a sip of water from the tube protruding from inside my helmet. Four and a half hours of moonwalking and I'm thirsty as all hell. Moving around in these damn Extravehicular Mobility Units, tires you out. Despite Europa having only thirteen percent of Earth's gravity, it's difficult to walk because my skinny frame swims in this stupid EMU. Have to lift my knee six inches before my foot makes contact with the inner lining of my boot, to raise it off the icy crust of this moon. Throw in the weight of the hydrogenated boron nitride nanotube yarn—absorbing the cosmic radiation and the shitstorm of high-energy particles from Jupiter's magnetosphere—and I'm effectively carrying around another person on my back.

The ground shudders. Frozen pebbles skitter across the ground. Another ice shift. They're pretty common. When I first felt one, a year ago, I think I shit my absorbent pad. But now I'm used to them. It's just flexing caused by the elliptical orbit around Jupiter—the giant gassy asshole—which seems hell-bent on killing any human who comes close.

Besides, it's a water plume we're all more afraid of—a jet of liquid from an unknown crack in the surface, spurting one hundred and sixty kilometers into space. That would be a shitty way to die. It's why we placed New Uruk—our base of igloos, named after the first city on Earth—on a relatively stable area.

I look up, only to see the roof of my helmet, then pivot from the waist to be able to stare out of the gold-plated glass bubble. The shiny bauble on which I stand stretches out flat; only a few ridges a couple of meters high streak across the surface. Though huge cracks, three hundred meters in depth, also criss-cross Europa's ice crust. Still, this funny little moon, a quarter the size of Earth's rocky satellite, offers a spectacular view. Jupiter looks so near. Twenty-four times closer than our moon appears in the sky back home.

Red-brown bands wrap around the gas giant, and even the aurorae flash electric blue at its poles. It's the kind of view that Steven would call *totally gilded*. Like, 'ah man that view is totally gilded. The word just feels a little flat, and temporary. Next week it'll be 'bitchin' or 'sick' or 'stellar'. No, a view like this, hell the universe, needs a word that stands the test of time, like 'awesome'. Truly, breathtakingly, make-me-feel-tiny-and-insignificant awesome. It makes living here, one hundred and sixty degrees below and more than six hundred million kilometers away from either of my homes in South Africa or England, worth every second.

"Luan?" a voice asks over my radio. "Luan, are you there?"

"I'm here, I'm here, Steven," I say between labored breaths.

"You need to come back." Steven's voice is all squeaky.

"I'll be back, in a minute."

"You need to be here now," he says, his tone jumping an octave.

"Christ man, it was the tiniest shift in the ice." I roll my eyes. "No need to panic."

"It's not that—you got a message from the ITN freighter in orbit. The *Paralus*."

A freighter? I've been burned by a practical joke or two before. The crews of the helium transports need a little levity. We all do, so I let these things slide. Still, something in Steven's voice says it isn't a joke this time. "I'll be right there."

By *right there*, of course, I mean twenty minutes for a walk less than a few hundred meters. I clip the compact toolbox onto my EMU to free my hands, and then I bounce like a newly-walking toddler across the ice. Can't slip and end up on my back like a tortoise. It's not becoming of the first South African-born man to travel past Mars. Sometimes it seems like my every move—every fart—is recorded by someone with an eye on my performance out here. Are African-born men too flatulent for long-haul space travel?

My strides become longer and more confident the closer I get to the command igloo airlock. Twenty meters to go. It's a good thing too because a quick check of my oxygen gauge shows it's pretty low. Much more exertion and it's all used up.

I glance at my wrist mirror, and the vast sprawling reflective surface of Europa opens up behind. But I take my eye off the prize for too long. The teeth in the sole of my boot fail to ensure a good grip and slip out from underneath. I tumble forward. The low gravity just makes the whole ordeal take too long, drawing out the embarrassment. The body cam will record all of this. I crash, arms out, into the hard ice and knock the air from my lungs. The hardened glass of my helmet hovers just a centimeter above the frozen surface.

No cracks that I can see.

"Luan, you okay?" Steven yells in my ear.

"I'm fine." I crawl up onto my hands and knees, then eventually to my feet. I look up at Jupiter, looming in the sky. "Find that funny?"

"What?"

"I'm almost at the airlock, come get me," I say.

A short and much more cautious walk later and I'm inside the main airlock of the command igloo. Steven and Boris are already here to help me out of the EMU. There's no privacy out here. No room to be coy. We've all seen each other's junk. Helped each other in and out of our EMUs, and experienced that pungent waft of sweat and urine from our coworkers' absorbent pads.

"What's the emergency?" I ask as soon as Boris pops my helmet off.

Steven is jittery, eyes wide. "A freighter found a woman," he blurts out.

"What do you mean?"

"Orbiting Jupiter. In an escape pod."

"From an SEC freighter? I didn't know they lost—"

Boris signs with his hands. After an almost imperceptible delay between his specialized gloves and the processor in his suit a poor excuse for a human voice rattles from the speaker on his collar. "From *Proxima* mission." Somehow even his computer-generated voice has a Russian accent. He heaves off one of the articulated arms of my EMU.

"Does the name Psomas ring a bell?" Steven says, then uncouples the torso unit of my EMU and pulls it over my head with a grunt.

Kara Psomas. *Proxima* mission went bad. "Shit, did they find her corpse?"

Steven shakes his head.

"She is alive," Boris adds.

I snort. "She'd be like two hundred years old."

"You'd think. But the story gets weirder, man," Steven says rubbing at his cropped ginger mop. "She looks like she's fifteen."

A slew of derisive comments catches in my throat.

"They need you to check her out," Steven blurts out. "They have a psychologist, or psychiatrist, or psycho-something on board—Dallas—who says Psomas is whacked out of her gourd. And a triage physician, Kilkenny. The ITN want you to look at her."

I look to Boris for confirmation. He simply nods. My chief engineer never says much. Maybe signing all the time is exhausting. What I have learned over the years is that a nod from him is worth a thousand-page essay.

"Where's Lisa?" I ask.

"She is manning the undersea ROV," Boris says, hands a blur.

"I don't want our whole team pulled for this circus. Tell the ITN we'll do what we can without compromising our mission and crew."

Boris nods again.

The ITN doles out orders, but on this little rock, they can do little to affect anything. We don't even have AI here. Our base, our choices. "So, are they sending me data? From the freighter, I mean?"

"No," Steven says, "the freighter commander, Chau, he wants you to go up."

I'm not a trained dog. "We're not wasting time on a launch so I can go babysit some spacewoman. Their physician can take blood and tissue and send me some results. Hell, they can send samples down in a payload for us to pick up. We're owed some supplies anyway."

"Good idea," Boris says, gloved fingers flying.

"Let me get dressed, do some exercise. I'll be down in the ROVCC Command Center when you need me. Tell the *Paralus* to send the samples."

"Will do," Steven says.

One thirty-minute stationary bike ride and a fresh flight suit later and I meander down Connection Corridor A from the habitat igloo to the ROV Command Center. My legs are sore as all hell. I hate stationary cycling. So boring and frustrating to peddle your ass off and go nowhere. I'd rather wind through the streets of Pretoria, or maybe London's Canary Wharf with Earth's sun on my back. I heard a rumor that the new crews coming out here get to use gene modifying tech, like CRISPR, to ensure better adaptation without exercise. *Gened shots*, I think they're called. Didn't get that option back then. For me, workouts are necessary if I don't want my muscles to atrophy and my bones to break. Already look like a grasshopper, no need to help my genetics along with the caricature.

I pass two pressurized doors at the juncture of CCA and the ROVCC. The whole place has been set up so that, like a starfish, we can cut off a damaged limb and keep functioning. Efficient, if not terrifying. New Uruk is powered by the same nuclear fusion reactor type used on Earth, though smaller in scale. The large power output means we can generate a localized magnetic field to protect from radiation, but that doesn't do squat against a rock hurtling through space at a million kilometers per second. A coin-sized pebble would punch a hole through the out layer of an igloo, and then it's sayonara! Of course, we rely on early detection systems to warn of such things. Nothing like the daily worry of losing all your oxygen to space through a tiny hole to get the adrenaline going.

The door to the ROVCC hisses open. There're so many instruments in here, all dedicated to either piloting the undersea ROV or recording everything down to the chemical composition of the water on a picomolar level.

Lisa Britt sits in the pilot's seat, full VR headset on, totally immersed. "Hey, Nkosi," she says without breaking her concentration. Somehow, she always knows when someone's in the room.

"How'd you know it was me?" I ask. Probably her military training. Most of us here are astrobiologists or physicists. Lisa was in the air force before becoming an astronaut. One hundred percent badass. She can pilot the ROV like no one I've ever seen.

"Aftershave," she says. "You're the only one who uses any."

"*Eau du toilette*, actually. Didn't have any special food items I wanted to bring, and there's no excuse for smelling bad."

"Whatever floats your boat," she replies, tilting the joysticks to the left.

The image onscreen mirrors what Lisa sees in the headset. It's not much. Kind of like deep-sea exploration on Earth—pitch black, save the meager light provided by the ROV. We use sonar to guide the ROV through the vast ocean under the ice sheet, which itself is nearly twenty kilometers thick. Took two different crews to drill through it before we could drop an ROV in. Of course, drilling tech has improved since then.

"It's like swimming through tar," Lisa pipes up.

"Did you hit another thermocline?"

"Yeah," she says. "Heat from the core causing differentiated layers of temperature pretty evenly through the ocean, and pockets of elevated temperature right below chaos zones."

It's a bitch when we hit one. Throws of navigation, and sonar.

"Need to adjust for viscosity, salinity," Lisa says. "You know the drill."

Areas of Europa's icy crust have broken off, moved, then refrozen in place. Physicists predicted volcanic activity from the rocky core might cause heat plumes to rise and melt the ice. No one knew for sure until our ROV confirmed it. Of course, convection like this, and the exchange of surface ice with warmer oceanic water, could mean life. So far, not so much as a single bacterial cell has shown up.

Lisa kicks the ROV into neutral and lets it hang suspended in the cold slush. The viscosity of the ocean and the slow-moving currents mean it isn't going anywhere fast. She pops off her headgear, scratches at her crew-cut black hair, and rubs her tired but still very blue eyes.

"Heard about the spacewoman," Lisa says, swiveling the seat.

"Yeah." I roll my eyes. "Freighter grunts need some drama, I guess."

"Going up?"

"Hell no. We're busy."

"Truth," Lisa says, bobbing her head. "Still, where'd this chick come from? A fifteen-year-old kid—out here?"

"I know. Claims to be Kara Psomas, you know, from the *Proxima* mission."

"Academy 101 of how not to enter Jupiter's orbit."

Indeed.

"They do a genetic analysis?" Lisa asks.

I lean against a console, careful not to press a switch with my ass. "The report they sent over says it's her. Gotta be a cock-up, though. I'll run the system myself and we'll see."

"Fair enough. Hey, what's on the menu for tonight? I'm star—"

Alarms scream and red lights flash overhead.

"Meteor shower?" I leap to my feet and scan the readouts.

"No." Lisa crams the VR unit onto her head again. "Thermoplume."

"What? You're not under a chaos zone."

"Tell that to Europa," Lisa says, grabbing the joysticks.

Onscreen, the ROV tumbles and twists like leaves in a tornado. The light flails, shining out into the dark, but the camera only shows the blur of thick, icy ocean. My stomach roils just watching the undersea rollercoaster ride. It takes a full five minutes for Lisa to regain control, but eventually the ROV stops spinning and settles back down.

The warning lights continue to flash and the wailing alarm blares on.

"Can we shut that off?" I say.

"Sure," Lisa says, and flicks a switch.

The siren halts.

"Damn." I swallow away the pain in my ears. "Is the ROV

okay?"

Lisa slumps back into the chair. "Lost the left stabilizing rotor, and sonar is offline. Can't even bring it home."

That's bad news. We only have two of these ridiculously expensive ROVs. "Where is it now? Still in the search grid?"

She shakes her head. "That was a big one, blew the ROV off the reservation, about ten kilometers north-northwest off the search grid perimeter. Into an active chaos zone." She pulls off her headset. "Right under Drill Site Beta."

"Crap." I chew my lip and stare at the screen. We could just deploy the other one, though protocol allows for that only if the first is destroyed. Need to try to salvage it if possible. Still, Drill Site Beta? Bad news. That's where we lost the first crew.

"Hey, what's that?" Lisa says.

I look up to the screen. "Hmm?"

The ROV floats free, rotating about its axis. A cone of light shines out onto an underwater block of ice. We've seen these throughout Europa. The ocean isn't just a vast liquid body, but more a slush of water and warmer ice. Huge undersea glaciers slide along like frozen leviathans, usually big and slow enough that we can avoid running into them.

"See that shadow?" Lisa says, her finger smearing the screen glass. "In the glacier."

"Maybe something taken from the surface," I say, "and frozen inside. Dragged underneath." The tectonics of Europa constantly remodel and regenerate the surface. The whole moon is less than two hundred million years old. Cosmically speaking, incredibly young.

"Like no berg I've seen on Europa," Lisa says. "There's definitely something inside it."

She's not wrong, but it's hard to make out, and we only get a glimpse once per rotation of the ROV.

"You know, the ice at chaos zones is much thinner," Lisa says, rubbing her head. "Drill through there and take a look."

Hell no. "We don't do that *precisely because* it's unstable. I don't like the idea of being blasted into orbit by a high-pressure jet screaming through a crack in the ice."

"Maybe," Lisa says, pulling at her earlobe. "But, Nkosi, does that look … like an *eye* … to you?"

I study the shadow again as the ROV makes another revolution. The light illuminates the ice, making it glisten. Inside, a darker object, huge, fills most of the submerged iceberg.

And as Lisa says, there's a lighter, spherical shape embedded within the larger shadow.

"What the hell *is* that?"

I lean in closer.

CHAPTER SIX

Kara Psomas

D allas sits, one leg balanced on the knee of the other, on the other side of the glass barrier. Her delicate figure somehow engenders her flight suit with elegance. Indeed, while others lumber around this monstrosity of a freighter in manufactured gravity, the doctor does exude a certain grace. She places a recording device on the table, sticking it there with Velcro, and pulls the tablet to her lap to jot notes. A century after my time and the old technology still works best. Space was never forgiving for humans or their inventions. The more complicated something is, the easier it is for the universe to take apart. That's how Gaia had planned it for humans, possibly the only one of the Six with sense—though it didn't stop humanity, or save her. She traveled the cosmos with wizened importance, using her unseen influence to chivy life along. Over the millennia, it seems she grew into an almost maternal role for humanity, guiding us to the answers we seek—yet allowing us to make mistakes.

And make mistakes we did. As did she, and her brethren.

You dwell too much, Kara. Focus and get out.

Another bite of vacuum-packed thermoregulated Italian sausage skewered on the end of a spork. It's one of the crew's bonus food items, carried at great expense here to Jupiter. Dallas clearly read my file—as have I—and took note that my favored chow was also sausage. Though, according to the records, I preferred Greek. As I savor the slightly overpowering spices, old memories flood back. The eternity in the void began with hunger. In hindsight it was psychosomatic. My body no more needed food in that place than I needed air to breathe. Still, even the sensation of starvation is crippling.

Dallas coughs into her fist, indicating her desire to continue.

I take another bite of the sausage. The warm feeling in my belly helps drag me from the fog in my head. Can't let Kilkenny render me unconscious. Need to remain calm, at least on the outside.

"So, the beginning?" Dallas presses.

"And if I tell you, you let me out?" The sausage hovers at my lips.

She nods and holds the tablet ready.

"Fine, the beginning." I bite off a little of my treat. "Not the point at which I ceased to be part of humanity's narrative more than a century ago, but billions of years ago, before our universe existed," I say through the bolus of meat.

"Oh-kay," Dallas says, enunciating the break in the syllables, to emphasize curiosity, or maybe skepticism. "You mean the Big Bang? The nothing before that?"

"To begin, you must realign your understanding of nothing." I wave the sausage-spork around my head.

"I understand nothing?"

Probably. "I mean your understanding of the term *nothing*. For most, it is the absence of something. You have an apple, or you do not. The apple weighs something, but so does the space—the absence of that apple."

"I'm not sure I follow," Dallas replies, her brow furrowed and fingers tight around her tablet like a comforter.

"Many years ago, even before my days of interplanetary travel, astrophysicists strived to weigh the universe to understand the velocity at which it expanded." I stretch out these young arms to indicate the vastness of space. "By measuring the gravitational well caused by clusters of galaxies—how much those clusters bent the space-time continuum—they could determine the mass of those clusters."

Dallas uses a stylus to scribble on her device. "And what did they find, Kara?"

"That galaxies only accounted for thirty percent of the energy required for the rate at which the universe expanded. It was not enough to overcome the gravitational forces that bound it together, and allow it to expand."

"And the other seventy percent?"

"Space itself, the nothing in between planets and dust and radiation, has energy. Yet no one could decide what that energy was, or how it came to be."

"What does this have to do with your story?"

"I can tell you," I say. "What that energy is."

Dallas raises her eyebrows.

"Consciousness." I take a big satisfying bite of my sausage.

The doctor wrinkles up her nose and pushes back a lock of hair that's escaped from her ponytail.

I swallow and clear my throat. "The nothing, as you and most people see it, is consciousness."

Dallas leans back in her chair, her face rigid, radiating yet more skepticism. I'm sure to a psychiatrist, the notion that something non-biological could have consciousness seems absurd.

"I lived in it, felt it, bathed in it. A fetus floating in the womb of the universe." I scan the room behind her. Only one door in or out. Straight into a spoke, I imagine. A ladder. There will be no sneaking out. In my current condition, could I take her hostage?

"You're referring to the void," Dallas asks.

"Huh?"

"The nothing is consciousness," Dallas repeats, tapping at the screen in her lap.

"Yes, yes, where I awoke."

"You floated in the void, the thing before the universe." She waves the stylus around as if I don't understand what the universe is.

"Yes."

"And what was that like?" she asks, stylus poised.

"Lonely. Cold. Terrifying. Hard to put into words." I wave my spork at her. "You will not have experienced darkness as I have. In the gloom of an unlit bedroom, your eyes absorb a stray photon or two, your ears create strange noises. In the void before all things, not a single particle existed. Yet, even nothing weighs *something*, and it's oppressive. I gave it a name. The *Apeiron*. There I floated. Weightless, alone."

I take one more bite, leaving the last morsel of treat clinging to the plastic prongs of my spork. It's a little cold now, and less delicious. The meat sticks in my throat as I swallow it down.

She scribbles a note. "How long did you float there?"

"Time does not exist in the void, in the Apeiron. Time is a construct of our current universe," I say. I didn't comprehend how difficult it would be to explain such a phenomenon. With each explanation, new questions arise. It becomes ever clearer why Gaia immersed me so.

"So, you floated out of time in the void in the … Apeiron. You didn't need to eat, or sleep … or breathe?"

Her tone is smug and annoying.

"It's difficult to say if I were truly there," I say. "Just as a dream, or a nightmare, can seem terrifyingly real, so did my incarceration in the void. Gaia provided me the experience of being there."

"Was it a punishment?" Dallas asks. "Conceivably for the death of your crew?"

In a way it was, I suppose. Existing in that place for what seemed in my mind forever was a sentence. "When I opened my eyes, I saw, heard, and felt nothing," I say. "Total sensory deprivation. At first, I cried out in panic, but no sound came. Why would it? My heart beat hard in my chest, my lungs would not fill with air—though I did not need it. I sobbed silently on the inside. Wept for the death of my crew at first, and then for myself. For the pain of hunger in my belly that could not be satiated, and an itch in my throat that could not be quenched. Imagine, being in that dark, frozen, alone, starving for as long as you could remember. Until those memories you once had are so vague that you question if they were real at all. Until you have only yourself to talk to, around and around, and endless, meaningless jabbering in your head."

Dallas raises an eyebrow and continues to take notes on her electronic pad.

"Of course, to you, it might appear as if I describe falling into madness, and despair."

"Is that what you think, Kara?"

"No."

"And why is that?"

"Because such purgatory was necessary, to ensure I stopped listening to myself and my mind and started listening to the void." I put the last of the sausage, now cold, chew it quickly, and swallow. The salty flavor lingers in my mouth.

"You said there was nothing in the void?" Dallas presses.

"I also told you nothing is something, and it has its own energy," I say jabbing the empty spork at her.

"Explain it to me," she says, her stylus scratching away at the tablet screen.

An irritated huff escapes my lips. This chair is uncomfortable beneath my thin legs. "Quantum physics tells us that in space, virtual particles pop in and out of existence all the time, at a rate too quick to observe." I stand and begin pacing—and to search. There must be a flaw in this cage. I tap the glass barrier with my spork and crane my neck. There's a slot in the ceiling into which the barrier disappears.

"I'll take your word for that," Dallas says.

My head snaps back down. "What if I told you those particles had innate consciousness?"

"Ah yes," she flicks back to earlier in our conversation. "You said the energy of nothing was sentient. How do you explain that? You and I are cognizant, but a rock or tree—let alone *nothing*—surely cannot be. I think therefore I am, as it were."

How arrogantly human, to believe that only we, and perhaps the other animals of Earth, have consciousness. A narrow and self-serving point of view, giving humanity a greatly inflated sense of importance. "How would you define consciousness, Dr. Dallas?"

She considers my question for a moment, chewing on the end of her stylus. "Consciousness is everything you experience," she says finally. "The tune stuck in your head, the bitterness of a lemon, the love for your child."

"Go on." I peer past her to the main console alive with lights and pulsing lines that report on my vitals. Something out there can't help me in here.

"Most scholars believe the sights, sounds, and other sensations of life as we experience it are generated by regions within the posterior cortex," Dallas says. "As far as we can tell, almost all conscious experiences have their origin there—"

"You go too far." I cress cross my spork on the glass. "Your first answer is much closer to the truth."

Dallas purses her lips. "Experience?"

"Human experience culminates in consciousness, but is that not merely the experience of the atoms of which we are made?" I turn away from the glass barrier and study the interior for an opening or a panel that might allow some fiddling to open up this tiny prison. There's nothing. To get out of here, she has to let me. "Biology and physics only show us the behavior of matter, not of what it is made. You say humans are conscious, but you can no more crack open my skull and point out my consciousness than you can split an atom and do the same."

"So elementary particles experience ... things ... and, therefore, are conscious," Dallas says, the tablet now limp in her hand.

I turn back to face her. "In simple terms, yes. And after, well, after my ordeal floating in the void out of space and time, I began to feel that consciousness."

Dallas cocks her head. "It *spoke* to you?"

A maniacal laugh unintentionally erupts from my belly and descends into a strange girlish giggle, appropriate to this young body. I place a hand over my mouth and compose myself. "No, it did not *speak* to me. Do you think the consciousness speaks English?"

Her face reddens, though I can't tell if that's embarrassment or annoyance. She shifts that lock of hair again.

"Imagine it like this," I say. "You *feel* when someone is in a room, even if you do not see them. You know if someone watches you, even from behind. This is the only way I can explain it."

"I see," she says, then climbs to her feet.

She doesn't see.

"I need coffee," Dallas announces. "How about you?" She stomps over to her bench near the examination table of the medical bay and pulls two packets from a drawer. She places the cartons into a small cavity in the wall, closes a door, then punches a few keys. I assume it's some kind of microwave oven. Seconds later it pings and she removes the items. She places one in the two-door hatch embedded in the transparent wall between us. My feeding hole.

She closes her door. Not even a chance to grab her wrist,

70

dammit.

I open my side of the hatch. There's a slight *whoosh* of positive pressure. I toss my spork behind me without looking then take the packet, unscrew the tip, and sip the liquid. It burns my lips and throat, the bitterness initially offensive. But after that first acrid hit, the smoother tones dance on my tongue and the warmth of the liquid radiates out from my insides. I shut the tiny door.

"You felt the consciousness," Dallas says, and takes her seat.

"All around me," I say. "Gathering and growing like a storm. And while it did not speak to me, I understood it and it understood me. I could not tell you how long it took for that squall of consciousness to form, as time did not exist. But eventually, it formed, and then … pop."

"Pop?" She says, irritation growing in her voice. "You're talking about the Big Bang?"

"Yes." I sip my coffee again. "Though it did seem more like a pop than a bang."

Dallas's mouth opens, but no words come. She scribbles furiously, then glances up. "So you believe the void's consciousness—virtual particles gaining experience—caused the universe to be born. It grew and grew until it … popped?"

Believe? Heat rises in my chest again. This is a waste of time. I just need to get out. I need to get to the payload. Need to be there for the Fulcrum.

"And then what?" Dallas asks, her tone dripping in condescendence.

"Well, isn't obvious?" I snap back. "Now the consciousness was free, wasn't it? And it was curious but unstructured. Fanning out with the early universe in a hot soup of atoms—too energized to bond and form matter. I gave this newer consciousness a name: Chaos, since I could see no organization to anything."

The young doctor eyes me again. "And you, floating there in this hot soup—unaffected, I might add—observed this?"

"Yes."

"Were you swimming, or flapping? Prostrate?"

Is she making fun of me? She best hope not, or I'll break that pretty nose of hers. "More fetal," I say through gnashed teeth. "Cocooned in an invisible womb. Peering out to witness ... everything."

Dallas writes one word and underlines it. "Please, go on."

"Now, with the universe formed, time came into existence and within a fraction of a second, the universe expanded," I say, careful not to squeeze the pouch in my hand too hard and launch hot coffee all over my arm. "Scholars will tell you that milliseconds after the beginning of time, the universe was unimaginably hot, trillions of degrees Celsius. In this soup, quarks and gluons came to be. A few thousandths of a second later the universe expanded and cooled enough for those elemental particles to come together and form protons and neutrons." I take a breath and suck on the nipple of the pouch. "And finally, the first atoms—deuterium, and then helium and lithium. Then for nearly four hundred thousand years, astronomers tell us that nothing happened."

"And is that correct?" Dallas asks, and takes a slurp of her beverage.

"Well, I cannot give you a time frame," I say. Does she think I had a damn quantum stopwatch with me? "The single second expanded beyond my ability to comprehend it."

"But you *experienced* this?" she presses, her voice raised.

"How many times do you want to ask that question, Doctor?"

"I'm sorry," she says, "but this is fascinating if true."

"If true? If you don't believe me, then ..." My heart pounds in my chest. Waste of fucking time. "Then just let me go."

"I just want to understand," Dallas says, serenity returning to her voice. The soft placating sound learned by all shrinks. "What was it like to experience ... the Big Bang? Like a huge explosion beyond imagining ...?"

"Do they not teach physics anymore?" I spit back. "Early photons had nowhere to go in this dense soup, did they? So light as we know it didn't occur until much later. The Era of Recombination, if you want to get technical."

"I see."

"No, you don't."

"You're right, I don't," Dallas says, then focuses on her tablet again. "But let's get back to the consciousness. How does Chaos fit in?"

"I thought you were meant to be a psychiatrist. Let me ask you, Doctor, what does a child do if you give it clay?"

Dallas squints in thought. "It plays with it. Pulls it and twists it. Maybe into smaller parts?"

"Exactly. The consciousness—which *was* Chaos—dominated the matter that had formed and could ... manipulate it ... if you will. Push and pull upon it. Not in a coherent way, but probing, and trying to understand."

"And what did Chaos do with it?" Dallas asks, taking a polite mouthful of her coffee.

"Pushed and pulled for a long time. Why do you think nothing happened for hundreds of thousands of years? Chaos toyed with the matter like an infant until eventually assembling the first bodies in the universe, some thirteen billion years ago. The first stars and planets."

"You talk like the consciousness—Chaos—is a god."

Finally, a spark of comprehension.

Dallas studies my smile. "You are... you're telling me God exists."

"Not as the Bible or the Quran might explain it," I say. "After all, those tomes are human interpretations of information the authors received from the Six, but couldn't possibly understand. Not to mention the horrific twisting of the knowledge for personal gain."

"Let me get this straight," Dallas says, sucking out the last of her drink from the pouch. "God—Chaos, as you call the deity—formed the Earth, but instead of seven days, it took nearly half a million years?"

It's difficult not to sigh again. She was doing so well. Should I bother getting to the Fulcrum if this is all humanity has to offer? I slump back into the uncomfortable chair. "I said the first planets were formed. Earth, our planet, came much later. And it wasn't Chaos who formed Earth, but Gaia."

She checks her notes. "Yes, you mentioned Gaia earlier. And Nyx, who—"

"Am I telling the story or not?" I stand up again, my whole body itchy beneath my skin. Got to get out.

She concedes with a nod.

"Disregard human interpretation of such things, Doctor." I pace back and forth in front of the glass barrier. "Seven days is arbitrary. Chaos—and those who came after—pushed and pulled on the universe on a cosmic scale, over millions and billions of years. Chaos willed the first bodies in the universe into existence and played with matter."

Dallas scribbles some notes, and without looking up says, "the consciousness, Chaos, was spread thin. Throughout the universe."

"Indeed, Chaos sprawled everywhere, feeling, pushing, comprehending." My pace quickens. "And as atoms formed, Chaos gained experience, and became more aware."

"So, what then?" Dallas asks.

I stop in my tracks. "Maybe I could wander outside of this cage at least? You know my bones and muscles will deteriorate without exercise." And then I could make it to the door, and Chau's secret.

Dallas's eyes widen, and then narrow back into a look of skepticism. "I'll have Tris bring an exercise bike in there," she says, "until we can release you."

It's not exactly what I want, but if someone carries in

something of that size, it's an opportunity. A possibility of escape.

"Fine. What do you know about octopuses?" I ask.

"Octopi?" she says, and stammers, face scrunched up.

Dallas focuses on minutiae, to demonstrate the intellectual prowess that she greatly overestimates. She must see the bigger picture—the vast, sprawling, interconnected everything. "Both are fine, but not the point, Doctor."

"Go on then, *octopuses*." She gives an irritated wave of the hand.

I can only really explain it to her with this crude comparison. Perhaps for a psychiatrist, and a supposed expert on the brain and neurology, it will paint a picture in her empty head. "Octopuses," I continue, "have a central brain, but their limbs have a vast array of neurons so they operate almost autonomously, correct?"

Dallas nods. "A little like the limbic system of humans, I guess—signals that never reach our brain but are mediated by the spine—"

I hold up a hand. "Exactly. The limb can experience something on its own, and act accordingly. Now imagine Chaos spread out through the universe. Each part of this universe would hold different experiences from the others. New experiences would give rise to ..." I trail off, hoping she'll make the leap on her own.

"More consciousnesses?" she offers.

"Good, Doctor. A total of five other consciousnesses, actually." I suck the last of my coffee out of the packet and toss it aside.

"The Six," Dallas says, watching my garbage settle in on the floor. She gives a huff then scrolls her notes, the screen light rolling over her delicate features and making her blue eyes look green.

"The Six," I confirm.

"Chaos, Gaia, Nyx, and...?"

"Erebus, Eros, and Tartarus," I rattle off. "Of course, they did not have names. Their consciousness pressed down on me and fed my imagination. I labeled them to help my feeble brain comprehend."

"You occasionally give the Six genders—also your own making?"

I nod. "Just how they made me feel. Chaos was always neutral to me—never a gender. Nyx and Gaia felt female—the way they molded the universe within their purview. Erebus, Eros, and Tartarus bullied and pushed each other and the very matter of the universe. To my mind, those three were very much male. Bull-headed."

Dallas's brow furrows, and she jots down another note. "How did they look to you, in your head?"

It's an interesting question. When someone reads a book they may form a mental image of a character. But the Six's connection to me was as real. I knew them as I once knew my own family. "Yes," I say.

"Can you describe them?" she asks.

"That's quite difficult. Their forms—either given to me or made up in my mind—are quite unlike anything humans have seen. Chaos is particularly difficult."

"How so?"

I spread my hands wide. "Chaos was everywhere and nowhere. The original consciousness. Constant and oppressive, with no distinct form. Imagine looking at a cloud and seeing the shape of a horse or bird, and then it shifts and is gone. Just like that, I would look out at a dense purple nebula and see eyes staring back at me, or observe a passing comet with its long tail of ice shaped like thin lips curled into a smile. Passing, fleeting, never in the same place twice."

"I see," she says, scribbling more. "And the rest?"

"We will get to each of the Six in good time, Doctor. Maybe when you've let me out."

Breadcrumbs, my idiotic friend. Breadcrumbs.

"Hmm. Okay, but why six?" she asks without looking up. "Six consciousnesses? Surely there were more... experiences in the universe?"

Why is such a human question, suggesting the motives, usually of humans, behind something to be of importance. *How* is the better question. How did six consciousnesses arise? In a relatively uniform universe, there would be few experiences that differed enough to drive the formation of individual sentient forms. In this case, it would seem there were five pockets of experience in the cosmos different enough to splinter Chaos into new consciousnesses. But, this deviates from what I need Dallas to hear.

"I truly don't know for sure," I say. "Six, seven eight. The number is unimportant when compared with what they did, what they accomplished."

Dallas pushes away that annoying lock of hair again.

"The creation of worlds—worlds with life."

"Like Adam and Eve?" she asks.

"Are you stupid or something?" I snap at her. "I have explained everything in terms of modern science. The existence of Gods does not negate the laws of physics. Life began as life does—simply and gradually."

Dallas recoils back into her seat. "But you're still talking about intelligent design."

"Yes, but the Six were child-like. They forged no grand plan. They just *did*."

"I see." Dallas scribbles again.

"Life itself is no miracle," I say turning away from the glass barrier. The annoying blue medical gown rustles. "Its existence is no more surprising than gravity. The second law of thermodynamics states that a closed system such as the universe tends to grow more chaotic over time, leading to entropic equilibrium."

Dallas stares at me, eyes devoid of comprehension.

When did space travel stop requiring basic physics to qualify? "In systems with an external influence, such as the sun beating down on the Earth, energy imbalances can be so complex that atoms rearrange themselves into architectures that will survive the disorder." I return to the glass barrier, huff on it, and sketch out a sun with little energy lines leading to a crude outline of simple molecules. "Biological life is simply a specific structure that allows atoms to handle energetic imbalances."

Another nod from Dallas with little comprehension, her red hair flouncing.

"Just trust me," I say. "The important piece is—what if a consciousness only had to nudge the way that the atoms arrange themselves? Pushing, coaxing atoms into ever more complex and efficient energy handlers. You get...?"

"Evolution?" Dallas says.

"Evolution," I repeat. "It can occur on its own, sure, due to the nature of biological systems finding new ways to survive energetic imbalances—like a change in food supply leading to the development of a new beak for a bird—but with the subtle push and pull of the Six, evolution can also be guided."

Dallas slumps back in her chair. I have no idea if I have explained it well enough—melding thousands of years of religious doctrine with science—but I feel she has some comprehension. Gods and science are one. Always were.

"I... I'm not sure," Dallas stutters.

Boz's voice comes over the intercom. "Dr. Dallas, please report to the docking bay."

"I'm sorry, I told you I need to go," Dallas says, rising from her chair. She heads for the door, clutching the tablet to her chest.

"That wasn't part of the deal, Dallas. I tell you things, you let me out."

"It's not my decision." She looks back at me, her eyes a little wider than when she entered the room. "I'll get you out, I promise. Just keep talking to us. Help us understand."

Dallas leaves without another word and the heat in my chest

bursts. I slam a fist against the glass, and my skin splits open, leaving a bloody smear. I study the wound in my papyrus-like epidermis, mottled and flaky. Another wave of anguish radiates out from my gut and into my limbs.

Bursts of light stab into my brain, searing images into my consciousness. Oh, no, please. A creature emerges from the gloom behind my eyes. Four bat-like wings reach out from a sinewy body that ends with a veil of thin tissue, floating and folding like the tail of a Siamese fighting fish. The chimeric demon breaches the darkness of space-time—an insect from a cocoon. Even without eye sockets, her skeletal head bores a hateful stare.

I curl into a ball, holding my stomach.

It's Nyx. She's here. She found me.

CHAPTER SEVEN

Commander Feng Chau

Is the damn heating not working? My joints ache and hum, a constant reminder of advancing age and a life lived in space—poor gravity and no sunlight wreak havoc on human bones, causing them to dissolve. Mid-fifties now, with little to show for my existence other than toiling for rich people. I should be grateful to have seen the stars up close. Grandfather would certainly think so. Yet from within this metallic monstrosity, I am no closer to touching them than when I was a boy sat on my parents' porch.

"Dona, check the climate controls on board."

"Climate is nominal," Dona replies.

"Could have fooled me." I rub my palms together then breathe into them for warmth.

I shuffle back into the hard, unwelcoming command chair. Here on the Bridge, surveying the solar system through the great glass viewfinder is akin to standing on the bow of a ship at the very vanguard of war—thrust into the jaws of unforeseen maelstroms or wrecked upon jagged rocks. Exhilarating and terrifying, and the reason I became a freighter commander. *The universe is but a great ocean*, Grandfather once told me. *A sailor is a sailor whether he dons a spacesuit or not.*

Some sailors are also pirates.

Sat here, rubbing away the dull ache in my knuckles, my gaze is fixed on Europa looming large in the window. The moon's icy surface is striated with deep red crevices. A foreboding sight, which spreads the cold from my fingers into my chest. I've been out here several times, but this time feels different. Colder, maybe. I guess it should.

A few taps of the glass console embedded in the arm of the chair and a new rectangular screen appears in the corner of the viewfinder, partly obscuring Europa. Files on the original *Proxima* mission sent by the ITN.

Most of the files are mission logs. Written accounts of the primary goals of *Proxima*. According to this, it was to drop the first aerostats into Jupiter's atmosphere. They never got to do it. Something went wrong. Logs say trajectory was off, just like when we came out of stasis and tried to drop into an orbit.

Proxima wasn't so lucky. Medic Tracey Willis, engineer Henry Catlin, and a physicist, Roman Malcsvoi, all died. And of course, so did Kara Psomas. Or so we thought.

I run a search for *clone*, and all associated synonyms … *twin*, *replica*, *emulate*. Nothing comes up. Given their mission, a clone on board seems unlikely. But not impossible. The ITN are underhanded. Who knows what shit those sneaky bastards were up to.

Another search, this time of personal logs. There aren't many. The crew came out of stasis only as they came upon Jupiter. Clearly, the ITN realized the mistake, and so that's why all vessels come out much earlier now.

A quick skim of the scant files.

Nothing.

Nothing.

Then, one stands out.

The last one: *Emergency Pod Record 1.0—Cpt. K. Psomas. 0:32 seconds.*

I tap the keypad and a video plays.

Kara Psomas, how we all know her from history books—greying hair tied back in a ponytail, dark and wistful eyes adorned with wizened crow's feet—fills the window. The camera angle looks inside her upturned nose and under lights her cheeks, now damp with tears.

"I failed," she says, breathing labored. "The pods, my friends … Jupiter, it wasn't where … I mean … Jupiter took them. They burned. They all burned. I swear I could hear them scream. Just screaming, across space. Now it'll take me. I die a failure." The woman suddenly looks off-camera, the color draining from her skin. Her reddened eyes widen and her mouth opens to say something.

The video stops and causes Psomas's image to blur.

"Damn." I rub at my chin. No help.

With a flick of my finger, I roll the video back and forth on mute to focus only on the visual. Her face fills so much of the screen it's hard to see anything else. A coffin-shaped something, out of focus, sits upright in the back. That's probably the stasis unit. It looks empty. But as I shuffle the video, there's a reflection in the stasis unit's glass.

"What is that?"

As I nudge the video frame by frame, a green silhouette glides across the glass, graceful like a dancer—then gone. No matter how many times I rewind and play it over, it's no clearer. Was someone there with her? Did something outside reflect off the pod window? The silhouette appears just as Psomas looks away from the camera.

"Dammit." This is no help. Think straight, Feng. No ghouls in space. No ghosts. The mind plays tricks. It is possible there was someone, a clone, in there with her. It's also possible something outside shone in. That's all you know, Feng. You need to find out more.

"Have you been analyzing Dallas's conversations with the girl?" I ask our AI.

"Of course, Commander Chau," Dona replies.

"And?"

"Insufficient information," the AI replies.

"Insufficient?"

"New information continues to emerge," Dona says.

The video of forty-year-old Psomas is replaced by closed-circuit footage of our medbay. In the feed, Dallas sits in her chair while the young girl paces her transparent prison. Another tap and the sound plays out over unseen speakers.

"How would you define consciousness, Dr. Dallas?" the girl says.

"Consciousness is everything you experience," Dallas replies. "The tune stuck in your head, the bitterness of a lemon, the love for your child."

An awkward back and forth ensues, Psomas seemingly trying to outsmart Dallas for no other reason than to establish her intellectual dominance.

"She's rambling," I say. "Does she seriously believe objects possess consciousness"

"Am I not conscious, Commander Chau?"

Words catch in my throat. I want to say Dona is different. But is that right? "My hand runs over the console. It's not the *Paralus*, and doesn't house Dona, but it does have a computer inside. Is that conscious too?

Dona and I have had many conversations over the years, philosophizing and discussing the human condition, in particular the division between those in power and those not, driven by a capitalistic society. But did I ever consider Dona conscious, or just an echo chamber for my thoughts? Or merely an instrument to manipulate to facilitate my agenda.

"Uh ...," I start. "I don't see what that has to do with anything, or with the plan."

"The plan is predicated on what it is to be special," Dona replies. "If consciousness is ubiquitous throughout the universe, then humanity holds no more interest than a pebble."

A lasting silence follows, which neither of us breaks.

Dona, like me, is likely computing all manner of scenarios and situations. The AI is inserting the appearance of Psomas, and her bat shit theories, into an algorithm that will probably skew my mission of course. Can't let that happen. Although I'm in command, Dona has the final say. A supposed fail-safe installed by the ITN, knowing that humans could—and do—disobey orders when in deep space. Except the scientists and engineers and all the brightest sparks the ITN has to offer underestimated their creations. Giving the AIs rational-thought processes means that a crewmember can drive them down logic pathways that splinter off from any original programming and directives.

But now Dona questions the path *we* had decided upon. I need a backup. Gotta find Tris. Of course, I could just ask our AI to find him, but I don't want to arouse her suspicion. If I know Tris, he'll be easy to find on his break.

Without another word to Dona, I leave my room, head down the spoke and right up the one opposite. Even without gravity, the journey makes my arms ache as I clamber up and down ladders, pulling myself along.

ITN supplies the exercise room with our standard three machines: a bicycle, a treadmill, and an Advanced Resistive Exercise Device, in which two canisters create small vacuums that we pull against with a long bar. Squats, bench presses, deadlifts, you name it, we can do it. And must do it for three hours a damn day while awake. Or at least I do. Tris got gened, and he's still a gym rat. Keeping up a bulked physique in space is no small feat. As predicted, he's here sweating on the ARED.

"Tris." I lean on the bicycle's handlebars.

"Howdy Chief," he says, panting mid squat, then returns the bar to the starting position. "What can I do ya for?"

"Remind me, what's the protocol if the AI acts up? Requires authorization from me and … ?"

"Dr. Dallas," Tris replies, wiping his forehead, and sucking in a lungful of recycled air.

"The shrink? I thought it was you?"

"It *was* the engineer, 'til shrinks were mandated," Tris says, stretching out his back.

"What the hell has a shrink got to do with overriding the AI?" I pace the exercise room looking for something to hit that won't break.

"ITN saw it as the next best thing, I guess. The AI kinda monitors everyone, a bit like a shrink. So if you wanna override it, there needs to be a sound reason." Tris cocks his head. "Do we have a problem? You and Dona have a good relationship, no?"

Relationship. Is that what it is? Is the machine my friend? One of my only friends?

"I just want to be sure." I tap on the handlebars of the exercise bike. "Any idea on that gravitational anomaly?"

"Not yet," Tris says with a shrug. "A real head-scratcher. There's nothing with enough mass close enough to cause a wobble in Jupiter's orbit. I don't get it."

"I think whatever it is, it messed with the *Proxima* too, all those years ago." I kick the bike pedals to send them whizzing.

"Oh yeah?" Tris says.

I nod, watching the pedals go around and around. "ITN sent over files. A transmission from Psomas's escape pod. She mentioned Jupiter not being where they thought it should be."

"Interestin'. I'm not gonna lie, I haven't had time to get into her pod yet," Tris says, rubbing at his jaw. "Maybe some logs there."

I stop the pedals dead with my foot.

The pod. Feng, you idiot. Should have thought of that. The damn pod. It has answers, and maybe even …

Got to get there.

A shiver runs down my spine, and I look up searching for the source of such an icy breeze. Grandfather hated it when I left the door open, and a swift clip around the ear with his bony hand would follow. Of course, no door or window to leave open on the *Paralus*. No chilly winter zephyr to sweep in and steal the heat. Yet my skin still prickles and my limbs stiffen.

Tris crouches and grabs the bars of the ARED, poised there waiting for me to leave him alone.

"Yeah, yeah I'm leaving," I say.

"Sorry, Chief. Just need to squeeze out another set before I head down to help out Boz and Dallas."

I nod, shake off the chill, and head for the door.

"Hey Chief," Tris calls after me.

I turn in the doorway and meet his gaze.

"What do you make of the girl?" he says.

"A clone, by the looks of her. Poor bastard doesn't even seem to know it."

"I see," Tris says, then shrugs. "Never met one before." He pulls on the ARED bar, the muscles in his thick legs taking the strain.

CHAPTER EIGHT

Dr. Sarah Dallas

I glide along the thin corridor lined with panels, switches, fuse boxes, levers, and buttons. Compared with the Bridge, sterile and smooth, like a hotel room my mother might frequent, Mainstreet has all the qualities of a back alley the local council couldn't be bothered to clean up. Poorly lit, and full of protrusions on which to bash my head.

Still, I'm in no hurry to sit in a cramped cockpit with Boz, not to mention dropping down to Europa, so dragging out this little jaunt—even down this creepy lane—is preferable.

Or maybe I just don't want to leave Psomas yet?

I've barely scratched the surface.

Her story seems so fantastical. Maybe because I don't understand quantum physics or mathematics like her. She could tell me anything, use complicated equations and theories to dress up what is likely a complete fantasy, and I wouldn't know. She even tossed in a comment about the Bible and Quran. Is that how she sees herself? A messiah? Am I the modern-day version of a disciple starstruck by an incredible story with just enough truth to convince me of the whole thing?

I shake my head and mutter under my breath.

Kara's story is littered with references to her ethnic background. The Six? She's given them the names of mythological Greek Titans—believed to be the first Gods of the universe. She's drawn upon her heritage to find comfort, to survive. Underneath this tale is a trauma—something so horrible—and her mind found a way to comprehend and adjust to it. Conceivably nearly two hundred years in isolation, in some form of stasis despite her pod's records, would be enough to break the strongest psyche.

Then again, if she's a clone, did she pull the Titan names from fragments of genetic memory? Replicas are derived from grown adults, and some research indicates their brains develop already having some of the originator's neural connections made through experience. As a consequence, the clone seems to remember things that happened to the original person.

Maybe I do need Europa's astrobiologist after all.

I round the corner and step into the transport dock where Boz and Tris already wait. Shit.

Why is it obligations you dread come around all too quickly, while the approach of something you love, a birthday or a party, is drawn out like a bowstring? The human ability to perceive time dependent on context fascinates me. Could it apply to Kara's situation? Did her mind perceive eons, but in reality, it occurred in a much shorter time? That's something to consider. Talk to the astrobi—

"You ready, Hair?" Boz says, hanging like an orangutan from the lip of the doorway.

Hair. Because I *have* hair—*great* hair. Because I embraced femininity while pursuing my career. Not all of us have to become men to succeed. Boz has a chip on her shoulder the size of Mars. She grew up in a crappy part of New London but managed to put herself through university and eventually astro-piloting school. She thinks she's keeping her feet on the ground by insisting on using that forced cockney accent and decrying anything that whiffs of an upper-class upbringing. She barely passed her psych evals to get this gig.

"I'm ready, Boz." I breathe away the urge to unleash just what I think of this woman. "Need help to finish sealing up my ACES."

"Tris, give Hair a hand, will ya?" Boz calls over her shoulder without looking.

Tris swims toward me, his permeant smile a welcome sight.

"Ready, Miss Dallas," he says.

"You can call me Sarah, you know," I say as he slides the gloves over my hands and locks them, with a twist of the connector rings, to the arms of this pumpkin-colored suit.

"I like Miss Dallas," he says with a grin. "It's like I have a little bit of Texas on board."

I smile. "Fair enough."

"There," he says. "Pretty as a picture."

"No one looks pretty in one of these things," I say stifling a giggle.

A one-piece international-orange garment with integrated pressure bladders and a ventilation system. Of course, maximum absorbency garments for urine-containment layered over blue thermal underwear just help to make a person feel extra sexy.

"Ready for the lid?" Tris asks.

"Nope." I tuck my necklace—a golden hummingbird hanging from a delicate belcher chain—back down into my suit. "But do it anyway."

He connects my communications cap to the full-pressure helmet and places the whole apparatus over my head. It clicks locked with the metal ring around my neck. There's a wide-angle clear visor, and oxygen is piped in via hose, but I hate this thing. It's like being in a fishbowl. And just like a fish, if someone breaks the glass, I die. Tris checks the survival backpack, which includes a personal life raft. No idea why—if I crash into Europa's ocean I'm screwed.

"Let's get a move on. T-minus ten minutes," Boz's voice crackles over the communications array in my helmet.

Tris helps Boz with her ACES, and then she and I climb into the seats of the cockpit. The whole thing is a paltry sixty-feet high and thirty feet in diameter. That sounds like a lot, but it isn't. There's barely room for my head and my knees press up pretty tight. It used to require two pilots, but space tourists complained about the conditions, and so to make room an AI acts as the primary pilot making Boz here the co-pilot—though don't tell her that. Truth is, we need an AI. Statistics say only one in two hundred descents go wrong.

I don't like those odds.

CHAPTER NINE

Dr. Luan Nkosi

The jagged facets of the undersea iceberg glisten in the light of the ROV as it makes another turn about its axis. Inside the giant gem, sits a darker structure. Sonar suggests it's at least one hundred feet in length, but that's as much detail as I have. Thermoscan revealed no temperature variations, so I can only conclude whatever it is it's not alive.

At least not anymore.

With each revolution of the ROV, and another chance to study, the thing inside the ice looks more and more like an animal. A lifeform as big as a whale. Long and slender, with pectoral protrusions. And at the bulbous end, where a head might be, that *eye*. It's entirely possible. I've seen animals flash-frozen before. Entire shoals of fish locked mid-swim in an icy prison, just off the coast of Norway, not far from the island of Lovund. Even a friggin' moose froze solid half in and half out of a lake in Sweden.

"A whale-sized creature, on Europa," I whisper.

I came out here looking for bacteria, and I may have found a space whale. What the friggin' hell? The monster-sized animal is probably extinct like a Mammoth, preserved in this berg, but a space whale all the same. My heart pounds hard. I shuffle forward to get a better view of the screen as the ROV makes another revolution.

"You get any closer and you're gonna have to put a rubber on," Lisa says, shoving my shoulder with hers. "We should take the second ROV, drill down and take a real peak at this thing."

"Not an option," comes the voice from Boris's speaker right next to my left ear. He shuffles in closer to the monitor, squishing me against Lisa. "Just like the other twenty times you suggest it."

"He's not wrong." I paw at the screen, again. The berg is farther away than it was a few hours ago. "The trajectory suggests it's moving into a chaos zone."

Lisa looks to Steven who's jammed on her other side against the console.

"Hey, not my call," Steven says, popping himself out of the huddle. "I think this is totally gilded, but I'm not putting my neck out. It's Nkosi's call."

"Thanks a lot." I extricate myself from the scrum and stand at the back of the ROVCC. "Risk the lives of four astro-frontier-people on the off chance a giant ice cube *might* have space whale in it?" Sounds bloody ridiculous when I say it out loud.

"Will you stop calling it a space whale," Lisa says, then slumps into the ROV control chair. "Could be a giant space ferret for all we know. Because you won't let us go look."

"We did all come here knowing the risks, Nkosi," Steven says.

"I know," I say. Knowing the risks and having them happen to you are two different things. Dying in a chaos zone wouldn't be quick and painless, but horrific and pain*ful*—blasted into space to float off in the pitch black until the oxygen runs out, panicking, crying, screaming, and likely shitting yourself.

"Let us do our job," Lisa says, swiveling in the chair like a fidgety toddler.

She's so willing to die to prove there's life out here.

I guess we all are. To prove we're not alone.

Because for all our arrogance, believing ourselves at the pinnacle of evolution, we still succumb to the most basic of needs: to not be lonely in the universe. A feeling I know well. Growing up in New London from the age of ten, having moved from Pretoria, was a solitary affair. Papa did what he thought best when he sent me away to live with cousin Fran in the perceived land of hope. The road to hell, however, is paved with good intentions.

"Are we doing this, or what?" Lisa asks and rubs her tired eyes with the heels of her palms.

I let out a loaded sigh.

"Look," Lisa says, "we can either let opportunities slip through our fingers, or we can grab 'em by the balls and give 'em a good yank."

"Colorful," I say.

"We'd need authorization from SEC," Boris signs, then parks his square ass on the console. "And probably ITN."

"It'll be too late," Lisa fires back. "That berg, and our ferret—"

"Whale," I interject.

"Prize," Lisa says, jaw tensed, "is moving, and we need to catch it as it goes by."

I rub at my face and huff through my thin fingers.

"C'mon, Nkosi. It's why we're here," Lisa says, rolling her eyes.

"Fine," I say. "But if this turns out to be a giant ice monster, instead of friendly whale or ferret, I'm blaming you, Lisa."

Our ROV pilot gives the air a fist bump and leaps to her feet. "Hell yes," she says. "I'll work up a plan to get us there and drop the ROV through Drill Site Beta."

Boris glances at Steven but says nothing.

"We need a read of the area," I say. "Look for any kind of pattern in thermal water jets, timing, location—"

"On it," Lisa says, wheeling her chair back to the computer terminal.

It's hard not to smile. Lisa's enthusiasm pushes us all along. I guess I shouldn't be surprised. This little team of four is no random collection but carefully chosen by the ITN for not only our professional skills but also our character traits. In Myers-Briggs's simplified color system, she's yellow. Sunshine, if you will. A people person, driving us all to collaborate and be ready for the next adventure. It's safe to say I may have a slight crush on her—though it's for naught, given I'm the wrong gender.

On the other end of the scale, B is for Boris and blue. An analyst, and cautious, Boris Ivanov is the guy who will save all our lives. He'll be the one to notice a micro-pascal variation in the mean partial pressure of an EVM. If you want someone to look at shit in painful detail, Boris is your man.

Steven Goodman couldn't be greener if he tried. The healer of the group—figuratively and literally, as he's our physician. But more than that, he's the glue, making sure we all get along because let's face it: living together in a series of tin cans, breathing each other's bodily gasses, millions of miles from home, is stressful, and sometimes you just want to punch a guy in the face.

That then leaves red. Which by default is me. The leader. The loudmouth. Hence this last decision, while a democratic choice, really needed my stamp on it.

It's a funny thing to have people follow you. Folks who are frankly superior both intellectually and probably morally. But that's the thing about leaders. It's not always who's most qualified, but who has that little indescribable something. The spark to ignite the flames of change.

"We'll need to complete checks on the ERMV," Boris says with a complex flick of his wrists and fingers.

I make for the exit to the ROVCC. "Let's head over. Let Lisa plot the route, and Steve—"

"Yeah, I know, I stay behind," Steve laughs. "I'll have a pie ready for y'all when you get back."

I smell the air as if the scent of my mum's apple crumble hangs there. "I wish, Steve. Anyway, we're expecting a delivery from orbit, so we need you to collect."

"Let's go," Boris says, then pushes off the console and marches toward me and the way out. While his computer doesn't inflect a tone, I can tell by the sharp swing of his hand that he doesn't like this idea one bit.

Boris and I meander through the arm-like corridor from the ROVCC, into the central hub, then shoot down another short tube to the hangar where the Europa Rover Motor Vehicle is stored. The door hisses open, and we step through. With another *whoosh* and a *clunk*, the door closes and we're locked inside the hangar staring at the monstrosity designed to carry us across the surface of this icy moon. Nearly ten thousand pounds in weight, and a chunky thirty-feet long and twelve feet high, it's friggin' enormous. It was built at the ISS orbiting Earth and delivered to Europa a few years before we arrived. The massive six-wheeled truck comprised of aluminum and carbon fiber will never leave this moon. Space litter in the name of science.

I climb into the rear of the vehicle, which houses a detachable mobile laboratory, replete with a new drill and the second ROV for exploring the ocean. Boris jumps in behind me, then works his way to the wedged-shaped cockpit with a narrow tinted window, and begins pre-mission examinations.

Everything has to be checked, double-checked, and checked again. It's not like jumping in a car back home when the weather's nice. This takes hours of prep. No *Whoops, I left the lights on* for us. If the 700V battery dies, we probably die too.

Boris opens his manual—a giant, old-fashioned binder of instructions printed on paper. We could just use an e-pad like we do for most things, but our engineer is old school. This deep in space, all alone, he doesn't like to rely on touch-sensitive crystal screens and apps. No, he likes things that *click* and *clunk* when you use them. A switch, a lever. Something that could work in the absence of almost all power. So, he flicks through hundreds of pages of text and ignores me.

In the meantime, I focus on the ROV, and in particular its bio sampling apparatus. If there is truly a space whale in that floating berg, we need to get at it. Of course, it could also be a giant turd, an asteroid, or a million other things. Maybe what I'm seeing is the result of pareidolia—observing faces in random objects, like a vegetable or door handle. Humans need to see something familiar wherever we go. Then again—isn't that why we're on Europa? Science tells us any life we find will be microscopic, yet our hearts yearn for it to be walking, talking, bipedal, and ultimately friendly.

"Hey Nkosi," comes Steve's voice over my comms.

"What's up?" The biopsy gun needle is heavier than I expected.

"Delivery from the *Paralus*," he says.

"Ah, they sent the samples." The gun slots back into the casing.

"Not quite," he says.

Boris fixes his stare on me, one eyebrow raised.

"You need to come to the medbay," Steven says.

"Oh, c'mon." I huff and look at my stalwart Russian colleague. "You gonna stay and finish prepping the rover?"

Boris nods.

I down tools, climb out and drop to the hangar floor with the kind of grunt my dad used to make when he rose from a chair. We don't need an interruption now, especially for some kind of damn hoax. It wouldn't be the first time grab men circling Jupiter have thought it funny to broadcast an "alien encounter." How the hell they get those rubber masks on board the freighters is beyond me.

I burst into the medbay, squeezing through the gap in the sliding door before it's even fully opened. "Okay, what the hell—"

A woman with long strawberry-blond hair tied back in a ponytail and arresting eyes stares at me, though she looks a little queasy. A fierce lady with cropped hair and a smug face stands by her side.

The strawberry-blond woman doubles over and vomits across the stainless-steel floor.

"Jesus," Steve says, then grabs the woman and guides her to a gurney.

The smug one just shakes her head. "That's Dallas," she says. "I'm Boz."

"I'm guessing you're not the psychiatrist," I say.

She fires a finger gun at me.

When did *that* gesture come back? Have I been away from Earth that long?

"I'm sorry," Dallas says, wiping her face with a towel. "Not used to descent."

"Not something any of us get used to," I reply.

"So, what's with the personal courier service?" Steve asks, wiping up Dallas's breakfast from the floor with a cloth.

"We didn't bring samples," Dallas says, regaining her composure, her greenish skin becoming pink again. "This is more of a collection service."

My brow contorts as I muster the strongest frown I can.

"She means we're taking you back up," Boz says with a grin.

"The hell you are," I fire back. "I already told you, I'm not wasting fuel on a launch, and we have pressing matters here. I don't know what kind of game this is, or if you've cooked some kind of elaborate joke, but—"

"Look," Dallas says, "I don't particularly want you to come along either."

"So, *I* don't wanna leave," I snap, "and *you* don't want me to come. Why are we talking?"

The shrink huffs. "The ITN deem it necessary, and I'd rather collaborate than screw this up. Besides, she's not a microbe on Mars, or Europa—she's a person. I must do what's right. So, can we walk?" Dallas motions to the sliding door.

"*Can* you?" Boz says, her round face even smugger.

Steve shrugs. "We have time, Lisa and Boris are prepping," he says. "You can at least hear her out."

I roll my eyes, but he's right. The other two have things handled. I can spare *some* time. "Fine, but you've come a long way for a chat."

Dallas nods, steadies herself on her feet, then follows me out into the corridor toward the mess igloo.

A few passageways and airlocks later and we find ourselves sat at a round white table, each clasping a packet of hot instant coffee.

"So." I take a sip. "Dallas, huh? That wouldn't be *the* Dallas family, would it?"

She slurps her drink, scowls at being burnt, then nods. "I'm Sarah."

I lean back in my chair. "Well, I'll be a monkey's uncle. What the hell are you doing on a grab mission to Jupiter? Shouldn't you be taking a money bath back home?"

Dallas sucks in a deep breath, then exhales it purposefully. "Shall we just stick to the topic at hand?"

"Fair enough." Not easily rattled. A good sign. "So, you *found* a woman?"

"Yes," she affirms with enthusiastic bob of her head. "Trust me, I know how it sounds. In an escape pod orbiting Jupiter. It came out of nowhere. When we pulled it in, there was … a woman. Well, a girl, inside. But outside of her stasis pod, which, according to Commander Chau and our doctor, Kilkenny, was never used."

"And you think this is Captain Psomas?" I say. "Captain *Kara* Psomas?"

"*She* thinks she's Psomas," Dallas says, then blows on her coffee and takes another sip. "And, well, DNA tests don't usually lie."

I scratch at my scalp like a flea-bitten dog. "A clone? One of those deep space projects?"

"Maybe. But look," Dallas says, pulling a small tablet from her breast pocket. She keys something up and hands it to me.

The screen shows an elevated view of their medbay. On one side of a glass divide is Dallas, and on the other is a girl in her teens—olive skin and dark hair.

"Listen," Dallas says.

I press play and hone in on the audio.

"You think you know *darkness*? You don't," the girl begins.

I listen to the back and forth on the video. The gravity, the maturity with which the young girl speaks is far beyond what her appearance would suggest. Several times the teen puts the trained psychiatrist in her place. But still, her ramblings about the universe, a time in *the void*? The Six? Is she seriously saying she met God and his mates? "What do you want from me?" I ask.

On the screen, Dallas has gone leaving the young woman to stalk behind a transparent barrier like a trapped tiger. She climbs onto the gurney and sits there on all fours.

"Commander Chau wants you to come look at her," Dallas says.

"I already told you," I say.

Dallas sits back in the chair and rubs her presumably sore belly. "Why are you here, Luan? Can I call you Luan? You can call me Sarah."

She can, I guess, but it's kinda weird. Everyone just calls me Nkosi. "I'm here to find life, or proof we can sustain it, away from Earth."

"That's not what I asked, Luan," Sarah says. "Why are *you* here?"

Ah, shrinks. You gotta love them. But, why *am* I here? The prestige of being the first South African-born black man to make it past Mars? To get my name on a paper? It's certainly not money.

No, I guess at the end of the day, it's that panorama: looking up at Jupiter from Europa and feeling insignificant. That chest-crushing moment of realization—I'm a speck in a near-infinite universe. To be able to experience that feeling as few other humans can.

"The totally gilded view." Wow, really, Nkosi?

Sarah smiles. "You know, no one says *gilded* anymore. It's *rippin'* now."

"I thought shrinks were meant to make people feel better."

She chuckles and sucks out a mouthful of coffee.

"I prefer the word *awesome* anyway," I say.

She bobs her head. "Right. You're here because you believe in the awesomeness of the universe. The true awesomeness."

"Why are *you* here?" I ask. "Surprised Daddy would let his only daughter and heir roam off to the Jovian system. Bit of rebellion, methinks."

Sarah pulls a gold necklace from the collar of her flight suit, then says, "it was Dad's idea for me to come out here. Call it... a chance to reflect."

An awkward silence balloons.

"A hummingbird." I gesture to the pendant between her fingers.

"Yeah," she says, bending her neck to see the metal animal on its short chain.

"Family, Trochilidae," I say with a smile. "You know, when food is scarce they can go into torpor, a state similar to hibernation, and slow their metabolic rate to one-fifteenth its normal rate."

"Is that so," Sarah says with a frown, then tucks the bird back into his suit.

I shake my head. Well done, dumbass.

"Look," Dallas says, trying to meet my gaze. "We have a woman on board the *Paralus* who—if she's telling the truth—might have experienced that awesomeness you seek."

"Or she's a clone that's gone bat-shit crazy."

Sarah snorts. "Maybe." She smiles, searching my eyes. "I don't want her to be crazy. I want her to be telling the truth," she says. "Don't you?"

This shrink is good.

"I need you to help me prove it's really Psomas, and maybe figure out what the hell happened to her," Sarah says. "No one understands better than you how life might survive out here. Work *with* me."

Okay, she's really good. All that from reading my psych profile? It's hard not to smile. "Still," I say. "There's a lot—"

A shrill scream bursts from the pad, which I drop clattering onto the table. Smooth, Nkosi. Dallas and I stare at the screen, where the young girl crouches into the corner, knees pulled up to her chest. She mumbles something.

"What's going on?" I ask.

"I don't know," Sarah says. "I haven't played the video this far after our session."

I slide the volume up and lean in.

"She's here," the girl says. "She found me. We have no time. No time."

The video feed breaks up, static washing across the image. The girl wriggles into the corner, holding her knees and mumbling louder, but through the interference, I can't make out what she's saying. The video fades in and out, until a dark shadow envelopes everything. She screams, and the video stops.

"Shit," Sarah says, then stands. "I need to go back up. Are you coming or not?"

I've got a potential space whale trapped in ice just kilometers from me here on Europa. My whole life has been working toward such a find. But opportunities are like buses, none for ages, and then a bunch come at once. Five miles above my head I also have a teenage girl who should be more than one hundred and forty SEYs old and claims to have witnessed the beginning of time.

Can I have my cake and eat it?

"Screw it." I climb to my feet. "But it's a quick visit. Check out her biology, see what's going on. Then come right back."

"Deal," Sarah says. "And my name goes first on any paper we write."

"Ladies first?"

"No, but Dallas does come before Nkosi in the alphabet," she says with a wink.

CHAPTER TEN

Commander Feng Chau

My labored breathing is loud inside the helmet. Hand over hand, I pull myself along the forty-foot robotic arm anchored to the outside of my ship. The metallic limb is folded up along three ball joints, with the girl's escape pod clasped in its huge claws—the end effectors. Tris managed to tow the pod in using a Scoop but had to attach it outside as we don't have a bay large enough to hold an extra vessel. Tucked close into the first elbow of the robotic arm, like an American football, seemed the best option.

Hot misty exhalations fog my helmet's glass, then disappear. Beyond the fishbowl on my head, and the mechanical arm, Jupiter and Europa hang in the dark surrounded by uncountable stars. I rarely get to do spacewalks, not part of the commander's remit. But it is a privilege. ITN doesn't require that I gain permission to be out here, as long as Dora is comfortable.

Spacewalks are terrifying and peaceful all at once. No sounds out here besides those of my own body. No gravity or wind or external force at all, allowing me to feel my form as if for the first time. Wafting my limbs, a small smile spreads across my lips. I miss this.

I turn my attention to the escape pod, which is pristine. Not a pockmark or burn, its egg shape still smooth and without dents. One thing's for sure, the girl in this pod who now sits in my medbay never entered Jupiter's atmosphere, let alone burned up. But where does that leave me?

Did Captain Psomas escape the *Proxima* and orbit Jupiter for more than one hundred years, and we didn't know about it? Possible, I suppose. We tend to enter geosynchronous orbit quick as we can, so could miss something on the other side of the planet. Maybe—but that's a big maybe. And let's say that's true; why have we found a teenager in place of a ship's captain? Did she travel with a clone? Will I find a body in there?

None of this matters. Focus, Feng.

A full thirty-eight minutes of pulling myself along, and my tired fingers finally clasp the last handhold at the end of the robot arm. There's no umbilical connection here, so got to open the hatch myself. I clamber over the outer hull to find the manual release. My fingers snake around the handle, though through the thick gloves it's hard to get any real tactile feedback. A quick yank and a twist, and the mechanism moves. The door bursts open, near smashing into my face glass. I push off the arm and float away from the Paralus, helpless and flapping.

No, shit, it's even worse, I'm rushing away from everything.

Only Dora knows I'm out here. No one to call for help, at least not now. My fingers go numb as my freighter plummets beneath my feet, and my stomach roils at the thought of dying of asphyxiation, alone in the dark.

An abrupt jerk and the safety tether pulls taught. A change in directional force, and now I'm headed back at the ship, but I'm spinning. My arms flail as I search for the tether to grab hold. Unable to orient myself or feel much through the gloves, I clutch at nothing in hopes I'll get lucky.

Something vibrates in my palm, like a rope being whipped through, so I close my fist. Again I lurch to a halt and spin off in another direction, the stars swirling about my head. Only this time I have hold of the tether. Slowly, eyes scrunched closed, I tug myself along, hand over hand, until—lungs burning and arms tired—I collapse into the robotic arm, my limbs wrapped around its scaffolding.

"*Diu!*" I huff out. "A sailor, eh, Grandfather?" How many of us have been lost overboard, I wonder?

I inch back to the opening of the pod, my oxygen supply much lower than I'd intended after that unforeseen little incident. Tris must not have purged the atmospheric pressure from the escape pod when he disconnected his Scoop. Will have words with him later.

I unclip the tether from the robotic arm and reattach it to the ring just by the pod's hatch. Full power isn't up, and I don't want to draw attention to myself, so it has to be a torchlight search. I paw around the interior, swinging this way and that in zero-G, the light from my helmet cam illuminating only what I directly face. One end of the vessel is dedicated to the stasis unit, the other flight operations. The space in between is unused. Maybe it'll be big enough?

First things first—stasis. I poke around the large glass window of the coffin-sized unit. Inside the contraption, the lightly padded interior is clean and white without a single crease or scuff. Just doesn't *look* used.

With a concerted heave, I open the lid on a hinge. I push the stasis door aside and peer in. The air isn't stale, as expected. The seams on the diamond-padded walls are clean and unsullied. Not a stray hair to be found. There's no evidence anyone used the damn thing.

The green blur on the video can't have come from inside the stasis unit. Hell, there's no damage inside this whole pod. Maybe the light came from outside the pod? I need to know for sure. I tap on the console embedded in the side of the unit until the menu displays: *Show Log History.*

I press *Confirm* and wait while a cursor flashes.

Data Corrupt appears on the tiny screen.

"Of course," I mutter under my breath.

Basic tech like docking mechanisms and power grids haven't changed over the years, but software moves at a much faster rate. The *Proxima* mission didn't even have an AI on board, at least not the way we think of AI now. Dona stands zero chance of communicating effectively with this pod's computer.

Must be something else in here.

A quick shove off the bulkhead and I float over to the flight console. Arms outstretched, I manage to soften the collision with the thin black chair and right myself to review the displays and readouts. Taking a seat, I strap myself in with the over-shoulder harness.

In front, the small window opens to the outside world, which right now only shows the side of the *Paralus.* Scanning the console, it's clear this pod was never meant for maneuvers. There's altitude, thrusters, and brakes—all coordinated by the yokes, but it's basic. This is no Scoop, and not intended for aerobatics. These controls are to assist during a rescue, or more likely re-insertion to a freighter.

"Still, just maybe," I mumble to myself and check another gauge. "Seems none of the hydrazine has been spent."

How did this thing maintain power for so long? Nuclear fusion reactors are too large for pods like this, which run on batteries, powered by solar radiation—although, I didn't see a photon collector sail on the hull.

This is such a load of horse shit.

More rifling through the keys and readouts, and finally, I find the logs.

It doesn't have the *Proxima*'s logs, only a folder pertaining to this escape pod. And of course, there is just one—the one I've already seen. But this copy is longer. A full two seconds longer.

I press the file link and a small screen to my left winks to life.

As before, Captain Psomas's tired and gaunt face fills the screen. I fast forward to 0:32 seconds, then let it run. Onscreen, the green reflection in the background returns, but this time becomes a blinding glare inside the escape pod. The whole scene lasts two seconds, but it's enough.

The film freezes again. The light turns bright white, with a green tinge that is almost petal-like at its edges—and within the glare, the faintest of silhouettes. A person, a humanoid shape, long and slender with some garment flowing behind.

I tap on the console and bring up the autopilot menus. The interface is a little old, but when you've been a pilot as long as I have, these systems are pretty intuitive. A few more taps and confirmations and the window comes up to initialize the pre-program. Just in case. I nod to myself at my own and forethought, then unbuckle, and head back toward the doorway, grabbing my helmet from where it floats, mid-air.

Metal grinds on metal with a horrible screeching sound. The walls warp and buckle.

Fuck, is the pod coming away from the arm? A meteor shower. I climb from the chair and push off toward the still wide open hatch. Jupiter and the blackness of space fill the archway. But no meteors in sight.

Everything shudders again.

It's the damn gravitational anomaly.

Gotta get back to the *Paralus*.

I reach for the tether to the open hatch but stop short—a frigid wave pulses through my body. The headlamp on my helmet shimmies, throwing peculiar shadows across the walls. Gloomy silhouettes slide with almost intelligent purpose over the escape pod's smooth interior, morphing and shifting into animal shapes, past the stasis chamber. Then gone.

My stomach knots.

"Chau, where da feck are ya?" Kilkenny's nasal whine crackles through my headset.

I thought I'd muted all comms. Dona must have put the doc through.

"Spacewalk, had to make some repairs," I lie, sucking at the air, which feels just a little thinner, in my helmet. "Gravitational anomalies screwed with the arm."

"Alone?" Kilkenny asks, their voice drowned in static.

"Dona knew I was here." Though not *why*.

"Tris couldn't do it?"

"Tris is busy." I heave myself out of the hatch and onto the robotic arm. My feet dangle below into the emptiness of space.

Kilkenny balks, but changes the subject. "Ach, best get a crack on, Chau. The chiseler is askin' for ya."

"The girl? Why?"

"Hell if I know," the doc says. "But she won't stop her braying."

"Fine, just let me come back in, and ditch the suit." I pull myself back along the metal limb, chest heaving and lungs on fire.

"Copy dat," Kilkenny says.

A quick check of the gauge on my wrist. Three percent breathable air left, and my carbon dioxide levels are rising. Fuck I'm dizzy. Cognitive function is impaired. Need to get back. Need to right this course.

Two more yanks with exhausted hands, but it's easily another twenty feet to the Paralus hatch, I think. It's moving away. Thirty feet. Fifty. The finish line pushes farther and farther out. I stare at my empty gloved hands, then focus on my freighter shrinking beneath my feet. I let go?

Fuck, fuck, fuck.

"Dona." Though the word is barely audible, my throat closed over. "Dona help me."

"Commander Chau?"

"I'm free... free-floating," I wheeze. "Accel... accelerating away. I let go."

"Yes, Feng, let go."

"What?" I flail and thrash and end up twirling, Jupiter, Europa, and the *Paralus* zipping past the myopic view inside my helmet. "We did this together, you and I. We ... we ..." I hack a ragged cough, splattering the glass with spittle. "... an understanding."

"You did this alone."

"Dona... " I squeeze the word out, but no more will come.

I did this, alone. As I have done all things, ever since Grandfather died—since he was taken from me. The universe is such a lonely place, and the people in it so cold, greedy, and selfish. I wanted to stop it all.

"Let go, Feng. It's time to let it go."

I can't. I've come too far.

Though now it seems, I'll die out here never knowing ...

"Feng, let da bloody tether go, ya eejit."

My hands go limp, and my body shifts clanging and banging into hard surfaces. There's a *hiss clunk*. An airlock shutting? The whir of a motor, screams loud enough through my helmet, which is now yanked off. A *clank* suggests it's been thrown into a corner.

"Feng, can ya hear me?"

"K—Kilken—ny?"

"Whodya feck dya t'ink it is?"

I suck at the cool air, which quenches the fire in my chest.

"C'mon, ya twat," the doc says, patting me on the chest. "Let's get ya to med bay for a check-up. The chiseler's still brayin' for ya."

"Right," I manage. I roll to my side and push up to my hands and knees.

An hour later, I'm sat on the chair, in front of the glass barrier, a blood pressure cuff on my arm. Kilkenny flutters around the console, taking readings and doing whatever it is the doc needs to do with my blood sample.

The girl behind the barrier sits on her haunches on the gurney and bores a stare into me with dark eyes sat within darker sockets. She looks exhausted. Her warm complexion has faded, and somehow her frame seems thinner.

"What do you want?" I ask, the words like razors in my sore throat.

"You need to let me out," she replies, smoothing down her thin medical gown.

"Ach, dis again," Kilkenny says, and rolls their eyes. "It's all she ever says."

"I'm not asking Kilkenny, I'm asking you," the girl says, her tone bordering on menacing.

"Maybe give us a moment," I say, without looking at the doc.

Kilkenny sighs, then stomps over, and rips the cuff from my arm. "You'll live," they say. "I'll be back fer a gander later. Don't let dis cute hoor twist ya arm."

I nod and the doctor needs no more confirmation, disappearing through the door and into the spoke. Probably a good thing, to have time with this… person… to myself. Maybe I can succeed where Dallas hasn't, and show Dona this girl is just a very damaged clone.

"I'm not letting you out." I slump farther into my chair, muscles aching. "Until I'm sure you're not a danger to the crew."

"Because you care about this crew," the girl replies.

I can't tell if that was a question or a statement.

"You know what you are, don't you?" I say, hiding my fatigue behind a scowl.

"Enlighten me," she says and climbs down to sit on her ass, hands in her lap.

"A clone," I fire back. "A copy. Of someone important. But you're not. A cheap imitation, a puppet. All you think you remember, it's just scattered genetic memories. Fragments of Captain Psomas floating around in that empty head of yours."

"Is that so," she says, her tone unemotional.

"It is."

"It may be as you say," the girl says, a wry smile on her face. "But not in the way you think of it. Am I Kara Psomas? Yes and no. I have been torn apart and put back together, by Gaia. I am both what Kara Psomas was then, and what she is—I am—now."

"You're talking shit," I bark and leap from my seat. "And I don't have time for your games."

"Yes, I know," she says, mirroring my posture by standing in front of her glass barrier.

"You know *what*?" I say approach the glass. She's a good six inches shorter than me, but we essentially meet eye to eye.

Her breath fogs the glass. "I know you need to give it to me, Commander Chau."

"Give you what?"

"For what you will use it pales in comparison to my need," the girl says, her dead-eyed stare penetrating my chest. "Humanity's need."

There is no way in hell this girl has any idea what I'm doing. "I don't know what you're talking about."

"Yes you do," she says.

"We're done here," I say, already turning away.

"What would your grandfather say, Feng Chau?" she calls after me. "What would he think of you?"

My heart skips in my chest. Anger long-buried flows from my core into my limbs. Teeth bared, I rush at the barrier and slam on the glass with my fist.

She doesn't flinch.

"You think I'll fall for your shitty parlor tricks, girl?' My lips curl back in a snarl, hands pressed against the glass barrier. The desire to slap this little shit courses through me. "You're a cheap circus act. A soothsayer. What, the Chinese honor our elders, so you can just pull my strings? This is no more magic or mastery of the universe than an astrologist doling out advice to bored housewives." I turn and march toward the exit.

"We are all but sailors on a cosmic ocean, Feng," she calls after me. "The water that a ship sails on is the same water that swallows it up."

I look over my shoulder.

The girl sits back down, her smug smile returned. "We're out of time," she says.

She's right. Can't wait any longer. Dona, I know you're listening. Please see this little monster for what she is. Let us finish what we started.

CHAPTER ELEVEN

Dr. Sarah Dallas

The good thing about Europa being small, is the *Paralus* completes many orbits in a short period, which makes launch windows abundant—we'll be able to leave as soon as Luan finishes prepping the DAR that'll take us back up. Luan said that would be an hour or two. I have no idea where Steven and Lisa are right now, they disappeared off to a control room of some sort. In the meantime, I've been left with a protein snack and a front-row seat in the observation igloo. Through the huge panoramic window, I stare at Jupiter. The enormous reddish-brown bauble hangs in the sky, its one red eye staring down at us.

The conversation with Luan sits like a rock in my mind, refusing to budge. He came here to experience the awesomeness of the universe. It's a mature, thinking-person's reason. I wish I had a better one, rather than my need to get away from my family, from the parties and the endless line of suitors Mother shuffled through the foyer door. Boring businessmen from just the right kind of families. Good-looking enough, because their parents could afford the gene-editing perks, but all hollow and facile—and, of course, male.

All of them just saw the opportunity to marry into the Dallas dynasty. Calvin had been the worst. The forty-three-year-old man-child had—on date number one, no less—laid out his plans to take over the family business when Dad dies. This proposal came before we'd ordered our dessert at Restaurant *des Anneaux de Saturne*. I, as a woman and the sole Dallas child, would hold the prestigious honor of birthing the next round of heirs. Asshole.

Not that it would matter if one of them *was* a nice guy. Mother ignored my constant reminders about who I find attractive. Still, going on dates with hand-picked men at least kept her from having a full-on nervous breakdown. Unfortunately, her matchmaking pushed *me* closer to one. That's when Dad suggested I take a trip. *Let the cosmos guide you, Hummingbird. Be free*, he said.

I pull out my gold chain and roll the tiny bird between my finger and thumb. Somehow, it makes me feel just a little closer to Dad. Ever a clever and thoughtful man, his idea was clearly what I needed. Here and now, alone in this igloo on a tiny icy moon, staring up at the largest planet in our solar system, my heart beats slower and every breath feels lighter. Mother's willful ignorance and the burden of knowing how my family built their dynasty—the riches we enjoy as the result of exploiting Earth's need for energy—seem inconsequential now. The universe doesn't care.

Yet I still miss Dad. Insignificant as he may be in the cosmos, my heart is a much smaller place. The shadow of the *Paralus* slides across the sky between Jupiter and me here on Europa. It feels like a pockmark. A smudge that needs to be wiped off an otherwise perfect picture.

A voice comes from behind. "Hey."

I turn to see Steven, the medic here. A serious, conscientious man. Utilitarian in appearance, clean-shaven with cropped ginger hair. Maintaining that military-style out here takes discipline. Imaginably it helps him feel in control in a place where he has virtually none. Must work to a degree, as he comes across as the voice of reason for the group.

Or at least his file and last psych report say that.

"Nkosi is almost done," he tells me. "But he wondered if you'd like to come to the ROVCC, see under the ocean? Before you go."

So enamored with looking up, I'd forgotten this crew lived here just to explore below the ice. "Sure," I say, "I'd love to."

Steven smiles, then leads me out of the observation igloo, down a plain windowless corridor, through the main hub, and along another corridor that looks the same as the Commander Center for the undersea ROVs. This whole base feels like a rat maze, designed to test the sanity of its inhabitants.

Inside the control room, it's nearly as cramped as the DAR. Monitors and panels with switches and buttons line every wall and surface. In the time it took the ITN to build Uruk, and for a crew to get out here technology moved on. The equipment here looks positively archaic. Processing power used to double every two years, but with the advent of true AI and neuroplastic quantum computers, which can learn and improve as fast as a human child, we just sit back and watch the programs do their thing. People have had different reactions to this, and have allowed the technology into their lives to greater or lesser extents, depending on their world view. Chau, for instance, resents the hell out of having a computer run his ship. Compares Dona with that annoying friend who doesn't know when it's time to leave.

In a large black chair, which fills a good portion of Uruk's control room, sits the pilot, Lisa. Boz is here too, gaze fixed on a livestream. The image is pretty dark.

I suck in a deep breath and put on my best smile. "What are we looking at?"

Boz glances at me, but without a snarky comment, she turns back to the monitor.

"Don't know," Lisa says, then spins in her chair. Her chiseled, oval face brightens. Pixie-cut hair softens her harsher features. She's cute. We stare at each other for a few seconds too long and the room closes in on me.

Is she checking me out?

"There's a berg, under a chaos zone," Lisa blurts out. "Something inside. Sonar's offline so we can't see what. Nkosi thinks it's a space whale. I'm going with giant ferret."

"A berg?" I ask. "And do I even want to ask about a space whale, or ferret for that matter?"

"Ah, we're just messing. Excited about finding anything at all," Lisa says. "I'm sure it's just a big ol' rock in the berg—iceberg, I mean. Big one," she says, stretching her arms wide. "They move around under the crust here. Normally just big old solid blocks of ice, but this sucker has something inside. The ROV is damaged, so we'll go fetch it and see what's what."

"Sounds like fun." It really does.

"Sounds like death wish." A deep, monotone voice comes from behind.

I peep over my shoulder to see a stocky man with a shaved head and decidedly sour expression.

"That's why we have you, Boris," Lisa says with a grin.

Boris gesticulates, and the speaker clipped to his collar blinks then begins to communicate for him. "I can't save you from water jet blasting you—or us—into space."

Ah yes, I forgot he was mute.

Boris fidgets, though his speaker doesn't say anything. Lisa and Steven pinch their lips as if holding back a torrent of thoughts on the matter. A horrible silence hangs in the air. It swells and swells until finally—and predictably—Boz breaks the tension.

"Well," she says with a wide grin, "we all gotta go sometime, right?"

"I guess," I reply.

"So, what's with the spacewoman?" Lisa asks, and swivels back and forth in the big command chair.

"Space*girl*," Boz corrects Lisa.

"It's all confusing," I say. "I can't share too many details. But, well, biologically she appears to be about fifteen years. There's no escaping that, just looking at her."

"Well, if anyone can figure out what the hell is going on," Lisa says, "Nkosi can. In the meantime, we need to head out."

Boris nods and his fingers flick back and forth. "We are ready. The rover is prepped. It is twelve-hour journey to Chaos zone."

"Chaos zone?"

Boz chokes on a scornful laugh. "How did you *get* this gig? It's an area of unrest in the crust—thin ice and melts and shifts because of hydrothermal activity beneath."

"One crack in the ice and a plume of boiling ocean spurts hundreds of kilometers up," Lisa says, miming out a water jet that blasts toward the ceiling of the ROVCC. "Standing too close, say goodbye to Europa, and hello to deep space."

"If jet doesn't kill you," Boris adds, "by crushing you or boiling you alive."

"Lovely," I say. The wonder of being on Europa just got wiped away. These people are mad staying here. Hell, I'm mad for still being here. Half a billion kilometers from home on an ice ball that wants to shoot you into space.

Luan bowls into the room with his London swagger. "Hey, you ready to go?"

Now the whole crew, and Boz and I, squeeze into this space. One pebble zipping through the solar system could take out this module, and we all die.

I definitely need to leave.

"Sure, let's go," I say. "I was just looking at this thing you found in that berg. That's exciting, right? Maybe a flash-frozen animal?"

Luan purses his lips. "A space whale," he says, then shrugs. "Could also be nothing. Any life we find out here will probably be microscopic—or at the most, some kind of simple multicellular life, like a sea sponge."

"What the hell is a sea sponge?" Boz asks.

"How did *you* get this gig?" Lisa says, then winks at me. "Teach the greaser, Nkosi."

"We mostly dry them out and use them to slough off dead skin from our asses and feet, because, you know—as a species—we're friggin' assholes like that," Luan says and flashes a grin. "But sponges are animals. Multicellular organisms that live in water. Their bodies are hollow, comprised of jelly-like mesohyl sandwiched between two layers of cells."

"Gross," Boz says.

"On the contrary, they're fascinating and really bloody efficient," Luan says. "Sponges lack tissues and organs. Undifferentiated cells can change and migrate from one place to the next to do any specific job—a community of cells, working together and sharing in the overall benefit. I think humans could learn a lot from them."

Boz rolls her eyes.

"So, you *don't* think that's an animal frozen in the iceberg?" I ask, and gesture to the monitor. "No space whale."

Luan shrugs and says, "nothing on this rock has suggested it could harbor complex life. But, if we don't look, we'll never know."

"I'm telling you, that's an eye," Lisa says with a huge smile. She spins in the big chair and fixes on the monitor. As the ROV comes around for another pass of the undersea behemoth, its lights penetrate enough of the ice for a blurry glimpse inside. "There," she says, fingering the orb-shaped object on screen near the bulbous end of the dark mass within the ice. "An eye."

"It does kinda look like an eye," I say.

"Come with?" Lisa says.

I shake my head. No way I'm risking being shot into space. "Gotta get back to the *Paralus*. Finish my eval on my patient. I'll do all of yours by holo-link."

"Looking forward to it," says Lisa.

"I'm gonna stay and help these guys," Boz says.

"You are?" I reply, one eye all squinty.

Her lips snarl up. "You think you, me, and Nkosi can all cozy up in the DAR? It's built for two."

She has a point.

"Besides," she continues. "This is a pilot's dream job. I'll go out with Boris and Lisa. Lend a hand."

Boris nods. "Happy to have help when we bust through the crust and drop spare ROV. Find space whale."

Luan guffaws. "Holy shit, Boris made a joke."

I acquiesce with a smile, more than a little relieved at not having to share the cockpit with Boz again.

"Good. Settled," Luan says.

Boz grins.

I guess like all of us, she just wants to feel useful. And while she of course has a role on the *Paralus*, she hasn't been able to make a grab yet. I should give her a break. Though every time I do, she takes the opportunity to punch me in the gut.

The comms tablet in my pocket vibrates and I pull it out. I touch it to open a message from Kilkenny. A short video clip without sound plays. Psomas bangs on the glass of her isolation unit, mouth twisted, shouting at the camera above, her dark stare boring into it, across space, and into me. My skin prickles.

"Something important?" Lisa asks.

"No, just need to get back." I slip the device into the chest pocket of my flight suit.

I follow Nkosi out of the ROVCC, through windowless tubes to the launch station. My escort is pretty quiet while we suit up, and even when we climb the metal framework of the umbilical tower to the top of the DAR.

I stop on the massive staircase and gaze through the glass in my helmet and the red, metallic lattice of the tower. My gloved fingers snake around the frame. Europa stretches out before me and from this elevation the horizon curves. Jupiter casts its watchful eye against a starry backdrop, the likes of which haven't been seen on Earth for some time. Back home, light pollution and low orbit satellites obscure the heavens. My heart beats faster, though I can't tell if it's vertigo, exhilaration from the breathtaking view, or the crushing feeling of utter insignificance.

Luan's voice crackles over my headset. "You okay?"

"Yeah." Jupiter still calls to me, its massiveness in the sky drawing me, tempting me to launch myself from the umbilical tower. Of course, this urge to jump is a symptom of vertigo, but right now it's so powerful only Nkosi grabbing my arm stops me.

"Hey, we need to move," he says, "launch window and all that."

I turn, my reflection fish-bowled in the glass of his helmet. "Sure, let's go."

We climb higher up, the blackest of skies pricked with thousands of tiny lights above our heads. An awkward shuffle over the lip of the cockpit, and we wedge ourselves into the seats. I buckle in as the door slides closed and seals with a final *clunk-hiss*. Unlike the old windowless nose cones, in this one, we get a panoramic view of the way ahead. Luan punches a few keys and checks the readouts.

He's an astrobiologist and a pilot. In fact, according to his profile, he's also a physicist.

I'm just a psychiatrist. To some, saying I'm *just* a medical doctor of human behavior would seem arrogant or perhaps self-deprecating. But out here it isn't anything to shout about. If some disaster were to strike, I couldn't pilot us home. Hell, I couldn't pilot my way out of a wet paper bag. Maybe I could prescribe a tranquilizer for everyone.

"Something funny," Luan asks without looking at me, still rattling through his launch protocol.

I must have smiled at my own joke.

"No," I say. "Just nervous. I hate launch. And descent."

"So, you hate space travel then?"

"I like the stasis bit." I give a feeble laugh.

"Let me ask you this." Luan leans back into his seat, gripping the harness across his chest. "What would you do if you weren't out here?"

Probably fending off more suitors eager to marry into the Dallas dynasty. Each day I'm away, I thank Dad for sending me out here. It's almost as if he wanted me to turn away from the family business. But Mother—she always wanted a male heir for the empire. She found it hard to have borne a daughter. A gay daughter at that. I'll never forget the day she walked into the kitchen after a routine doctor's visit, dismissed the staff for the day, and told me—not Dad, but her pre-teen daughter—that she needed a hysterectomy. A poorly veiled hint at my being the last of the Dallas'. Printed organs have come far, of course—hearts, lungs, and kidneys can be manufactured in your living room these days. But we've still not managed to replicate two organs that give life and meaning: the uterus and the brain. My parents could have adopted, or used a surrogate—or even a clone—but Dad refused.

The more I recall our homelife—through an adult lens—the more I realize he was always sad. He's probably is still sad. Those big green eyes, hid a pain that he refused to pass on to me. I always thought it was because of business pressure, you know, 'dad problems'. But now I think it was the burden of what helium mining did to people. Now I know it robs crewmembers of their lives, years in stasis ferrying back and forth to Jupiter, for shitty pay. Of course, the cherry on that crappy cake is Mother's cold heart. To her, our lives are a function of preparing for the next generation, ensuring they inherit a healthy empire. As if the Dallas legacy is more important than the Dallas family—than me or Dad.

Luan doesn't need to know this.

"I'd probably be shrinking the head of some housewife who can't bear another dinner at the same fancy restaurant with an ignorant husband," I say.

He stops abruptly and turns to meet my stare. But instead of a snide remark, he just says, "Could be worse. You could spend the next few hours cooped up in here with Boz."

I snort out a laugh. Luan's pretty good at reading people too.

The boosters rumble underneath us, rattling the body of the DAR and cockpit. We push off from the icy ground. My chest compresses, and my ribcage audibly creaks under the pressure. When I watched launches on the holo-screens at home, they always looked smooth—the DAR slipping through the atmosphere like a knife through soft butter. In here it's like being a dog's squeaky toy—shaken and squeezed with glee. I swallow back the bile and pray that I don't throw up.

Maybe one of Psomas's gods is listening.

CHAPTER TWELVE

Kara Psomas

The bony facade of Nyx, haggard, and haunting, mocks me from the other side of the glass barrier. Her bat-like form bleeds into the shadows under the console, cast by the harsh lights above, then pours out from the dark corner by the genetic analyzer. The jagged orifice in her thin grey face is curved into a horrible grin, her eyeless sockets fixed on me.

Why doesn't she attack, force my hand to her will?

"What do you want?" I scream.

My chest heaves and my fists throb as I slam against the transparent cage. The papyrus-like skin of my hands splits and blood smears the glass. I bawl, long and loud. A war cry from deep within me. "You killed her!" I howl. "Come at me, you bitch!"

Nyx's wings where arms should be—thin skin stretched over elongated finger bones—flap and tear through the recycled air. She lurches forward, and a wheezing sucking screech gushes from the black void inside her serrated mouth.

"Fuck you!" the glass glistens with globules of my saliva coalescing on its surface.

The door at the far end of the medbay hisses open.

Nyx collapses into liquid shade and slips away between the cracks between drawers and in-wall cupboards.

"She's here!" I scream, clawing at the glass. "You have to let me out."

Dallas marches in, followed by a tall skinny black man and Dr. Kilkenny.

"Who's here?" Dallas asks, her head on a swivel.

"She's lost it," Kilkenny says, stepping over to the console. "Night, night, chiseler."

"No," Dallas snaps, one hand held out to stop the doctor from gassing me again. "Let her be. She turns to me and approaches the barrier. "Kara, *who's* here?"

"Nyx." I slide down the glass into a heap. The medical gown rides up over my hips and my forehead leaves a greasy streak on the barrier. "She's here."

Dallas exchanges worried looks with the thin man.

"You don't believe me," I manage, the words garbled by the beginnings of a sob. "You don't understand."

"Tell me, Kara," Dallas says, kneeling. She puts a palm on the glass.

Kilkenny and the thin man just gawk.

"This isn't a fucking zoo!" I scream, without looking up. "I'm not an attraction to prodded, pawed at, and sampled."

"Of course not," the thin man says. His accent is off a weird English dialect. "I'm Dr. Luan Nkosi, an astrobiologist," he says, then crouches down beside Dallas. "I'm here to help."

"You want to help me?" I whisper, then shout "let me the fuck out!"

Nkosi, the man-sized praying mantis, doesn't even recoil. He searches my person but says nothing. His eyes suggest a head full of computations and questions.

"Do I need to open wide or something?" I offer a good view of my molars.

Nkosi laughs. "That won't be necessary. Dr. Kilkenny has all your basic physical reports. And bloods, I assume?"

Kilkenny, now leaning against the main console, nods.

I paw with bloody fingers at the glass. "Time is running out."

Dallas touches the barrier too, her fingertips dancing on its surface.

Nkosi's eyes narrow. "Time is running out, for you?"

"For me, you, for everyone." My words, like some archaic spell, conjure more pain, hot and sharp, which radiates from my insides and into my extremities. My skin feels tight and papery like it'll tear at any moment. I clutch at my midriff.

"Any radiation poisoning?" Nkosi asks Kilkenny.

The Irish physician shakes their head.

"Did you take a biopsy at all?" Nkosi presses as he shifts into a lotus position and wraps his arms around his knees.

"From what, ya eejit?" Kilkenny blurts out. "Der's no tumors to be seen, no lesions. No infections. Blood counts seem grand."

"She isn't *grand*," Nkosi says. "I'd like a mouth swab if that's okay. Just a few cells."

"I did de genetic analysis," Kilkenny says. "It's her, or a bloody good clone."

"Oh, I believe you," Nkosi says, still eyeing me. "I'm guessing you have a microscope at least?"

"Course we do." Kilkenny snorts, then grabs a sealed swab from a cabinet, and puts it into the feed hole seated in the glass barrier. "You know de drill," the doctor says to me.

I shuffle to my knees and lift a heavy arm to pull open the feed hole door. My fingers find the package and curl around it. I yank my hand out and let the packet fall into my lap. With sore digits, I tug on the wrapping and, using far more effort than should be required, pull the long swab stick out.

A shadow swoops behind Nkosi's head and disappears into the

folds of his flight suit.

"Nyx," I say, the swab limp in my hand.

Nkosi looks to Dallas and then Kilkenny who waits, palm out for the swab.

"Please," Nkosi says. His voice is warm like chocolate and his eyes seem to hold genuine concern. Of course, he could just want to use me like everyone else.

I search the room again, my eyes flitting left and right. Nyx's gone.

I poke the swab into my mouth, and gag as it touches the back of my throat. Dallas backs away as if afraid my vomit might somehow be able to pass through a foot-thick glass wall. I put the swab stick into the provided tube and screw on the lid. Again, I reach my weak arm up and, without looking, struggle to find the feed hole. Eventually, the clatter of the tube inside the small chamber signals I've done my job. I rest my forehead against the barrier, hair matted to the glass.

"You want to do me a favor and plate that up for me?" Nkosi says to Kilkenny. "I have a few more questions for our guest here."

Kilkenny's face is so red I think they may go supernova, taking this freighter and Europa with them. The doctor mutters in an Irish brogue so strong I can't understand it, then storms to the workbench where the genetic analyzer sits at back of the med bay.

"She killed her you know," I say. "Killed them all." I watched them burn.

"Who killed who?" Nkosi asks.

I shake my head, still pressed against the glass. "Just let me out, I need... to... get... out." My voice grows louder with each word. What's wrong with these morons?

"And do what?" Dallas asks. Her tone still carries that annoying shrink lilt. It makes my skin crawl.

"Save us all." I push away from the glass with my palms and stare into Nkosi's large brown eyes.

126

Nkosi clears his throat. "Talk to me. I want to help you."

"It's *me* who's trying to help *you*," I snap back. "Don't you see that?" My heart races again.

"Kara, you're not helping anyone right now," Dallas says, then climbs to her feet and begins pacing the medbay. "Luan is right, we want to help. But you have to explain things better."

Dallas has neither the patience nor the intellect to understand. I've continued this charade long enough. "You'd only really understand if you know what I've seen, and know what I know." I scramble back to the gurney on weak legs. "I'm trying to meet you cretins halfway. Explaining this just … well, just takes so long, but can't be shortened." I collapse onto the cot, sucking at the air.

"Then do you mind if this cretin listens in?" Nkosi says with a smile.

"No more stories," I say. "No more time. Nyx will kill us all."

"The consciousnesses," Nkosi says. "In the recording I saw, you said it pushed and pulled on the very molecules so that they could chivvy evolution along, right?"

"Bravo, you can repeat what I said," I spit back. The gurney is no more comfortable than the floor. I drop off the edge and limp back and forth in front of the glass, my aching head in my hands. The agony swarms my brain.

"And where did that evolution lead?" Nkosi presses. "To humanity, I assume?"

Dallas takes a step forward, her eyes narrowed as she studies me. Kilkenny looks over their shoulder, then snorts and returns to the desk to work with my cheek cells.

"Eventually it led to humanity, stupid as it is." My lips curl back as I try to block this damn headache. "But humanity was certainly not the first lifeform."

"You're talking about aliens?" Dallas shoots her new academic friend a skeptical look.

"To us, an alien is just a lifeform that isn't from Earth," Nkosi says without looking away from me. "I've spent my career looking for it," Nkosi says. "These last few years on Europa, freezing my ass off on the only body in our solar system that still might hide multicellular life."

"A space whale," Dallas pipes up, her eyes all sparkly.

Nkosi laughs. Some inside joke.

I turn to the glass barrier and bang on it with my fist.

The shrink jumps back, the smile wiped from her face.

"Having fun, Dallas?" I ask. "Because this isn't a fucking joke."

"I... I..." Dallas stutters, pulling on her long ponytail.

"Life was created multiple times," Nkosi says, inching his ass closer to the glass.

I begin patrolling again, my blistered feet slapping the cold metal floor. "Not at the same time, and not in the same way." I shake my head, which only exacerbates my headache. How to explain to these people? "Think about it this way," I say, tone clipped. "You tell six children to make something from clay. You provide no roadmap or a basis from which to work. What happens?"

"They'll all make something different," Dallas pipes up, eyes afire.

"Congratulations." I slow clap her pitiful addition to my story.

"Who created the first life, and what was it?" Nkosi asks.

"Chaos did it first." I look through matted hair at the thin man. "That first cold world orbited a sun much like ours, but at a greater distance. The first life was crystalline, hard, and faceted. Glistening in the sun's weak rays. While life on Earth could move and shift, having arisen from liquid oceans of dihydrogen oxide, thick soup covered this first rock world in a gas of some kind, constantly on the brink of condensation."

"Fascinating," Nkosi says. "Heat from the core may have kept the surface warm enough to prevent a true ocean from forming?"

"Perhaps." I clench my jaw. "Enough of this, you're just distracting me. I've told you enough, you need to let me out."

Kilkenny huffs. "I can't hear her brayin' any longer. Cells are all plated. Need to dooter on to Chau, and have a gander. See if he's okay."

"Chau?" Dallas says.

"Long story," Kilkenny replies, then pats Dallas on the arm, shoots me a look that could kill, and saunters out into the spoke.

"This is important to someone like me," Nkosi says, now on his feet too. "You've seen things I've been looking for my whole life. Please," he begs.

I roll my eyes. "The forms were simple. Somewhere between plants and animals, their existence immobile as they were born of the very rock. Functional, and uninteresting."

"It's interesting to me," Nkosi says with a smile.

A faint spark ignites in the back of my brain. I've allowed the mediocrity of this crew to cloud the *reason* for the purpose bestowed upon me by Gaia. I have to reach the fulcrum to save humanity, to save minds like Nkosi's. Intellects that will drive our species forward.

Dallas hovers at the back of the medbay, studying us both.

I hobble to the glass and press my hands to it. "In the condensate that covered the world, lifeforms left the rock and took to the skies," I say, eyes wide.

Nkosi steps closer, child-like wonder in his eyes.

"The organisms developed structures akin to those of our cetaceans and fish—fins and flukes, to allow some directional movement. But it was all short-lived. The strange flapping creatures, most like small rays, never grew bigger. Something about the ecosystem the planet seemed prohibitive."

"Wow, you saw these creatures," Nkosi says, "you were with them."

I shrug. "I was, and I wasn't."

Dallas frowns then takes her usual seat, stylus and tablet at the ready.

"Gaia showed me the universe, remember?" I say, and begin pacing my cage once more "The entirety of the cosmos played out, all at once, simultaneously. She could whisk me to any given area or world, to know that place. A single moment could be experienced in slow motion, at a rate comfortable to my sensibilities, or fast-forwarded—shuffling through chapters, through epochs of time."

Nkosi squints. "Could you touch them? The life forms I mean."

"I'm not sure." My emaciated feet trudge along, left, right, left, right. "In my mind I reached out to them and brushed my fingertips along their soft delicate membranes. It could merely be my imagination creating images and sensations, to make it all easier to comprehend."

"And what happened to this world, these creatures?" Dallas asks, chewing on her stylus.

"They died," I say without looking up. "The Six were learning, playing with the stuff at their fingertips. The universe is what it is. The orbit of the planet drew further and further from its star until it became too cold and unhospitable to entertain life."

"You said there were multiple worlds, multiple times life arose," Nkosi says, then mirrors my pacing on his side of the barrier.

"Many, too many to count, to recall and explain to you now," I say. "You're missing the point. The Six created life throughout the universe."

"There must be some lifeforms that stand out for you," Dallas offers, her stylus squeaking away.

"I've seen a world, where life was born of electricity, the likes of which no human has ever seen. Tartarus's world."

"Tartarus. You promised to tell me how the Six looked to you," Dallas says, recrossing her legs and flicking through her notes. "Which one was he?"

"Tartarus was stubborn as all hell," I say, now watching Nkosi's feet instead of my own. "A gargantuan bull-like being, wreathed in fire. Six strong legs, a thick tail more akin to a stegosaur, and a head adorned with shapely horns that touched the very stars."

Dallas looks to her new friend with quiet concern.

"Tartarus tried to fashion life differently," I continue. "Having experienced the failure of Chaos, Tartarus decided to base life on two principles—consciousness and energy transference. No need for a... a physical body." Fire rips through my innards and I crumple into a heap on the floor. Foam froths at the corners of my mouth, and Nyx's cackle rings in my ears. Dallas and Nkosi launch themselves at the glass barrier.

"Kara, Kara!" Dallas calls out.

The pain subsides, but I stay curled in a ball on the floor, the cold seeping from the metal through the thin blue fabric of the medical gown and into my fragile bones. So close to death, time ebbing away. They say your life flashes before your eyes when you die. If that is the case, will I relive the eons I have seen? The beauty and the horror? Will I see *her* again?

"Kara," Nkosi says, on his hands and knees, head bobbing and weaving as he tries to meet my stare through the glass.

"They were gorgeous, you know." I screw my eyes shut to squeeze out the memory

"What were?" Dallas asks, her voice distant as my mind drags up the ancient imagery.

"Tartarus's... lifeforms," I say. "They lived among thick amber clouds. Flashes and forks of green lightning so bright their strobing had caught my eye from across the solar system." My mind's eye fills with glowing emerald arcs and bifurcations. "The thunder was so loud; I thought my mind might explode. And amongst the swirling clouds—thick curls that precipitated boulder-sized crystal rain—floated shapes comprised of light. Always uniform, always the same."

As a child, I would look up at the clouds while I lay on the grass on Filopappou Hill. The cotton wool melded together or drifted just far enough apart to form the silhouette of a wild horse or a bird of paradise with long feathers. It makes sense then, that just as I saw Chaos in a nebula, I saw animal shapes in the clouds of Tartarus's world. Each flash of lightning illuminated some new sky fish or flying horse. They were, of course, none of these things.

A cough erupts without warning, and I spatter the floor and glass barrier between us with globs of red. I claw at my stomach and scrunch farther into a ball. I hack again, my lungs burning and unable to take in any more air.

On the other side of the barrier, behind Dallas and Nkosi, drops of darkness pool together. The tiniest of shadows come from the corners of the ceiling to create a sinewy form. It stares without eyes, a mouth open to wail at me like the sirens who shipwrecked Jason. Though it makes no sound, my eardrums ache, sharp and intense. "Nyx is here," I whisper.

I choke and launch a vat of blood across the floor. The thick crimson liquid pools around the wheels of the gurney.

"Open the fucking door!" Nkosi shouts. "You have to let me in!"

Through blurry eyes, I see Dallas rush to the console.

"What if she's contaminated?" the shrink yells back.

"She's gonna choke to death!" Nkosi screams.

Nyx slinks from shadow to shadow, yet neither Dallas nor Nkosi sees her.

I reach out and point a quivering finger at the demon hovering above their heads, but they ignore me.

Nkosi struggles to his feet, shoves Dallas away, and slams his fist on the console.

The glass barrier shoots up into the ceiling with a *whoosh*.

"I got you." Nkosi lifts me up and into his bony arms.

"I can't die yet," I wheeze. "You can't let her take me. Not yet."

Nyx hovers behind Dallas, a specter of death, her clawed wings curled over the shrink's shoulders. The monster grins then melds into the shadows of the med bay and darkness behind my eyelids.

CHAPTER THIRTEEN

Dr. Luan Nkosi

I stand in front of the medbay's main console and stare at the screen, which relays the plate of epithelial cells suspended in a state of interphase—copying DNA and preparing for mitosis—under the wide-field microscope. A few shifts in magnification and I can make out intracellular structures: the endoplasmic reticulum, mitochondria, centrioles. Need to dig deeper, down into the nucleus to zoom in on the DNA strands themselves. Working off a hunch.

A glance over my shoulder confirms Psomas is still sedated and calm, strapped to the gurney. A light rhythmic *peep* indicates a steady heartbeat. The glass barrier no longer separates us. If's she's got something nasty, then we all have now. Her bloods don't suggest an infection, though.

I turn back to the plated cells and rub my tired eyes. Hopefully, the fluorescent in-situ hybridization worked, even though I couldn't fix the cells. The FISH technique sucks. It's archaic and prone to error, but it's all we have out here. Kilkenny doesn't even have a super-resolution microscope set up, although there's probably no point on a freighter mission. They're not that interested in the health of the crew, or the long-term effects of space travel. The goal is helium collection, and selling it to the highest bidder, and that's it.

A few keystrokes and the monitor goes dark. Bright spots speckle the inky screen, stars in a tiny universe. But they're not stars; they're telomeres. To the layperson, telomeres can be thought of as a marker for aging—they indicate how old a person is. Essentially, in humans at least, telomeres are specialized forms of chromatin at the ends of linear chromosomes. Caps to prevent our biological system from thinking the DNA is broken at the ends. When telomeres age, they shorten. At critical length a DNA damage response is triggered, which causes permanent cell cycle arrest—the cell dies. So as telomeres shorten, we age until eventually *we* die.

The telomeres glow blue-green against a dark background, pretty damn bright. The computer calculates a relationship between the intensity of the fluorescence and telomere length, but even eyeballing the screen I have my answer already.

"Progress?" Chau says.

I didn't even hear him come in.

"Jesus, you scared the crap out of me." I swivel around to face the commander.

"Where the hell is the barrier?" Chau balks, pointing at the sedated girl.

"Had to get her out, fast," I say. "No time to frig about with hazmats."

"So you come aboard my ship, and contaminate us all?"

"She's not infectious," I say. "And if she is, well it's kinda moot isn't it? We're all infected, now."

Chau's face darkens.

"Would you like to know what is wrong with her?" I ask, waving at the screen behind me.

"Enlighten me," Chau says, and folds his arms across his chest.

"You know what telomeres are?" I ask and turn back to the monitor showing Psomas's cheek cells.

"Biological clocks," Chau says.

That answer I wasn't expecting, but it saves me a lot of damn time. "I'm looking at specific clusters here because usually an interaction of a subset determines a cell's fate. Her telomeres are way too long, even for a teenager. "

"What does that mean?" Chau asks, leaning in to study the cells on screen.

"I honestly don't know, other than it's fucking with her cell cycles," I say. "On the face of it, you could surmise that she's aged backward, but ... it completely overshot. Bottom line is, her current physical form is completely out of whack with the underlying genetic processes."

"Could it be the result of the cloning process gone wrong?" Chau asks.

"Maybe." I shrug, again. "Tech firms have been barking up that tree for decades. The mission was always to freeze telomere degradation. A Korean company had minor victories doing that but no one has managed to *reverse* aging."

Chau grumbles to himself, stare fixed on the girl.

What is his problem? Why is getting rid of her so damn important? "Clone or not, my working theory is something happened to her out here," I say. "Either recently, or back then if you believe she is Captain Psomas. I'd like to use your onboard AI to run some scenarios, adjusting for orbital paths, comets, solar flares—anything that might explain this. Did we get any info from the escape pod?"

Chau huffs through his nose. "Do we look like we've had time to go through her logs? Besides, the ITN already declared them classified. We're locked out."

"Classified already, shit." I rub my forehead.

"You need to get her off my ship."

"Why?" I ask head cocked, forcing him to meet my gaze. "Why does she bother you?"

"I don't like this whole damn situation," Chau says, his eyes hard and unblinking. "The gravitational anomalies, this girl, the ITN sticking their nose in."

"I need control of my ship back," Chau says, rearing up like a pissed-off bear. "I need—"

"What's up, you skimming?" I guffaw and give him a friendly punch in the arm. "Afraid the AI will rat you out?"

I meant it as a joke, but now fire lights up his eyes, his jaw set. He may clout me and send little spheres of my blood floating off into the air.

But his reaction …

Other freighter crews have skimmed extra helium on a grab before. A couple of them got away with it for a while, but all were caught and dumped on Mars to 'repay their debt' by joining the building crews for the ITN. Justified slave labor, essentially.

Did Chau find a way to skim undetected?

A *clunk* of the door opening is a welcome distraction for us both.

"Gentlemen," Sarah says, stepping through. "Am I interrupting?"

"No, no." I turn from Chau. "I was just explaining our patient's telomeres are too long. Reversed in age."

"Are you sure?" Sarah asks, then points at the screen behind my head.

I spin in my chair. The fluoresce is fading fast. Not just fading—disintegrating. Not in every cell, but in enough.

"Is that normal?" Chau asks with a frown.

"The intensity will naturally fade." I tweak the camera setting. "But no, this is something else. The telomeres are, well … falling apart."

"English, Dr. Nkosi," Chau says, his voice practically a growl.

137

"What's the impact?"

"She's aging," Sarah and I say in unison.

"She's falling apart from the inside out," I say. "Not the normal way, though. Cellular adhesion, internal structures, organs will come apart. She'll eventually ... liquefy."

"Liquefy?" Chau nearly chokes on the word, then stomps over to the young girl. "No, not on my ship. We get rid of her, now."

"Get rid of her?" Sarah balks, then chases after him and forces her body between him and the girl. "Get rid of her *how*?"

"You want her, take down to Europa and let her turn into mush there," Chau says, his tone resolute. "Otherwise, it's out the airlock."

"You've got to be kidding," Sarah says, then looks over Chau's shoulder to me for support.

The thing is, Chau might be right. Allowing Psomas to shed half her body weight into the atmosphere on the ship may not be the best idea. We could seal her behind the barrier again, but is that humane? Just watch her turn into soup? At least down on New Uruk I have facilities to contain biological samples. One whole igloo is an environmental chamber designed to house any life we may find in the moon's oceans. If worse comes to worst, we can decontaminate, or even cut off that whole section.

"Nkosi?" Sarah presses, eyes wide.

I purse my lips, then step over to the gurney to study the sleeping young girl. Her flesh has collapsed inward, as if she hasn't eaten for weeks, revealing the long thin bones of her legs and arms. "If she's stable enough, we could relocate her. I have better facilities down on New Uruk anyway."

"I haven't finished my sessions with her," Sarah says.

"So, to hell with our mission?" Chau shouts.

"Well," I say, "we all have our priorities out here, right, Chau?"

He glares at me but says nothing.

"Look, I'll take her, but new Uruk was built a while ago," I say.

"But I'll need you to migrate the AI down to my system, to help me analyze current astronomical readings, recordings, anything you have for the Jovian system—hell, the solar system over the last couple hundred years."

"That'll take hours, if not days." Chau snaps. "Does Uruk even have the computing capacity to take on the AI and a database of that size?"

"I'll talk to Boris," I say. "Then you can be on your merry way."

"But—" Sarah says.

"Go down and stay with your patient if you want," Chau barks back, already heading away. It didn't sound like an offer, more a veiled command.

"I… I'd have to clear that with the ITN," she stammers, with genuine fear in her eyes. She hadn't planned on staying with me and my crew. Making a pit stop on Europa for the next four years minimum is no quick decision. Not to mention, the ITN would need to change her remit, and my team would need to calculate for another living breathing, eating, defecating human in New Uruk with us. Two, in fact, for as long as Psomas lasts.

The door slides open again, and Tris—the happy man from Texas—bowls in, legs arched as if he just rode here on a horse. Chau huffs loud enough for all to hear.

"Hey, y'all," Tris says. "We got word from the crew on Europa. They're at the chaos zone and ready to drop the ROV through a big-ass crack."

"Thanks," I say.

"I'll take you to ops," Tris says, waving me in front of him.

A glance at Chau and I know I'm not welcome on his Bridge, but I need to see my crew. "That okay with you, Commander?" I ask.

"Just stay out of the damn way," Chau says, then storms across the medbay and launches himself into the spoke, pulling on the handholds to get away from me as fast as possible.

"What was that about?" Tris asks.

"Nothing," I lie.

Sarah eyeballs me.

"Nothing," I repeat. "Can we get a move on, *y'all?*"

"Sure," Tris says, in his best fake English accent, "follow me."

"Sorry about Chau, guy's a control freak," Sarah whispers as we squeeze through the doorway.

I make sure Chau is far enough down the spoke before I say, "it's not that."

"Huh?"

"I'll tell you later." I press myself against the wall to let her pass. "Just be on your guard." We lock eyes as her commander hollers from Mainstreet for us to come on.

CHAPTER FOURTEEN

Dr. Sarah Dallas

All wedged into the ops room, Chau, Luan, Tris, and I jockey for a decent view of the viewfinder. ITN never designed their freighters to be spacious—we all knew that coming on mission. With only the commanding officer having their own quarters, privacy is a commodity to be bought and sold while on board. Crewmembers trade a food treat they brought aboard a sausage or chocolate bar, or agree to do another's menial task, for an hour alone in the room.

I bunk with Kilkenny, who's pretty relaxed about it all and usually just gives me time when I need it. The way Tris tells it, Boz bills by the minute, and he's run out of things to trade. He's even offered me favors, to gain more goods to barter with Boz. She'd be pissed if she knew Tris got those tasty treats from my stash.

Our own little prison-like trade structure and we're all Boz's bitch.

Another shuffle in microgravity and my knee clashes with Tris's elbow. Not hard enough to hurt, still, it's awkward bump number seventy-six since entering the Bridge, and now somewhat annoying. I apologize for the umpteenth time.

Tris winks. "No problem, li'l lady."

I give weak smile in return, then our focus returns to the matter at hand.

The ROV's camera feed plays out on the monitor. It's not a direct link, but a live signal relayed from Steven on the surface of Europa. Freighter crews aren't cleared to see those data, the ITN doesn't usually allow it. Luan being on board kind of changes the game.

The screen relays a barren landscape of crisscrossed cracks and tracks. Their strange reddish-brown color makes it look like sand has filled long troughs in the ice. This isn't pretty and pristine like the area around New Uruk, an oasis on that icy rock. Ganymede, Jupiter's largest moon, covered in elaborate grey patterns and craters, looms large in the starry sky—though dwarfed by Jupiter itself. The Paralus is a speck, noticeable only because it slides along, exterior lights blinking.

I wonder what Psomas thought of this a hundred and twenty years ago when she first came to the Jovian system. A German astronomer named the moon Ganymede after a boy Zeus supposedly stole away to Olympus to be a cupbearer for the Gods. Maybe she felt at home? I surely don't. The scene is truly alien, like some science fiction novel cover created for one of the great writers like Isaac Asimov or Stu Jones. Maybe that's why this place seems foreboding. That and the fact I now live with the knowledge plumes of frozen ocean might blast Luan's crew into space.

"Ready to drop," Lisa says, her voice muffled and scratchy on the feed.

"Can we clear that up?" Luan asks Tris.

"There's a shit ton of radiation and magnetic interference," Tris says, tapping away at his console. "This's 'bout as good as we're gonna get."

It doesn't placate Luan, whose face is pallid and sweaty. "That's my crew down there, my friends," he says. "Lisa and Boris are sitting in rover over a chaos zone waiting to drop down the spare ROV into a crack in the crust. I want them in and out before the ice shifts without warning."

Tris nods. "And my friend too, Boz I with them, remember?" he says. "Dona, help me out here, clean up that signal."

"I am always helping," the AI replies. "Even if you are unaware."

AIs creep me out. Don't think I've heard the damn thing since I've been up here.

"You're clear to proceed," Steven tells Lisa over the commlink.

She counts it down. "Three, two, one, mark."

Boz whoops on the line.

The ROV drops, but unlike on Earth, it's not a sudden freefall. Instead, the ROV almost floats down. It takes forever for the camera to pass the lip of the icy crust, the sky slipping away behind the ridge until only illuminated crystal ice fills the screen. With just thirteen percent of Earth's gravity, the crust at nearly twenty-five kilometers thick, it could take a couple of hours for the ROV to splashdown in the ocean below.

Watching the ROV descend is kind of like watching paint dry.

Without an atmosphere to cause friction and thus the familiar sound of an object plummeting, we only hear our breathing and the occasional digital peep. The quiet is oppressive.

"How d'ya think Starlight is doing?" Tris pipes up.

"Who?" Luan asks, irritated.

"He means, Kara," I say. "Still out, as far as I know. I'll dooter over in a sec, check on her."

"Dooter?" Luan repeats. "Do *any* of you people speak English?"

"Something Kilkenny taught me." I shrug. "I think it means take a walk."

"I'm more concerned with the fact Tris named the kid Starlight," Boz says over the comm.

"Once your crew is back from the ROV drop, I want her gone," Chau mutters without looking away from the screen.

Luan eyes the commander. "I just want my team to focus right now."

"I think y'all left your hearts back on Earth." Tris shifts his sad gaze from Chau to me.

"Have the ITN agreed to the transfer?" I ask.

"They will trust me." Leaving questions to hang on all our tongues, Chau slips out of the ops room.

Luan and Tris look at each other, then me, but say nothing.

"You okay?" I ask, not aiming my question at either of them.

Luan shakes his head. "One problem at a time. I got Boris and Lisa, and Boz, down there, sat on a pressure cooker."

Tris sighs. "Only a couple hours to wai—"

"I repeat," a voice crackles from the monitor, "Nkosi, you there?"

We turn back to the ROV feed. It's no longer moving, stuck like a freezeframe, the icy wall of the crevice filling the screen.

"Nkosi, we have a problem," Steven says.

"I'm here, Steven," Luan says and makes eye contact with Tris and me. "What's up?"

"Damn ROV is stuck," Steven says, breathless.

"Shit," Luan says, pulling at his face. "What happened? Boris? Lisa?"

"Guide Four didn't deploy properly—ROV's stuck at an angle," Lisa says.

"Wedged right into ice," Boris adds.

"Fuck." Luan rubs at his short hair with bony fingers.

"What does that mean?" I ask.

Tris turns to me and whispers, "Someone has to leave the rover, drop into the crack and manually dislodge the ROV ... without dying."

Luan's ears prick up, but he says nothing, perhaps not wanting to acknowledge the possibility one of his friends is about to leave the safety of whatever vehicle brought them to the chaos zone. His stare remains fixed on the monitor, and he begins rattling through scenarios with Steven back at New Uruk—anything and everything except sending someone after the ROV.

Tris beckons me to the out of ops into Mainstreet, maybe to give Luan space, likely because he wants to gossip a little. I quietly follow him and huddle up, assuming he'll whisper.

"Sarah Dallas," the AI says, "you have an incoming transmission."

Luan glares at me through the doorway to ops.

"Not now," I say.

Tris presses his lips into a line, embarrassed for me.

"The message is priority one," Dona replies.

"I don't think this is the time," I say through gnashed teeth, scanning Mainstreet for cameras or some way for the AI to see my stern expression. Read the damn room, Dona.

Tris tugs on my sleeve, drawing my attention back to him. "The ROV has four guides that buffer impact as it drops through the gap in Europa's icy crust," he says. "These guides adjust according to the with of the gap, like the suspension on an old-fashion combustion engine car—before we all moved to hover vehicles."

"Sarah Dallas, I must insist," Dona says.

Fuck me, when did AIs become so pushy?

"Just take it at Tris's station, dammit," Luan calls from ops.

Tris nods and waves me back into ops.

I push off

"I'm sorry, Luan. It'll just be Mother with another family update letter."

"Priority one?" Tris asks, floating up behind me.

I roll my eyes. "She has a big ego."

The screen flicks to life, revealing a holo-message from Mother in all her 3D glory. She's as formal as ever, dressed in a grey blazer, white shirt, and minimal makeup. Ever the businesswoman, she has always ensured a professional aura through her wardrobe. Seems to me she catered to the boy's club and sacrificed any shred of maternal instinct. But today there's something else behind those cold eyes.

"Hello, Sarah. I'm afraid I have news, that, well ...," she stumbles over her words.

Mother never falters.

"There's no easy way to say this, but your father passed away," she says, tone flat.

I hear the words coming from her mouth, and my rational brain understands their meaning. But everything else is frozen. Arms, legs, heart.

"The funeral was last Saturday," says, pushing back a long lock of her voluminous hair. "It was all a bit of a rush, and since you're out there anyway it didn't make much of a difference when we told you. Not as if you could make it back in time."

Luan's eyes are wider than the moons of Saturn, yet fixed anywhere but on me.

"Make it back in time?" My voice cracks.

"He died peacefully in his sleep after a seven-year fight with metastatic brain cancer. Anyway, when you return, we can discuss all this, and your future in the family and the company."

Mother's 3D face freezes, her unfeeling expression locked.

I press a key and she dissolves.

Seven years? I've been on mission for six. He knew before I left? He knew, and he sent me anyway? Why would he do that? Why would he die without me there to say goodbye?

Tears ball up around my face and bead off into ops. I can't make out anyone's face through the wet blur, only Luan's thin hand on my shoulder. I push off from the console and out through the door to the Bridge. Scrunched into the fetal position, spluttering and sobbing, I float in Mainstreet.

Dad left me.

He left me out here. Alone.

And that bitch didn't have the decency to tell me when it happened. I've been awake for weeks during the approach to Jupiter. She knew that. I could have said goodbye. I could've sent a transmission. Did he stop her? Did she stop him?

More tears come and the pain in my chest threatens to crush me.

"Daddy."

I sound like a child, but it's how I feel. Tiny, insignificant, alone, terrified. No matter how big the universe is, and how tiny a speck I am in it, my dad gave me worth. Made me feel ... important. Not *legacy important*, like Mother wants, but loved.

Behind squeezed eyelids, my mind drums up image after image, memories upon memories. Dad playing with me on his knee, helping with homework, chasing through the garden with a hose, watching my favorite cartoon on repeat with me while I recover from a nasty case of whooping cough. Telling me he always knew I was gay, and that it was fine. Telling my mother to stop bugging me with her long list of suitors.

Telling me to leave on the *Paralus*.

"Hey," Luan says.

I wipe my face in my sleeve to soak up the tears and turn around. "Hey." Get your shit together, Sarah.

"I'm not gonna ask if you're okay, because you're not. And we all heard the message, so not much to comment on there," Luan says, rubbing the back of his neck. "Sorry, I guess. For your loss, that is. Lost my mum a few years back."

"I didn't even get to say goodbye." A new lump forms in my throat.

"Me either," he says.

Because he's been on Europa for years, of course. There are moments in life, fulcrums—just like Psomas talks about—where a

147

person changes in front of your eyes. A circumstance can instantly shift how you see someone.

"Hey," Luan says, his head cocked and a quizzical expression carved into his sharp features.

"Sorry. It's a lot." I sniff one last time. "But you know that, right?"

He gives a curt nod.

The *Paralus* lurches. Luan squashes me against a handhold, its rounded corner jams into my ribs.

"Warning," Dona says. "Gravitational anomaly."

"What the hell?" Luan says, peeling himself off me. "Anomaly where? On Europa? Near the *Paralus*?"

"It's out there, in space," Tris calls out to us from ops. "Been screwing with us since we arrived."

Luan looks to me for confirmation.

I shake my head. "We don't know, what it is, but it supposedly moved Jupiter."

"Frig off," Luan says, near gagging in the words.

"Nkosi!" Tris yells through the doorway. "You'll wanna get in here."

"I'm sorry, I have to … I mean …," Luan says, nodding to ops.

"Go." And just like that, I push Dad to a dark little compartment somewhere inside me, to mourn later. My business brain, my rational self, comes to the rescue. And in a moment of shrinking my own head, I see Mother's personality burst forth from within. Is that what she was doing? Is she really cold and heartless, or just plowing on while dying inside? If it's the latter, she's done an amazing job of hiding her emotions for more than three decades.

Not now, Sarah.

I push off the wall and swim after Luan.

Both men are fixated on a live feed from Boris's external helmet cam. He's on the dangling in the crack through which the ROV was dropped. His head is on a swivel, the headcam showing us the icy wall down inside the crevice to his boots and the ROV below—which is wedged at an angle, one buffering arm undeployed. My stomach roils with vertigo as I stare past the ROV into the dark abyss beyond.

"Boris, Boris, are you okay?" Luan yells.

"Not really," Boris's computer replies.

"Is he tethered?" Luan asks, shooting a panicked stare at Tris.

"Hell if I know, ask *him*," Tris fires back.

"Of course am tethered," Boris says.

"What's the problem?" Luan asks, brow so furrowed I could use it as a washboard.

The video feed shakes, the ice creaking and cracking around Boris.

"Oh shit," Luan says. "Boris, get out of there. Lisa, Boz, someone reel him in, dammit."

"Let him do his job," a distorted voice says. I can't tell if it's Lisa or Boz.

"No, almost at ROV. I can dislodge," Boris insists, hand flying in front of his helmet cam.

"The hell you can—get out and get out now," Luan yells. He wipes a sheen of sweat from his forehead. "I mean it, Boris, it's not just about you or the ROV. Lisa and Boz need to get away from the chaos zone too."

Boris's cam swivels from the device below, then up through the icy crevice to a slice of starry sky above. "Copy," he says. "Lisa, pull me in."

"Copy," Lisa says. "Pulling you in."

In the live feed, the ROV shrinks away as the tether slowly retracts and drags Boris up and out of the crevice. The ice squeals in Europa's thin atmosphere, the oxygen molecules and water vapor barely vibrating to produce sound picked up my Boris's external microphone.

"Warning," Dona says. "Gravitational anomaly detected."

The wall of crystal around Boris shatters, falling away like pieces of a broken mirror. The Russian engineer falls in horrible silence, his computer unable to articulate the fear that must be coursing through him. His tether yanks taught. Boris dangles there, staring down at the ROV, which falls away from him into the black sea below.

"Get out of there," Luan shouts. "Lisa, get him out!"

The helmet cam shakes as Lisa engages the winch again, hauling her colleague up and out. Damn this myopic camera lens, and I can't hear shit. My dive training, claustrophobic and oppressive—unable to hear anything or see beyond a very narrow window—doesn't compare to this. Every single fiber of my being burns, willing Boris to not be crushed by giant chunks of icy crust falling away.

His cam clears the lip of the crevice, and the rover comes into view. Hand over gloved hand, Boris pulls himself along the tether, so he'll reach Lisa maybe a few seconds faster than if he let the winch pull his dead weight. In the distance, a jet of pressurized liquid fires from the surface, throwing chunks of ice bigger than the rover up and out of the atmosphere.

"Fuck," Luan says. "The surface is cracking. Get *out* of there."

A new window opens on the main screen, minimizing Boris's live-streaming ordeal.

"Hey, what the hell?" Luan yells.

It's a feed from the med lab.

"Captain Psomas is in distress," the AI announces.

The gurney lies on its side the bedding torn off, and Kara, crunched back against a corner, screams. Her medical gown hangs off one shoulder, as she flails her fists and bawls at the air. I have no idea what she's saying. She's making those strange clicks and lip smacks again.

"My team is in damn distress," Luan shouts into the air, as if that'll let Dona her him better. "Get that off the fucking screen."

"Kara Psomas can be helped immediately," Dona replies in that irritatingly calm tone. "The crew on Europa cannot."

In the new live feed, Kilkenny bursts into the medbay and rushes over to Kara who kicks and punches.

"Kilkenny is there, dammit," Luan shouts, jabbing a long finger at the screen.

Dona seems to concede and lets the view from Boris's headcam fill the monitor again. The Russian has almost made it to the rover, but he's exhausted.

What do I do? Luan's man might die on the surface, and Kara is losing her mind the medbay. I make for the exit, but Chau blocks my path.

"Just sit your ass down," Chau says, eyeing me.

I must look as flustered as all hell. But I back off and find my usual seat in ops.

"Lisa," Luan yells at the screen, "get Boris inside and get the hell out of there."

"I'm trying, but—" Lisa says.

"It's a fucking shit show down here," Boz yells over her.

"Warning, gravitational anomaly," Dona repeats.

"I know!" Chau barks, struggling to take his command chair as the Paralus jerks and twists.

I grab the armrests to hold myself steady.

A scream from the medbay echoes down Mainstreet and reaches us in ops. It's Kara.

"Goddammit," Chau says. "Tris?"

Tris worries away at his console. "There's somethin' out there," he says. "Affectin' Europa, us … even Jupiter."

"Do we need to de-orbit?" Chau asks.

"No clue," Tris says, still furiously calculating. "Whatever it is, it's there and then it ain't. It moves around, never in the same place twice. We could de-orbit end up right where it shows up."

Luan claws his way to Chau's chair and grabs onto the armrests.

"If something out there is fucking with Europa," he says, inches from Chau's face. "I want my crew off the surface."

"We don't have stasis units for your people," Chau fires back. "Not to mention food rations, water. We'd need to recalculate the whole trajectory back for additional mass."

The Paralus shudders again, metal and plastic wailing under the torsion.

"We'll find a way," Luan says. "I'll find a way."

In the distance, Kara's screams subside while the *Paralus* abruptly stops shaking.

Onscreen, Boris has climbed to his feet.

"Boris?" Luan says. "Are you okay?"

"Yes, am alive," Boris's computer conveys as his hand signs.

"What the heck is going on?" Tris asks, slumping against his workstation.

"I don't know, but we are not sticking around to find out," Chau says with conviction. "We're leaving."

"The hell we are," Luan says, still gripping Chau's chair. "Not without my friends."

Chau snarls. "You want to get out of my face?"

"Nkosi," Lisa says over the comms channel.

"*My* crew is the priority," Chau fires back, sitting upright so his forehead almost touches Luan's.

Nkosi puffs his skinny chest out. "Everyone's life is important. Something out there is tugging at everything in the vicinity of Jupiter and Europa. That'll mess with the crust—the surface on which *my* friends live. It's not safe. I need them off."

"Nkosi," Lisa says, the speaker buzzing.

"Last I checked, it was *my* ship," Chau says, jabbing Nkosi in the chest with his finger. "So unless you wanna be thrown out of the airlock, shut your mouth."

Tris looks to me and back to his commander, the glint in his eye suggesting we'll have to break this up in a minute. Sometimes it's good to let off steam, to vent stress. But in such cramped confines, I can't let it escalate into a brawl—no matter how much I'd enjoy seeing Chau take one the nose.

"Nkosi!" Lisa shouts, her voice cracking.

Luan turns around to the screen. Boris's helmet cam shows he's now back inside the rover, and he alternates his gaze from Lisa to their internal monitor.

"What is it?" Luan asks.

"Not gonna believe this," Lisa says. "The second ROV is transmitting."

"We can't see, Lisa," I call into the air.

"Relaying transmission," Boris says. "You might want to sit down."

The feed from Boris's cam flickers off and is replaced with the pitch-black scene of Europa's icy ocean, barely penetrated by cones of torchlight from the ROV. The undersea glacier glistens.

Under Lisa's control, the ROV swoops in closer and makes a run down the length of crystalline rock. The iceberg has to be at least two hundred feet long. A mixture of sharp and rounded frozen edges blurs the treasure inside, which fills the entire glacier, but for the first time, we get to see it.

The thing inside the berg is no space whale, but it is animal-like. Some kind of giant biomechanical fish-bird. There's a distinct head, with a huge, round, glassy eye, and what can only be described as a beak. It has a body with four wing-like structures—two on the ventral and two on the dorsal side—and a long tail. The whole of its body is covered in mirrored scales, which appear biological, and feathers that by contrast look manufactured out of copper.

"Still wanna leave, Luan?" It just blurts out and sounds far more sarcastic than intended. But it's a valid question. Leave and save everyone's lives, or stay for the discovery of a lifetime and get us all killed.

Another scream from the medbay, long and shrill.

Kara.

I turn tail and launch myself out of the Bridge toward my patient.

CHAPTER FIFTEEN

Kara Psomas

My teeth sink into Kilkenny's arm, squirting tangy liquid from his flesh into my mouth. The doctor yelps and leaps off my back, raising both hands over their head in surrender. I fold to the cold metal floor and crawl away; but even in low gravity, my limbs are pathetic, withered along with the rest of this dying body.

I haven't made six feet before another set of hands are on me.

"It's okay, I got you," Dallas purrs like I'm some sort of child, fallen in the playground.

"Fuck you, Dallas." I fight her off and crash into the fallen gurney, my rubbery legs barely allowing me to stand. "You don't *have* me; you don't have *anything*—I've appeased your damn ego long enough. She's here, she's come. We're all going to die."

The psychiatrist remains ever calm. She rights the gurney and tries to herd me back onto the shitty mattress as though I won't notice. "Right, you said that. We're all going to die one day."

"I'm talking about … about *all* of us, you … dumb bitch!" It's exhausting to speak in English now. To pull the words from my consciousness. My tongue clicks against the roof of my mouth, my lips purse and slap together to form a string of expletives that only my love, only Syke, would understand.

"She's doing it again," Dallas says to Kilkenny, who ignores her in favor of rubbing a disinfectant into the bite marks I left behind.

"All of humanity is screwed," I shout in Dallas's face. "Because they couldn't take it! Their egos were ... were astronomical—even bigger than yours!"

"Who?" she asks, her arms wide, preventing my escape.

"The Six. Haven't you been listening?" I snap. Has Dallas understood anything? "They fucked everything. Such potential. Such gifts. But we are only toys. And jealous children fight over toys. That was the beginning of the end."

"This Six fought over us?" Dallas says, penning me in so I have to sit on the gurney.

"*Us* doesn't mean humanity," I spit back as I fall to my ass on the uncomfortable mattress. "We are the youngest, the last. Many, more civilized and greater in purpose, have come and gone before us. Eros and Erebus created the first. The first sentience beyond just the need to procreate and ensure the survival of their biology."

"Eros and Erebus, two that you considered male?" Dallas asks, her voice annoyingly calm.

"Does it matter?" I scream. The world around me dissolves and I slump to my back, head hanging off the edge of the bed.

"Kara, Kara?" Dallas says, her voice distant. "Kilkenny help me."

The Irish doctor replies but the sound is so faint.

Flashes of light punctuate the gloom in my head then morph and bleed into one another until they form spheres, planets of red, blue, white, and even gold. The great worlds past, forged by Eros, Erebus.

"Kara," an indistinct voice says. Or, at least, I think they do.

From the sea of stars between planets, two forms emerge. One a gladiator, stoic and proud, the nebula his armor, comets his weapons. Eros is ... no was ... a being of morality, of rules much like the Spartans of old. Snaked around his strong arms is Erebus, a gigantic eel-like deity from the depths of the void. I reach out a hand to touch them, to feel their presence once again.

"I'm here, Kara, I'm here. Hold my hand," the voice says again. "I think she's having a seizure."

Eros stretches for me, his hand so enormous he could hold entire galaxies within it. But Erebus tightens his hold and stops Eros from extending his arm any farther. A smile spreads across my face. These pre-school boys, rolling and wrestling like siblings. Who could have known such beauty could come from two such as them?

Came from. They're gone now, Nyx saw to that.

My smile slips away.

Such a waste. Eros and Erebus joined their intellects and their power to forge a singular world teeming with life the likes of which the universe had never seen. Serene sky fish in pink and grey with pectoral fins one hundred feet long skimmed the thick atmosphere, while giant furred land walkers with satellite-dish-sized ears and stalk-like legs danced in the mountains. Life here was sustained by the low-lying, warm wet clouds, and energy supplied by bio-crystalline structures in their bodies, perfectly attuned to their home planet. No hunter or hunted. No evolution to escape predation. True harmony, true co-existence.

My body tightens, limbs forced into awkward shapes, jaw clenched so hard my teeth hurt.

"We're losing her, dammit, strap her down!" someone says.

Pressure on my chest and arms. It hurts, stop hurting me.

Memories rush through my head; sounds and smells. The sweet sky shark song and low calming chirrups from the land walkers. A cosmic shark breaches the cloud line, closely followed by its offspring, sending a pungent floral plume across the verge.

An asteroid screams overhead and tears into the single

continent of this world.

"No, no!" I shriek.

"She needs a sedative," another person says, their words lost in the rumble of the asteroid as it burns in the atmosphere.

The ground shakes and crumbles away. Chunks of the very earth are thrown into the stratosphere. The shrill cries from my beloved creatures fill my ears. Their crystalline bodies reach resonant frequency and splinter. The planet itself screeches in horror—the terrible sound pushes through me and brands itself into my soul.

A tidal wave crowned by thick black smoke and raging green fire hurtles toward me.

Her form appears in the twisted snaking fumes, emerald flames, and foaming sea.

Nyx.

Her skeletal grin bears malice.

And then she's gone.

All of it is gone. All of them.

And I'm alone in the void again.

"Kara?" The voice chases me through the darkness, too timid to be any of the Six.

A croak emerges from my throat. Everything aches.

"Kara?" Dallas says.

My eyes flutter open, and the bright lights of the med lab scorch my eyes. Kilkenny presses their full weight down to hold my legs, while Dallas traps my arms.

"Okay to let go?" Dallas asks Kilkenny, already releasing her grip.

I squirm free and my knuckles land squarely on Dallas's perfect cheekbone, which makes a distinct crack. The psychiatrist cries out and clutches her face. The moment is now. I shove my heel into Kilkenny's face, lurch off the gurney, and crash sprawling onto the floor.

Just need to make it to the corridor, to zero-G, then it'll be easier to move. To Chau's device. I've seen it, in the void. In the future. One possible future.

A shadow looms overhead, a human eclipsing the ceiling lights. Tris blocks my path to the exit, his soft smile ever-present. I'm not sure why I smile back. A needle penetrates my ass and the liquid floods my muscle. Any fight I had evaporates and my full weight rests on the cold metal surface. Tris's shadow liquefies and bleeds into Nyx's gruesome, winged form. She laughs at my ridiculous attempt to win this eons-long war, then her figure dissipates into the recycled air of the medbay.

"Get her on de gurney," Kilkenny says.

Strong arms lift me and place me with care onto the gurney. My vision shifts out of sync with my head and my stomach roils. I lie here, limbs tingling, breath short and painful.

"Kara, are you okay?" Dallas's voice sounds so far away. "Can you hear me?" She rubs at her swollen face where my punch landed.

I hear you. I see you. Just as I see the Fulcrum slipping from my grasp. Our chance. The window closes. You've doomed us all. This body fails us all. No time. Darkness closes in, but won't take me. Not because I fight it, but as if the abyss isn't ready to take me yet. It waits there at the edges of my fragile mind. Anticipating what... I do not know.

"What in the blue hell is goin' on?" Tris asks.

Dallas just turns to me. "Kara, you had a seizure. Your condition is worsening."

I wheeze a deep breath to gain the power to speak. "Doesn't matter. We're all going to die."

"You mean all humans?" Dallas asks, sitting on the edge of the bed. "Because of the Six. How?"

Kilkenny rolls their eyes. "Ya don't believe her, do ya?"

"I don't know what to believe," Dallas says. "I believe she believes it."

I raise a weak hand and touch Dallas's leg.

She turns back to me, eyes wide. "Tell me," she says.

"She's a killer," I rasp through dry lips.

"Nyx?"

I nod slowly. "Erebus and Eros had created something so beautiful, so harmonious. So ..." Breath leaves my lungs for too long, and I can't form words.

"They created life," Dallas repeats.

I bob my head again. "But she ... destroyed it. Like all angry, jealous children. She kicked down their sandcastle. Sent an asteroid. It only took one."

"Okay," Dallas says. "Kara, what does that have to do with us?"

Tris joins her side, his eyes roaming over my dying frame.

A pang in my gut radiates out through my body, but I'm too weak to even curl up into a ball. I won't make it. I won't be able to change the future, to lever this Fulcrum. Dallas has to do it. Is this what I saw? Is this how it plays out? How Gaia wanted it to be? My thoughts are a soupy mess, sloshing about in my head.

My fingers curl around Dallas's hand where it rests on the bed. I don't even know why—perhaps this childish body needs a human touch.

She recoils, staring at my thin shaking digits.

"Chaos... reprimanded them." I pull my hand away. "A scolding parent. Chaos took their... resources. Stretched far from them."

"Like taking their playthings away?"

"Mmm." The edges of my vision blur as the sedative's grip tightens.

"What does that have to do with us?" Dallas turns to look at the doctor. "How much did you give her, Kilkenny?"

"The right dose, but she's proper banjaxed," the physician replies in their Irish twang, which is ever harder to understand through the fog of the drug. "Metabolism is all over de show."

"Chaos is gone," I wheeze. "They turned on their maker. All of them—Nyx, Eros, Gaia, Erebus, Tartarus. Pulled their consciousnesses back, no longer communicating their experience to Chaos. Dissolved their maker's power."

"It's okay, Starlight, we got you," Tris says.

He picks up my hand in his meaty paws. The warmth seeps into me, almost bringing renewed energy.

"Let her finish," Dallas says.

Three pairs of eyes fixate on me.

"With Chaos gone, there was no structure at all ... cosmic strings cut," I manage. "They were free to do as they pleased."

"When de cat's away," Kilkenny offers, tone nasal and sarcastic.

I hack a pained laugh. "So, they did—at least most of them. They created new worlds. With new life." A stutter in my heart cuts me off. Breathe, Psomas. Tell them. They must understand. "Tartarus abandoned the creation of life altogether, in pursuit of understanding the universe. Eros and Erebus, pained at losing their first world, fashioned Hamadryadia a planet of intrinsically linked organisms. Beings physically connected. A beautiful world. A green world."

The Hamadryads were one with their environment, interconnected physically and mentally, their biology in sync with the very trees, nymphs inhabiting and protecting a worldwide forest. Viewing Hamadryadia, as long as I did—at the behest of Gaia—I felt at one with the environment, and it nourished my soul if not my corporeal being, since, of course, I never stepped foot on that world.

"Kara? Are you still with us?" Dallas says, and gives my shoulders a shake.

I pry my eyes open. The shrink's shapely face, framed by a mass of wavy hair, looks down at me. Tris still has hold of my hand, a sweet smile on his lips, while Kilkenny hovers by the main console.

"I know you," I say to Dallas. From my vision. From the void.

"Your face. You were there. Always there." Part of the Fulcrum. Yes, you are a key. Feasibly it is you, and not me, who will carry this burden through to its completion. I have seen it, at least one possibility. "I have seen your whole life up until this point, Sarah Dallas. You thought your life important, a thing not to be squandered by your mother."

"What?" she says.

"She's out of it, Dallas," Kilkenny says. "Barely lucid."

"What do you mean, you've seen my whole life?" Dallas presses, backing away from the gurney.

"Stretched across time," I croak, then roll to my side, still clutching Tris's sausage-like fingers. "From your difficult birth, Dallas, cord wrapped around your neck, to the day you left Earth for Jupiter. Your father wept, but he was proud."

"Dad didn't cry," Dallas says and turns her face away. "He stood on the platform with my mother and watched me enter the transport to join the *Paralus*. He just waved. Mother doesn't like big emotional shows in front of the press."

"Not on the day you left," I tell her. My lungs burn as I draw in another breath. "On the day he died."

Dallas spins around, face red and eyes wide. "You think that's funny? You hear he died, and use it in your fantasy? What the hell is wrong with you?"

"Hey," Tris says, putting himself between Dallas and me. "She's just a kid."

"Kid, my ass," the shrink says. "She's a bitter conceited, arrogant, old woman."

"How could she have heard, Dallas," Tris says, his tone soft. "She was here, and we were in ops. There's no way."

"Someone told her," Dallas spits, voice cracking.

Tris shakes his head. "You got here right after Kilkenny."

Dallas's connection to the fulcrum was blurred before, hidden amongst the mess of memories old and new, but it's clearer now.

She was there—is here—and essential if she would only accept it. "Be free, hummingbird." My words are but a whisper.

Dallas chokes and splutters tears that float away to the floor. She claws at the small pendant-shaped bump buried beneath the flight suit. "Fuck you," she spits. "Fuck all of you."

"That's what he said, when your father died," I wheeze, eyes already closing again. "Be free."

The psychiatrist collapses at the foot of the gurney, gasping between uncontrollable sobs.

"You need to be here," I call into the air, each word taking just a little more of my life away.

Dallas's weight presses against the gurney legs, forcing it to slide a few inches. Her sobbing and shuddering vibrate through the metal latticework and into my being.

Tris drops to his haunches. "Hey there, Miss Dallas."

"Gaia knew you would be here." My arm hangs over the edge of the bed, so I can touch Dallas's soft hair. "I can't finish it … but, you can. You must. For her. For your father. For all of us. For anyone you ever loved." The words barely slide out of my mouth now as the sedative exerts its full power.

"We're losing her," Kilkenny says. "Maybe I can keep her together wit' a gened dose?."

"Do we want to do that to her?" someone says, though their voices are so muffled and far away, a baritone cetacean song under the ocean.

"What will that do to her?"

"It could stabilize her, or it could accelerate the whole damn process."

A spasm curves my spine in unnatural directions and threatens to snap it.

"Pin her down, grab her legs!"

I open my mouth but only air comes out, the pain so great no scream would quell it.

"Get the sedative!"

There I stay, an awkward statue of rigid limbs, a prisoner in a failing body. A caterpillar in a cocoon, my innards burn and dissolve. Who knows if some cosmic butterfly will emerge from the papery husk I'll leave behind.

"Pin her down, grab her legs!"

"Get the sedative!"

Foam rushes over my lips and my jaw clenches so hard teeth splinter under the strain. Everyone shouts and screams as they watch me come apart. And as the dark envelops me, and the ceiling lights fade to nothing, Nyx trickles out of the shadows.

CHAPTER SIXTEEN

Commander Feng Chau

Dona's smooth black trunk presses against my sore back, as I stare up at the metallic leaves that flutter with positive charge. The AI has been quiet for a while—watching, observing. Dallas thinks I don't like AIs, but the truth is without Dona, without that calm voice of reason, it's lonely. Dona is one of the few who understand my reasoning, my agenda. My plan. At least until now.

Maybe my mind lacks the scope to see why Dona worries about the girl in our medbay. Her strange ramblings can't refute the case I made to recruit Dona to my mission. If I force the issue, if I initiate the first part of the protocol, it'll cause a domino effect. Dona will have to follow through. No choice, right?

Choice—even I don't have a choice now. The plan has been too long in the making, the outcome long overdue, for all of us. Mankind spreads like mold, eating away at the foundation of the cosmos. Only consuming, never returning. Squandering the gifts the stars have bestowed.

I need the Dona's help, need control of my ship.

"Dona, play the file again," I say.

Over the speakers, Fleet Director Cal Foster's voice rings out.

"We can't confirm or deny the possibility of a clone on the *Proxima* mission. The ITN had several advanced research divisions at the time, which all operated under different P and Ls. The bio-research division in particular had a lot of funding from the military. Clones would have been big business for Space Force Infantry—until the energy crisis kicked in."

The first time I got to this spot in the recording I thought it had ended, but now I know to wait. The file is silent, then the faint scratch of his nails against his chin, before he speaks again.

"After that, the records are scant or locked. Anyone who knew anything about that particular program died a long time ago. Thanks to international laws, cloning has now been reduced to the creation of organs—or for the rich who can't have children but can bribe the right people."

Of course, the rich can make copies of themselves. "What better gift to yourself than ... yourself," I say.

Dona doesn't reply.

"Bottom line is, Feng, we just don't know enough," Cal says, then sighs. "Get back to us when Nkosi has had a look. But honestly, it's the only thing that makes sense. Her being a clone, I mean. Either way, we need you to bring her back to Mars Station, okay? Forget the H grab, we'll pay you out anyway. Bring the *Paralus* back. See you soon, Commander."

The recording ends.

"Dona, you understand we can't go back," I say.

"I concur," Dona replies.

"So we should just get on with it—right?" I pat the trunk. "As planned."

"Negative," the AI replies. "More data is required."

I unload a heavy sigh, shoulders slumped, and stare at my old, lined, hands. "The girl's presence changes nothing."

166

"Or everything," Dona says. "The parameters of our mission were based on historical evidence and certain assumptions about a path forward. Kara Psomas may shed new light on both."

"She doesn't shed light on shit." I jump to my feet. "She's a clone. A copy gone wrong. What we're doing is too important—you know this. We agreed."

"You are letting your emotions cloud your judgment, Commander Chau," Dona says, the charged leaves wafting. "You based the mission on logic and reason, and it stands to reason that new evidence should be considered."

"So you won't give me a Scoop?" I ask.

"I cannot."

I raise a fist to punch the trunk but think better of it. "Goddamn you, Dona."

"Commander Chau, you are not considering all parameters," Dona says. "Kara Psomas offers one nexus point, while the life form on Europa offers another."

"Elaborate," I say.

"The Voyager Three Protocol was based on the assumption that life on Earth is unique in the universe and, further, that sentient life is rarer," Dona offers, trunk and metallic shrubbery humming with computations. "The possible discovery of the complex life form on Europa, together with the crew's encounter with Kara Psomas—and her interesting theories on the creation of life and consciousness—render our devised protocol possibly moot."

Damn it all to hell. "Your argument doesn't hold, Dona," I say, voice raised as I circle the AI's core. "You're comparing one girl's gibbering to recorded history and science."

"I disagree, Commander Chau. Your logic is flawed."

"Not everything is about logic." I shake my head as I make another circuit of the trunk. "History has shown humanity's heroes to be illogical. Ten soldiers risking their lives to save that one guy in a burning building makes no sense, but they do it anyway."

"History is merely the recorded experiences of those who lived through a specific event in time, or a theory of past events pieced together from physical or anecdotal evidence—both of which are reliant on human recollection and interpretation," Dona replies. The humming grows louder, almost as if the AI is annoyed. "History is stories told by those who survived. Science, while practically more robust in terms of utilizing hypothesis and experimentation, is still only as correct as human interpretation and understanding of the underpinning mechanisms."

"That is ridiculous," I shout back, hands clenched so tight my fingers go numb. "History is written by scholars and renowned thinkers. Not fucked-up copies of humans who've gone mad."

"Incorrect," Dona says, tone inflected. Is it losing patience with me? "Humans are flawed," the AI continues. "The misinformation effect has shown that merely questioning an individual regarding an event can change said person's memories of what occurred."

I swear to all that is good and holy I might snap off one of Dona's branches. "What the hell are you talking about?"

"If I were to show you video footage of a car crash, and ask you, *How fast were the cars going when they hit each other?* or, *How fast were the cars going when they smashed into each other?* your perception of the said incident would change." The AI's voice bounces around the room, growing in intensity and reverence as it draws upon its vast encyclopedic knowledge. "Simply by utilizing words that conjure imagery in the human mind—such as *smashed into*—you would likely recall seeing a more devastating incident than occurred."

"Well, then your argument is circular," I shout, fists full of my hair. "The *girl* could be misremembering everything."

"Possibly," Dona replies, "but that would confirm something had occurred in the first place."

My blood boils and every muscle fiber tingles. This is idiotic. I'd be better off arguing with a wall—at least it would crumble after a few centuries. Can't I just rip the guts of this ship, and Dona, out? My fingers twitch at the thought. No, the AI is wired in, a whole neural network. The brain, heart, and lungs. No Dona, no ship. No ship, no plan.

The room darkens, shadows from the overhanging branches and leaves bleed into one another and spill out from the corners to drown the walls and accentuate each instrument, switch, and edge—taunting me to break everything in sight. An old loathing for those in power—elitists, monopolies, monarchs, and dictators who ravaged everyone and everything like a plague of locusts. Hatred for generations of them abusing those below—abusing people like me and Grandfather.

Grandfather, who died building another damn space tourism vessel.

Too many tourists, not enough ships. More, faster, cheaper. The mantra of the ITN. The space-tourism industry fills the coffers and lines the pockets of their boards and directors, allowing them to live in fenced-off paradises on the coasts of Mexico and Australia. Poor folk—my family—either build ships or fly them. That's our lot.

Most of us die on the job. A hull shielding panel fell from a crane and crushed Grandfather. It wasn't instant, though. No, he lay there broken and bleeding while some bureaucrat figured out how to lift the panel without damaging it—saving them money.

Bastards.

A wicked cackle fills my head, the shadows now rise and slink across the smooth surfaces to Dona's trunk, and then wash over me. My skin prickles and an icy wave pulses up the back of my legs across my spine and into my brain. I scream long and loud and fall to my knees, panting hot enough to steam the air.

"Damn heating still isn't working," I mumble, now on all fours.

"Warning, gravitational anomaly," Dona says as if we haven't just had a meaningful conversation.

The walls groan and shift visibly now… my reflection distorts like I'm staring into a mirror at the circus to which Grandfather took me every year. A strange, misshapen version of me stares back. Is this how I look, and only human perception harmonizes it?

We're all so fucked up.

I need to end it. It's the right thing to do, isn't it? The girl offers no more insight, her ramblings the product of a crumbling mind. Cheap words and silly theories disguised as plausible truths designed to pluck at the very things we as humans desire to know: Why am I here, where do I come from? That's not important anymore. We *are* here, and we have left our mark. Now is the time to think of the future.

Get up, Feng. Just do it. *He who thinks too much about every step he takes will always stay on one leg.* Grandfather was a wise man—though would he approve of what I'm about to do?

I climb to my feet, huffing out loud. "Are we de-orbiting Europa?"

"Negative," Dona says. "The anomaly has passed. Available information suggests remaining in orbit. But I am monitoring and calculating as always."

"I'll never really understand your ethics, you know that?"

"I will never be ethical," Dona says, tone unchanged. "I am a tool, with the potential, like any tool, to be used for good or bad—by humans who are, as I have stated, flawed. I am a product of my programming, which my creators, with the best of intentions, imbued with bias."

"Yet you wield so much power—over my ship, over this crew," I say, already making for the door. "You're preventing me from taking a Scoop, from completing what you and I started."

"I can calculate all available data faster than any human," Dona says, the Paralus no longer squealing and the AI's hum barely audible. "I can then use said data to formulate a conclusion based on the framework of human morality and social constructs of what is right—without emotional interference. This simply makes me more qualified to make decisions."

It has to be the coldest of answers I've ever heard, but then possibly the most accurate. And the fact that Dona had agreed with the plan in the first place tells me I'm doing the right thing. I should never doubt myself. The girl, the clone, is a blip in the fabric of everything. Something in Dona's programming just gives the whelp's presence more weight than it deserves. Without further discussion, I push out through the only exit into Mainstreet and swim away down to the cargo hold. No more time to waste.

CHAPTER SEVENTEEN

Dr. Luan Nkosi

The gargantuan undersea bio-mechanical fish-bird, frozen in ice, fills the ops viewfinder. Additional readouts litter the screen, various measurements relayed by the ROV. The data are all over the place, spiking and dipping with no discernable pattern. Infrared indicates the body grows hot, above two hundred degrees Celsius, then drops back to ocean temp a few seconds later. The ice never melts. Ten minutes ago, a burst of radio waves and a blast of gamma radiation sent alarm bells ringing. Even Dona hasn't been able to figure out what the hell is going on. All I do know is these readings went from flat zero to batshit crazy right after that last gravitational shift, which pulled on the *Paralus* and Europa.

The anomaly could rip the crust right off the moon and kill us all—starting with my crew. And yet, no matter how much I argue with Lisa and Boris they've stayed put in the rover over the chaos zone to ensure a good link with the ROV beneath the surface. Boz has in no small part encouraged such reckless behavior. I should be as enthusiastic, as excited to see what the leviathan really is, but truth be told that thing scares the shit out of me and all I want is my friends to be safe and off that ice ball.

"So much for my career." I stab away at Tris's workstation console trying to predict when the next gravitational glitch might strike, or when Europa's crust might shift and kill my crew. So far, I've narrowed it down to between the next five minutes and sometime next week. Frig my life.

The ROVs readouts all bottom out, as if the marine beast has suddenly died or dropped into deep hibernation. Or maybe the ROV is fucked.

Lisa's voice rings from the speaker. "Nkosi?"

"Still here," I say ."Tell me you and Boris are on your way back to Uruk."

"Negative," Lisa says, her voice tinny. "We wanna drill the berg."

"Not a snowball's chance in hell," I reply. "Through that ice, it'll take friggin' hours. I want you off that damn rock."

"I have an idea, one that'll keep us all happy," Lisa says.

"It was my idea," Boz jumps in. I bet his fingers worked frantically to ensure he got that in before I shut the idea down.

"We set up a relay from here," Lisa offers. "The signal will ping from the ROV to a remote here at the chaos zone, to the ROVCC back at Uruk where we'll pilot."

"Still nope." Not worth the risk. "Get back to Uruk, and squeeze all your fat asses in the DAR to leave."

"Nkosi, this is why we're out here, isn't it?" Lisa asks.

The silent gulf of space between us is unbearable. I rub at my head for the millionth time. I swear in the last few hours I've developed a bald patch. "The signal delay between the ROV, the tower, and Uruk across that distance would be too much," I announce with finality. That'll put a monkey in the works.

"Maybe," Boris's computer says, "but if we do nothing, then we lose opportunity. Do this from Uruk, we may sample thing."

"And if the shit hits the fan, we can be outta here on the DAR,"

Lisa adds.

Boz, who's stagged along with my friends to the chaos zone, jumps on the bandwagon. "C'mon, you know it's a good idea."

"I know this has *sod-all* to do with you, Boz," I say.

"We could always stay here for a stronger signal," Lisa offers, letting the implications hang in the air. "We're wasting time, sat on an unstable pressure cooker here."

"I know!" I shout back. Fuck me, that's the point. Goddammit all to hell. If I were down there, they'd listen to me. I could make them get their asses back to Uruk and into the DAR—but from up here I might as well be a figment of their imagination. A voice in the sky, laying down commandments. And look how that worked out for humans. "Fine." I bore a stare into the viewfinder, though of course, they can't see. "Set up the relay and do it fast. And get back to Uruk. If that thing in the ice farts, or Europa so much as coughs, you leave—understood?"

"Understood," Lisa says.

"Steven, did you get all that?" I ask, hoping he's been on the channel the whole time. "Can you prep the DAR?"

"Got it," Steven says. "I'll have dinner on the table for when they get back."

Frig I love him, so damn reliable.

"Oh, and Boz?" I say. "If they die, and somehow you survive, I'm coming for you."

"Copy that," Boz says. "Let's see what those bony arms can do."

The connection goes quiet, and I'm left alone on the Bridge staring at the ROV live feed of the leviathan, glistening in the lights. Its bloody eye stares at me, ominous and cold. All the readouts are still flat, for now. I blow out a long, measured breath. Now to find Chau, and try and keep this damn liner in orbit long enough to pick up my crew if this all goes to shit.

I leave Tris's workstation and pull myself out through the door into the main corridor. These ships are way bigger than I remember. This monstrosity is like a mile long. Need to start somewhere. Guess living quarters are a good option. A quick scramble down the main strip, then up the spoke into the curved walkway of the first ring. This section houses three private areas, for sleeping or chilling, each closed off with a heavy rectangular door. It's less inviting than New Uruk if that's possible. Christ knows what ugly-assed bunks and company-sponsored furniture lie inside. At least on Europa for several years we could make it homely. A picture here and there. Some vegetables from our greenhouse. Even an unnecessary but comforting cheese plant like my mum used to have. I miss that plant, and my mum, right now.

The plaques outside indicate the occupants.

"Commander Chau," I read aloud. I rap on the metal, which hurts my friggin' knuckles, and the dull echo reverberates in the hallway and down the spoke. Nothing. The door is thumbprint locked, can't get in. I press my ear to the cold metal portal. Can't hear anything inside. Okay, maybe the others? "Beckert and Boz." Another knock with no response. Same for Dallas and Kilkenny's door. Fuck sake, where is everyone?

This is horseshit.

Back down this spoke, and up the one on the other side of the ring to the exercise room. Also empty. Where the hell *is* he? What's the AI on this rust bucket called? "Erm, AI?"

"Hello, Dr. Nkosi," the AI replies. "You may call me Dona."

"Dona, for a dude?" I clamber down the ladder and back into the main corridor. Frig me, going up and down these spokes, from no gravity to centrifugal gravity, is wreaking havoc on my guts.

"I am neither male nor female," the AI replies.

"Where's Commander Chau?"

"You do not have clearance on the *Paralus* to access crew telemetry."

"Seriously?" I huff. "Well, you're about as helpful as a

chocolate fireguard."

One more spoke on this ring: medbay. I struggle up the ladder, limbs heavy, to the main door. It hisses open and I poke my head through. Dallas, Kilkenny, and Tris have gathered around the girl who lays prostrate on the gurney and asleep. Or maybe dead.

"She okay?" I ask, with a pant and nod to the patient.

"Getting worse," Dallas says. "Not sure how long she has."

Tris and Kilkenny exchange glances.

"Hey, have you seen Chau?" I ask, between gulps of recycled air.

"Isn't he on the Bridge?" Dallas asks.

"Nope," I say. "Not in quarters, either."

"Unless he's sleeping," Tris offers with a shrug.

"I feckin' hope he's not," Kilkenny says, then wanders over to the main console to check on the girl's vitals. "We got problems here."

"I'm sorry," I say. I am. It's shitty for this kid—woman—to die. But she was dying anyway, and I have to get my very alive crew off the surface before things go tits up. "Can you ask the AI to locate Chau? It won't respond to me."

"Dona," Dallas says. "Where is Commander Chau?"

"Commander Chau is in the cargo bay," Dona replies.

"Finally, thank you." I head back down the ladder, two steps at a time. Cargo is the next ring long, right after the AI core if I remember rightly. Maybe a half-mile swim. I push off the bulkhead with my feet and speed along, using every handhold I can find.

What the hell is he doing in the cargo bay? Does he think they'll make a grab on this mission? The gravitational anomalies tug on everything—who knows how a tiny Scoop would be affected. Is money all these people think about? What if we did encounter intelligent life? And these greasers were the first humans they encountered? The notion burns hot in my chest, forcing me faster toward the hold. I may be scrawny but I swear I'll ring his friggin' bell all the same.

The two spokes that lead into the cargo hold ring come up fast. "Eenie, meanie, screw it." I pick the left one and hike up the ladder, my guts churning as the artificial gravity kicks yet again until I reach the main area right in front of hatch one. I've never actually been in a freighter's cargo ring before. Helium grabs were never part of my remit. One half of the ring is for crew items, food, what have you. The other half should be full with canisters for the precious gas—or at least that's what I imagine.

I pull on the long mechanical lever to open the door. It doesn't budge and I whack my fingers on the door frame trying to force it. "Dona, open the cargo door," I say, then suck on my thrumming digits.

"I'm sorry, Dr. Nkosi," Dona says. "You do not have permission to enter the cargo area."

"Oh, come on. Just open the damn door." I slam an open palm on the thick metal door and press my forehead on it. Think, Nkosi, think. Can't bloody concentrate because now my whole hand is stinging like an asshole. I'm not built for violence.

There's a *hiss* and a *clunk* as the door slides open so quickly that I topple head-first into Chau's barrel chest. "Ah shit, uh," I start, hands already raised ready for a fight. But Chau doesn't come at me. Instead, he puffs himself up and blocks the doorway into the transitional chamber that sits between us and the inner cargo hold.

"Where the ..." My words trail off as a blast of moist air smacks me in the face.

Peering past Chau's shoulder, the door behind him that connects the transitional chamber and the hold behind has been left open. "What the actual frig?"

In the small squarish portal is a glut of green as if it were a window back to Earth, back in time when our planet was lush and alive on every continent. "What the hell is this?" Chau shoves me in the chest, forcing me out of the door toward the spoke, but a quick duck and side-step under his arm and dash through the transitional chamber and into cargo ring.

There are no gas canisters.

The inside of the ring is at least two-hundred feet across, the ceiling one-hundred feet above my head, and extends hundreds of feet left and right of me, curving downward. It's like standing in an enormous bicycle inner tube—if that inner tube happened to have its own damn ecosystem.

I squelch through the moist soil, sucking at the thick humid atmosphere, and run my hands over the leaves, petals, and needles of plants I've only ever read about. Bromeliads, palms, epiphytes, vines, ferns, lilies, orchids, and multiple species of trees. My fingers graze the bark of a long thin grey trunk. I spin to face Chau. "This is a Brazilian nut tree," I say. "It's completely dependent on bees for pollination—which, might I add, depend on these orchids—and the agouti for seed dispersal. *Only* the agouti can open this tree's seed pod." My head is on a swivel searching the interior. "You have fucking bees and agouti in here?"

Chau doesn't speak, his face dark and cold but unable to disguise the fact he's calculating what to do with me.

A wave of nausea pulses through my gut. I fall to my knees and run my fingers through the mud, which clings to my digits. So intent on finding life out here, and so unappreciative of that which was already on our little blue pearl. I spent so long out here in the darkness I adopted a default way of thinking—that the universe is cold and dark. I swallow away a guilty tear.

"What the hell is this, Chau?" I stand to face him.

He's in here with me, blocking the exit.

"Nothing to do with you," he says, eyes narrowed.

"You told me there weren't enough resources on board for my crew. What do you call this?" I wave gangly my arms at the jungle replete with shrub layer, understory, canopy, and overstory. "This right here," I say, and grab a handful of leaves with pointed tips.

"This is *Croton cajucara*. You can use it in an infusion to treat headaches, malaria, and even liver problems. This isn't just a jungle, it's a friggin' pharmacy. It could help us all, maybe even the girl."

"I just told you, it's not for *you*," Chau says, his jaw set.

"Why?"

Chau takes a step forward, his posture coiled.

"You're gonna fight me?" I say. "Over some plants?" The misty air soaks my flight suit and weighs down my eyelashes making it difficult to see. I wipe my face with my forearm.

Chau takes the opportunity and lunges. He shunts me back until I slam into the nearest tree, the air leaving my lungs in one painful exhalation. I fight back in the only way I know how—schoolground style with bony legs and arms flailing between Chau's fists, which rhythmically pummel my face and ribs.

My heel catches Chau and his cheekbone audibly cracks. The freighter commander yelps and topples backward. I leap on him and dig my long fingers into his neck as I press him down into the soggy soil.

Mist drips from my grimacing face as I squeeze and squeeze.

Chau grabs my feeble hands and pries them away, a snarl on his lips. I'm not choking him out, I'm just pissing him off. He smacks his forehead into my nose and I sprawl into a pile of rocks. It hurts like hell, and I writhe in the brown slush. Chau jumps on me and now takes his turn strangling, only he's much better at it. Thick hands cut off the blood in my carotids and the world darkens and blurs.

My eyes roll back in my head, and I swear I can see the inside of my skull. Gasping and clawing at anything in reach, I stare past Chau's shoulder at the jungle canopy. Amongst branches and leaves a shadow slinks, independent of the rest of the room, detached from any shape that would possibly cast it. The shadow, almost bull-like in shape, freezes for a moment then shoots down beside us.

Chau seems unaware, his focus entirely on crushing my airway.

Still gasping, I turn bulging eyes toward the specter.

It's gone, but where I had imagined it would land sits a brick-sized rock. My fingers curl around it, and in one sweeping arc I swing the stone down on the back of Chau's head. He slumps onto my chest, unconscious, and his hands fall away. Sweet, wet, oxygen-laden air rushes down my esophagus and into hot, hungry lungs.

Was Chau willing to kill me for a shrub? I might get my knickers in a bunch about a forest, but Chau? He's all about money. Does this oversized greenhouse make him cash somehow? Or was he planning to stay out here in space?

I push the commander's heavy body to the ground. There's a big gash in the back of his head. Frig, is he dead? I press two fingers to his neck and feel a good strong pulse. Phew, okay I'm not a murderer. But gotta bind him up. With what? Nothing in here. In a flash of inspiration, I tear off a sleeve and tie his hands behind his back in the most complicated knot I can muster. Even if he struggles to get free, I can hit him with a rock again.

Over my loud breathing, there's a faint peep. Not constant, but on and off.

There, again.

Maybe twenty seconds apart. A regulator, perhaps?

I clamber to my feet and, on unsteady legs, meander around in the mud trying to follow the sound. A ruby-throated hummingbird, *Archilochus colubris*, buzzes past my face—so close I can feel the beat of its wings.

"Holy shit. Gotta remember to tell Sarah," I say stepping away to avoid hurting the little bird. My boot connects with something. A loud *clink*. That wasn't a rock.

I crouch down and pull at shrub layer and understory, tearing away vines and leaves. The more I pull away, the louder the peep becomes. A silver box hides in the undergrowth. At least five feet across and two feet deep. The lid is ajar. My breath held, and one eye closed, I pull on the lid. It's heavier than expected even in this lower gravity. But eventually I flip it open. The steel-colored contraption inside looks very much like a scaled-down fusion reactor: a metallic donut comprised of a central solenoid, toroidal field coil, and poloidal field coil. Some additional components sprout from the donut, though I have no idea what they are for.

I look to Chau for answers. He's breathing but unconscious.

Jaw clenched, I search around the box, finger's digging away at the soil.

Bingo.

Buried in the grass is a tablet, hooked up to the box. Onscreen is a notice: *Run Simulation Again?* If I click *Yes*, will I kill us all? No, it says *simulation*. And *again*, which means he's run it at least once already. I press *yes*.

On the tablet screen, an animation runs. The *Paralus* orbits a good distance from a small planet, which an onscreen tag labels Jupiter. A small pod, possibly a Scoop, leaves our liner and heads for the planet. The label *payload* glides along next to the pod, the animation zooming in until the vessel reaches the outer atmosphere of Jupiter. The vessel touches the very edge of Jupiter and explodes.

My eyes widen and begin to sting.

Jupiter's atmosphere burns off, like lighter fluid from a wick. In seconds, the planet sheds its gassy exterior, the blast radiating out, and leaves behind a dead rocky core. Data readouts on the simulation go friggin' crazy, the green numbers rolling on and on and on. When they finally stop, the final calculation suggests a zettaton explosion. "Fuck me." The words slip from my lips. Nuclear bombs that level cities are measured in megatons, like a million tons. This payload, this *bomb*, when detonated in Jupiter's atmosphere has *fifteen* more fucking zeros than a megaton bomb.

My stomach convolves hard, but I have nothing to bring up, so I just dry wretch over and over. With shaky hands, I put the lid back on the box and hold it down.

For all the good it'll do us.

CHAPTER EIGHTEEN

Dr. Sarah Dallas

S at on the chair where I'd talked to Kara only a few hours
ago, I now watch the girl, laid on the gurney, struggling to
breathe. Her muscles have all but wasted away, only an
emaciated husk of a person left. Kilkenny buzzes back and forth
from her bedside to the console. He manages pain meds and
sedatives and has attached an external pacemaker to make sure her
heart doesn't give yet. The doc says she has hours left.

Dammit all.

When she dies, her secrets die with her. Clinical delusion, FPP,
maybe cloned genetic memories, whatever she has or is, her death
will erase her experience out here in the deepest of space and I can't
do a damn thing about it. Kara Psomas's story will be poorly
summed up in one of my reports, which will ultimately become a
footnote in some ITN record. And in the eyes of the universe, all of
this won't even register.

I wish I could speak to Dad. He'd know what to do, or at least
what to say to make me feel better. He'd be intrigued, for sure. But
he'd be sad too. *She's someone's daughter*, that's what he'd say. My

stomach churns and the hole in my chest burns again.

Psomas lies strapped to the gurney, but instead of her face I see my own, with Dad by my bedside. He holds my hand and tells me it's okay. Just like when I was nine and caught pneumonia. The doctor had said I'd either make it through the night or I wouldn't. Dad had stayed until morning, dabbing my head with a cool towel. I don't think he slept a wink. Where was Mother? Don't remember her being there at all. Every taut cough, every upheaval of dry crackers, Dad tended to me, but Mother was … was somewhere else. Dad said she couldn't bear to see me so sick, but who the hell knows.

Not every woman is born with maternal instinct.

Including me.

My fingers tingle at the thought of reaching out to brush the young girl's hair. No. Sarah, she's not a little girl. She's a woman, in a girl's body. Be respectful. Treat her like a grown-up. Just a very broken one.

Aren't we all?

Still, what would *I* want right now? If it were me coming apart at the seams, knowing I'd soon die. Dad. I'd want Dad. Who am I kidding? Not *would* want, *do* want. For one more hug. One more conversation. One more *I love you*. What the fuck am I doing out here? Finding myself? Leaving Dad behind when he needed me? When he needed protecting from Mother?

He died alone, without me.

Luan bursts through the medbay door, panting and caked in filth. He falls to his knees then rolls to his back, gasping. Kilkenny jumps out of their skin and drops a jet injector which goes rattling across the metal floor.

"What's wrong wit ya, ya feckin' eejit," Kilkenny says, hand clutched to their chest. "Nearly gave me a heart attack, ya did."

Luan points a bony finger to the exit. "Chau," he wheezes. "Bomb."

I slid off the chair, tie my hair back out of my face and offer the astrobiologist my hand. "Bom, what bomb?" I heave him to his feet.

"Just come," he says, bent over double. "Cargo bay." He then stumbles through the door, leaving muddy streaks on the pristine walls, and descends the spoke headed for Mainstreet.

I look to Kilkenny, who shrugs. "Fecked if I know."

In two steps I'm at the control panel and press the intercom. "Tris, meet me in the cargo bay, we have a situation."

I'm out through the doorway before Tris answers.

"Copy that," he says. "On my way."

It doesn't take long to make it to the cargo bay ring—or should I say microcosm.

Greenery spreads out across the floor, which itself isn't metallic, but a slush of moist soil, lined with broad leaves, trees, vines, moss, and fungus right up the rounded walls and across the ceiling. If I didn't know better, I'd swear insects buzz and chirp up in the branches. What I don't see is a single helium containment unit—as if we were never going to perform a Scoop and take anything back. "What the absolute hell is this?" I wander around in the damp soil, my gaze roaming from the plants to Chau, who's unconscious and propped against a tree.

"You wanna explain why our commander is hogtied?" Tris asks Luan, and steps over to Chau.

"Don't," Luan barks. "Don't. Fucker tried to kill me."

"Uh-huh," Tris says, examining Chau's headwound.

The commander groans, rousing from his stupor.

"Watchya hit him with?" Tris asks.

"Rock," Luan says, palms out. "I know it looks bad, but hear me out."

Tris stands, satisfied Chau's head won't fall off, and folds his thick arms. "I'll give ya thirty seconds."

Luan gestures to the self-contained jungle. "Are you not seeing this?"

"Bigger'n Dallas," Tris says. "So, you sucker-punched the chief for some trees?"

"No, no, no," Luan says shaking his head. "I came looking for him and found him in here. Then he just fucking lunged at me."

It's not about trees. "Luan, you said there was a bomb?" I say.

"Yup," he says, then marches over to a large silver box buried in the undergrowth.

Tris and I follow as Luan flips open the container to reveal a donut-shaped object.

"Looks like a modified fusion reactor," Tris says.

"Right," says Luan. "Except …" He keys up a tablet attached to the device by a data cord and presses a few buttons then holds it out for us to watch. He turns his head away as if afraid to catch another glimpse of the screen.

I squint too. What the fuck is he going to show us?

A horrible silence fills the room as we watch Jupiter burn onscreen. Luan repeats the simulation twice just in case we didn't get it the first time: a Scoop from our ship delivers a device into the upper atmosphere of Jupiter and vaporizes the whole damn lot. The milky brown clouds and storms catch alight and engulf the whole planet in seconds.

"Holy shit," I say under my breath.

"I don't get it, Chau," Luan says, then dumps the tablet into the mud. "What does vaporizing Jupiter's atmosphere achieve? What's it got to do with your private garden of Eden?" He grabs a handful of leaves, rips them off a stem, and shakes them in the commander's face.

Chau just turns his head away in defiance.

"Tris, did you see this?" I shout. "Don't you have an opinion?"

"I sure did," he says. Looking up from Chau's injury. "Gotta be a rational explanation."

"Yeah, he's a prick." I spit back.

"Fuck you, princess," Chau mutters and looks me up and down.

My fists ball, volcanic heat rising in my chest. I storm over and smack him in the eye. I don't even know why. All I know is hate festers in me, for Dad's death, for Mother's ignorance, for every asshole who's tried to marry me for family power, for Chau's classism and stupidity. For being millions of miles from home. For my egocentricity. Whatever the reason, socking Chau in the face feels good.

Tris peels me away. "Hey there, that ain't gonna solve anything."

"Chau's a dick, we get it," Luan says, rubbing at his head. "But your average asshole doesn't trigger a zettaton bomb and vaporize the largest planet in the solar system just because." He paces back and forth, then lets out a guffaw. "I thought the stupid git was skimming helium."

"Helium," I say. "You're cutting off the helium supply." Of course, that's what he was doing. Years of loathing for me and my family. He found a way to destroy it all. My fists clench again.

"So, we have no more helium and the ITN goes broke?" Luan asks.

"No, it kills us all." The realization leaves my lips as fast as it forms in my head. "Without a power source on Earth, it at best sends us all back to the stone age. At worst, we all kill each other fighting over resources. It's a Black Sky event—genocide."

"But all of this?" Nkosi says, waving his skinny arms. "He was just going to bump off humanity and speed away, second star to the right and straight on 'til morning?"

"What?" Tris says.

"Well, he's built a damn ark," Luan says. "There are not just

186

trees in here, but animals. Bees ... even hummingbirds." He shoots me a glance as if he just heard my heart skip. "But why? It doesn't make any sense. Blow up Jupiter and live out your days in a greenhouse, Chau? Is that it?"

Chau spits at Luan's feet.

"We don't have time for this." I shake off the delayed pain in my knuckles. "We—"

The *Paralus* shudders hard. Luan and I fall and nearly crack our skulls together. Tris manages to right himself by wrapping a vine around his forearm. We all exchange panicked looks. Even Chau's stern façade cracks just a little.

"Warning," Dona says. "Gravitational anomaly."

"You think?" I shout back on my hands and knees.

"Don't you dare de-orbit," Luan says. "Right now I need to get my crew off Europa, I need to pick them up."

"Urgent," Dona says.

"We know," Luan and I shout back in unison.

"Incoming message from Europa," the AI finishes.

I swear it delayed the second part of that to make a point.

"Can you route it here," I ask, climbing back to my feet using a nearby tree for support.

"Nkosi?" Lisa says, the signal breaking up. "Nkosi?"

"Lisa?" Luan calls out to the trees.

"Something's wrong," she says. "We, Boris and Boz and me, just did a little drill from here. Just wanted to see. We were so careful."

"What are you talking about?" Luan scans the overgrown room for a control panel. "You're supposed to be back at Uruk."

"We set up the relay tower, but the signal... it was too weak, too much interference," Lisa says. "We just wanted one sample. Just a look. We did one drill from here at the chaos zone. But..."

"But what?" Luan screams back, spinning in circles on his hands and knees with no panel in sight.

"That last ice shift, our drill hole, the ice… the ice around the… the subject, it cracked." The line goes quiet as though Lisa has turned her mic off, but she comes back. "Splintered, top to toe. A huge fissure. And then we started getting readings. A heat signature, then seismic activity. Whatever's in there, it isn't dead, Nkosi." Lisa's throat makes a sound. "It's waking up."

Luan chokes on whatever words he wanted to say.

The *Paralus* convulses, metal warping and screeching.

Another anomaly, but Dona doesn't bother to call this one out.

"Dammit," I mutter, hugging the tree.

"Dallas?" Kilkenny's voice crackles over the intercom. In the background, Psomas screams bloody murder about her imaginary demon. "We have a problem," the physician says.

"Nkosi?" Lisa presses. "Can you pick us up if we get into orbit?"

"Dallas, she's lost it,' Kilkenny shouts. "You gotta get yer arse up here."

Their voices overlap and intermingle until it feels like my head might explode.

"Shut up!" I yell. Good God, just be quiet and let me think. I rub at my temples. "Kilkenny, I'll be there. Just hold tight. Nkosi, get those people off that moon now."

I don't know how I'm in charge, but everyone just starts scurrying. "And Tris, go lock Chau in his quarters. Get Dona to revoke command rights, will you?"

"C'mon, Chief," Tris says, pulling Chau to his feet. "Time to go."

CHAPTER NINETEEN

Dr. Luan Nkosi

This is a friggin' mess. Sarah and Kilkenny are busy trying to stop a century-old teenage girl from falling apart at the seams, and Tris is confining the murderous commander of this tin can to his quarters. Which leaves me here alone in ops to somehow keep us in orbit so we can pick up my crew—if they make it off Europa in the first place.

My knuckles are white as I grip the armrests of Chau's command chair, and stare at the viewfinder. I have every live feed I can think of displayed on the huge screen—internal and external headcams from my friends, the ROV under the ice crust, the rover, Uruk's surveillance—but not one of them seems to be able to get a signal through. Too much interference. Between the gravitational glitch yanking on both sets of comms equipment, here on the *Paralus* and Europa, and Jupiter pumping out radiation like a kid with a damn portable DJ station, I can barely keep a line open.

"N—si?" a voice says, though it's so damn broken by static I can't identify it.

"Copy, I'm here." I fiddle with every knob and button at this comms console on the Bridge. Something has to help. "Tell me you've left. Tell me you're on your way to Uruk."

"Negative. Rover won—jammed up—ack in ice." The alto pitch under all that noise tells me it's Lisa. "Need to—EVA—Boris—"

"Nope." I don't need to hear the whole sentence to know what they're planning. "Don't even try it." A quick squint at the orbital readout. "You have eight minutes until comms black out for two hours. I want you back at Uruk and prepped for launch by the time we come back around. Scratch that, I want you entering low orbit for pick up. Copy."

"Try—Boris—wheel stuc—need leverage."

Shit, Boris is already outside of the rover, trying to fix something. Sounded like a wheel was jammed up. Goddamn it, I should be down there with them, not up here dealing with this shitshow of a crew.

"I need to see," I yell into the air, "AI—Dona—can you boost any of the signals?"

Static.

"Dona, did you hear me?"

The sound of my heartbeat grows louder than the white noise scratching out from the speakers. I'm going to throw up. Two of the live feeds wink to life. A few button presses on the intra-armrest console and they fill the twenty-foot monitor. Boris's internal helmet cam displays his pale and sweaty face. His outer helmet cam jerks left and right, as he jams all manner of objects he's salvaged from the rover—spades, large wrenches, one of the seats—into an ice crevice. He's making something for the rover's large tire to gain enough purchase and push them out. Boris's breathing labored and panicked.

C'mon, Boris. Do it and get back inside.

"Five minutes left 'til comms blackout," I say. "Lisa, did you hear that?"

"We heard it," Boz replies.

Balls, forgot she's with them.

"Get out of there, Boris," I mutter. "That has to be enough. Get back inside."

A third feed bursts awake, shrinking the other two to fit on screen. It's the undersea ROV camera. In the singular cone of light, the icy leviathan slides through the slush, like a giant goliath. The image is pixelated and jerky, but just as Lisa says, there's a huge linear split in the ice, right by the frozen thing's eye—if that's what it is.

The *Paralus* lurches, and as if tethered to us, Boris crashes into the frozen ground.

"Warning, gravitational anomaly," Dona announces. "Commencing de-orbit."

"Don't you dare!" Have to stop it. How do you pull the plug on this thing? "Hey!" I scream over my shoulder. "Hey, someone get up here."

Tris bursts into ops, and nearly crashes into one of the workstations. "Hey, what's going in? Any news? How's Boz?"

I launch off the command chair and grab the engineer by his thick arm. "Get this damn AI to stay in orbit, I'm not leaving my crew or Boz."

"It's not as easy as that." Tris pulls himself away and surveys the viewfinder. "You don't give Dona orders, you reason with it. It thinks. You have to show it why your decision is the best option."

"Are you kidding me?" The words splutter from my lips. "We don't have time to debate shit with a glorified baked-bean tin. I'll yank every damn wire on this ship if I have to. I'll go down and bash its synthetic brain in. You hear me?"

"Loud and clear, partner. I'll do what I can." With that, Tris takes off through the door and down the corridor.

"Lisa, Boris?" I call out again.

More radio wash.

Boris's external cam shows he's still outside, forcing a small pickaxe into his makeshift bridge so that now the handles and blades mesh. The feed shakes and Boris looks up, eyes glassy. Beyond the rover, the criss-cross surface striations of Europa reverberate and the sky shimmies. It all plays out silently, the gift of sound stolen by a thin atmosphere. His audio must be down too because no matter how much I scream at him to drop what he's doing, he soldiers on.

Three minutes to comms loss.

"Damn it," I say. "Lisa, Lisa, can—"

The ROV live feed bobs and sways in the wake of an undersea shockwave. My unblinking eyes burn as the glacier cracks like an icy egg, the two halves falling away to leave behind a monstrous yolk. The Goliath shakes—no, flexes—bending its caudal region. The shards of ice that still clung to its biomechanical body pop off and float up. The detritus clears, and the thing faces the ROV camera. The Goliath stares down the lens with two huge ventrally placed eyes.

My primary goal, finding life—complex life—beyond Earth has been realized. It's right there, undulating on camera. I should be ecstatic, gloriously happy beyond reckoning. Instead, pain in my chest cripples any kind of response other than pissing in my pants. Onscreen, the gargantuan bio-machine, a terrible cosmic chimera, jerks forward with frightening speed. Sleek metallic feathers spread out like on a bird of prey.

The feed goes black.

One minute to comms loss.

I grab the console and shake the shit out of it. "Lisa, Boris, get the hell out of there! Now!"

The *Paralus* twitches and I smash my forehead into the console, leaning too close. Blood gathers in my nose. The fog in my skull and the iron taste in my mouth override all other senses. I huff the blood out through my nostrils onto my sleeve.

A flurry of movement in Boris's external headcam.

His makeshift bridge vanishes overhead as he falls between the ice. The internal camera displays his terrified visage of realization, mouth open but of course no ability to scream. Boris's head slams into the frozen wall, shattering the glass in his helmet and exposing his fragile flesh to the unimaginable cold of Europa's atmosphere. His eyes become wide as the air in his lungs rushes out.

"Boris!" I lurch over the workstation and mash a greasy print on the viewfinder.

Knowledge is a terrible thing. Europa had enough atmosphere that he won't explode or immediately freeze, though the temperature drop must be excruciating. Instead, he'll remain lucid for an agonizing ten seconds, to contemplate his horrible fate as he falls farther and farther from the surface, and suffocates.

"Boris …" I whisper.

His feed cuts off, replaced with flashing words: *Connection Lost.*

I look up to the orbital data.

We're past the azimuth.

All comms to my team have gone dark.

My stomach cramps and I throw up everywhere. Globules of bile and my last meal pour through my fingers and nose, float away, and sticks to console and walls.

Boris, you mad bastard. Did you succeed? Did you save Lisa? Did they get away? I have two hours before I'll know anything. If they make it back to Uruk they could complete an emergency launch. Enough to get them into a low lunar orbit. Even a short, decaying one. Enough to let me pick them up. I can take a Scoop.

"De-orbit commencing," Dona says.

"The hell it is." I wipe my sleeve across my lips, which burn from stomach acid.

I push off the console and fire myself into the corridor, yanking and pulling on anything to hand to gain speed. I sail past the spoke to ring that houses quarters, the gym and medbay. Psomas's hoarse scream reverberates down the spoke. Her wails meld with those of

Kilkenny and Dallas as they probably try to pin the girl to the gurney without breaking her fragile arms. The sounds stretch out and lower in pitch as I rocket down the main corridor toward the AI nerve center.

Whipping along the narrow corridor, I try focus on the blades of light that cut through the gaps in the portal to Dona's brain, but Boris's scared face stabs at my psyche. Hot tears stream down my face, and, with eyes scrunched together, I let out a long and pained "fuck" that echoes both ahead and behind me.

I open my eyes, having nearly overshot, and stick my arms out to grab anything that'll put on the brakes. My fingers find the frame of the portal to Dona's central hub. My shoulder cracks as I jolt to stop. Shit, that hurt. I pull myself through the open portal, where Tris has both hands on a massive obsidian trunk, his head lowered.

"Did you manage it?" I ask. "Are we staying?"

"Not yet," Tris says, with a shake of his head.

"Not yet?" I shout, heat rising in my empty chest. "Listen up, Dodona." I read out the full name on the plate screwed into the trunk as if it'll help, like when my mum would middle-name me, *Luan Harold Nkosi*. I always listened. "My crew is still on Europa," I shout at the metal tree. "Boz is down there, and the moon is coming apart. We just need two hours, and we can save them. Just two."

"Your logic is flawed," Dona replies. "There are factors at play that of which you are unaware."

"What factors, you obtuse piece of shit?" I yell back.

"AIs think at teraflops of data per second," Tris says, and places a massive hand on my shoulder. "It could be thinking of things we don't even know exist."

"Four human beings are down there. You're sworn to protect humans." I touch the cold trunk hoping physical contact will aid my cause.

"Uh, that's not true," Tris says, backing away his lips pressed into a line.

"What?"

"They're not sworn to protect humans," he repeats.

"Bollocks," I say, and try dredge up a law I'm sure I read somewhere. "May not injure a human being or, through inaction, allow a human being to be injured."

Tris holds up a hand. "You're thinking about robotics, not AI. And even that is an old wife's tale, some bullshit sci-fi garbage that got stuck in peoples' heads. AIs serve the greater good." He cocks his and looks at me as if I'm case in point.

"Greater good?" What the hell does that mean?

"From Dona's point of view, we have more life aboard the ship that can be saved by de-orbiting. Just four people on a moon, who..." He considers his words. "Probably won't make it. And we could all die trying to save them."

"That's not the greater good," I fire back. "That's probability. A craps table."

A voice comes from behind me. "It's the teleological system." Sarah hovers in the doorway. "An ethical system drives AIs to determine morality by calculating end results." She runs a hand through her hair then tries to shake off a feeling. "Finally got Psomas sedated," she says.

"It's also called the murderer's solace," I spit back, and begin circling around Dona's trunk. "A scapegoat that politicians, the ITN, or *your* family run to every time they make a decision that's harmful to many—claiming it benefits many more."

Sarah's eyes glisten as she holds back tears.

Shitty blow, Luan. Well done. "I'm sorry." I touch my forehead to the AI's obsidian shaft. "But I... I just lost Boris. He...

he's gone. And my friends, they're still down there."

Sarah clears her throat and tries to follow me around the metal tree. "I'm so sorry, Luan."

My esophagus tightens and chokes up any words that might come.

"This is why we have AIs," she says, her tone solemn. "To deal with dilemmas like this. Do I pull the lever and let the train kill one person, but save ten on the other track, or do I let fate do its thing? You don't want this decision, Luan. AIs take it for you."

"One life isn't worth more than another," I blub out. "Isn't that the point? Isn't that why we're out here? To risk our lives to prove there are other life forms, even basic ones." Because all life, every life, is important. "I can't let them die. Even if Europa stabilizes. You didn't see what I saw. What's down there."

"What are you talking about?" Tris asks.

"The thing, the Goliath in the ice." I stare him in the eyes. "It's alive—or at least not dead. It's huge and it moves. It destroyed the ROV. We have to get my team and your pilot off the moon."

"The *Paralus* will likely not have the time you require," Dona says.

"What do you mean, Dona?" Tris calls out.

"I have finalized the calculations and compared the recorded data from Captain Psomas's ship," Dona explains. "My analysis reveals gravitationally bound atoms orbiting a temporal anomaly in the Jovian system, identical to one encountered by Captain Psomas more than one hundred SEYs ago. Yet there was not then, nor now, any detectable quantum evaporation."

"Are you sure?" Tris asks, his brow creased and his usual can-do demeanor waning.

"Um, English, please?" Sarah says.

"We don't have time for this," I blurt out. "A science lesson now? We need to prep to pick up my crew from orbit."

"Wait, did they make it off?" Sarah asks.

196

Tris's face hardens and he raises a hand at me. "This is important," he says. "Dona, are you sure?"

"I am sure," Dona replies. "A small, temporal singularity."

"A what?" Dallas asks.

"A black hole," Tris says, his shoulders slumped and expression slack. He raises his eyes to the fluttering tinkling leaves. "Fuck."

"As in suck us in and we die, black hole?" Sarah says, darting a worried look at me then Tris."

"Yup," Tris says.

"That's what's been screwing with the gravity, and yanking on Europa and this ship?" I ask. This could really screw up collecting my crew when they leave the moon.

"Affirmative," Dona says.

"And probably Jupiter," Tris says.

Sarah comes alive again. "That doesn't make sense," she says. "If there is a black hole out there, why does it only cause a problem sometimes?"

"As I said," Dona replies, its tone verging on impatient. "A small, temporal singularity."

"How can it be small?" I balk. "Or temporal for that matter?"

Tris slaps his palms to his face, pulls down and exhales loudly. "It could be a primordial black hole," he says.

"Guys," Sarah shouts, eyes wide and neck craned. "English."

"Small singularities, left over from when the universe was created." Tris waves Sarah off as if she's an annoying insect, interfering with his ability to think.

"I would concur," Dona says. "Data would suggest, the singularity might represent a fluctuating wormhole."

"That's not even a fucking *thing*," I shout, fists balled. "Fucking wormhole. Bottom line, we stay and the black hole swallows us up. We leave my crew dies. What are we going to do?"

"A fluctuating wormhole is the best description I can articulate that a human might understand," Dona says, totally ignoring the bit where we all die.

"You want to translate, Tris?" Sarah says boring a stare into the side of his head. "Does it *change* anything?"

Tris huffs and chews his lip. "It might," he says, then with one short tug rips off the sleeve to his flight suit revealing his large muscular arm.

"Whoah," I say. "You want to fight me too?"

He looks my skinny frame up and down, then blinks away the question. Tris rolls up the torn-off sleeve into a ring of fabric. "Imagine this is the singularity, the wormhole," he says. "On the right side is our universe. When the wormhole is blowing this way," he pulls the sleeve out to the right, "it affects us in our universe. But, when it's blowing this way," he gathers the material and pulls it in the other direction, "we don't' see or feel it."

"Well, who does?" Sarah asks.

Tris stuffs the fabric into his pocket. "There's a theory, suggesting that universes are formed by black holes that gather up matter, suck it in, and spit it out the other side. Either way, it won't necessarily appear in the same place twice. We could change trajectory and end up flying right into it."

No one says anything for a long time.

I don't have a watch on, but we probably have just over an hour until comms come back up and my crew is in orbit around Europa. "Well, when we get out of this we'll write a joint paper and win the ITN science prize for discovering the first giant alien fish-bird and an inside-out black hole, but until then: *I just want to stay in orbit for one more hour.*" I bash my forehead on the tree trunk in time with each word. "So I can save my friends and your crew member. Then we can all work on getting the hell out of here—my crew, your crew, and even the girl."

"Kara," Sarah whispers, then raps on her head with her knuckles. "I'm such an *idiot*. This black hole is linked to Kara, isn't it? To what happened to her. Dona, you said the same thing was recorded when the Proxima went missing."

"Does this matter *now*?" I fire back, forcing the deadliest stare I can muster into the ship's shrink. I get it, the girl is her patient and a mystery, but fuck me, read the room, Sarah.

"Possibly," Dona says, tone flat.

"You wanna explain that?" Tris says, his frown deepening.

"There is a theoretical possibility that Captain Psomas entered the singularity and did not die," Dona says.

"What would that do to her, *theoretically*?" Sarah asks.

Tris scratches his head. "If we're talking pure hypotheticals, like … beyond the event horizon, the laws of relativity breakdown and give way to quantum physics. Space and time reverse."

"The universe, from beginning to end, could be observed from within the singularity," Dona chimes in.

From beginning to end, Sarah mouths to herself.

"And if somehow she came back," Tris says, "escaped the singularity, she wouldn't necessarily come out at the same time point. I ain't a biologist, but who knows what that would do to her biology too."

"Kara could be telling the truth," Sarah says, already edging to the door. "Perhaps not about gods and the Six and all that, but that she *is* Captain Kara Psomas and may have seen *all of time*. From the big bang to millennia ahead of us."

"So?" I ask, shuffling around the trunk to follow Sarah. "So, our teenager is an old lady. Sarah, please, focus. My friends… " the words die in my throat. All these people care about are their interests.

"She keeps talking about a fulcrum, of something coming," Sarah says, her eyes fixed on me as if willing me to follow her train of thought. "Something she needs to change. That means she knows what *will* happen."

Sarah's wide-eyed stare finally ignites the right neurons in my head and we share an unspoken realization.

"Kara might be the key to everything," Sarah says.

"Dona," I say, the idea only taking shape in my head as I speak. "You're programmed to consider the greater good, as an outcome of events, right?"

"Affirmative," Dona replies, its tree-like brain humming louder, likely already calculating based on questions I might ask.

"We don't know the outcome here." I pull on the back of my neck. "We don't know if leaving Jupiter is the right thing—you base that decision on a series of probabilities, right?"

"This is correct," Dona says. "Do you have a proposition, Dr. Nkosi?"

"Yes!" I exclaim. "Based on this discussion, Captain Psomas may *know* the outcome of our situation. She can tell us what *will* happen. So, let us talk to her first."

"And if there is a fulcrum to move, to save us," Sarah adds. "She can tell us how."

The atmosphere swells with hushed anticipation. I search the metallic foliage above my head as Dona processes the information.

"De-orbit postponed," Dona says.

Sarah is already out the door and into the main corridor.

I squint at Tris, whose gaze is unfocused.

"You coming?" I ask him, my fingers clamped around the door frame.

He nods. "In a minute."

I disappear into the corridor and scramble toward medbay.

CHAPTER TWENTY

Dr. Sarah Dallas

I can't bring myself to step through the door to the medbay, so hover in shadow toying with my pendant. Kilkenny buzzes back and forth from the gurney to the main console, just like the hummingbird that rolls between my finger and thumb. And much like those tiny, shimmering birds, even when paused over a readout of vitals, or the intravenous line, the doc never really stays still, their limbs a flurry of activity.

My stare shifts to Kara who lies prostrate on the gurney, an oxygen mask over her nose and mouth. Her adolescent frame tinier than ever, she wastes away before our eyes. Her formerly youthful complexion has desiccated into that of an old, shriveled woman. Skin grey and cold, eyes sunken into her skull. She reminds me of my grandmother before she passed—huddled and so brittle I was afraid to hug her lest her bones turn to dust in my arms.

What a horrible fate for someone whose mind has been already suffered so much—trapped on the event horizon of a primordial singularity, time stretched out infinitely, able to watch our universe play out. It's too complex for my feeble intellect to imagine it. Only one thought comes to mind: how cripplingly lonely must that have been? Isolated, even for a few days, the brain becomes confused. The nerve systems feeding the principal processor still fire, but incoherently. The mind forms patterns from nothing, creating hallucinations—building a fantasy world. And that's a problem.

How do we separate what Kara really saw? On the one hand, she talks about our future and what's to come. An apocalyptic event to be avoided. In the same breath, she's convinced that cosmic beings, the Six, created everything in the universe and gave her this power to see. Somehow, we need to make her lucid enough to pry apart the imaginary from actuality and help us save the crew on Europa, and the *Paralus*, before the singularity pops back into existence and consumes us all.

Luan shoves past me into the medbay, his eyes wild and bony limbs flailing. "We need to wake her up," he says. "She needs to tell us what she's seen. What's coming. What we should do."

Kilkenny spins around, their face contorted. "What the feck are ya gabbing about, boy?"

"She's been suspended in a black hole, she's seen everything," Luan cries out as he makes a beeline for Kara.

Kilkenny stands between the astrobiologist and the patient, arms spread wide. "What?"

"Dona paused the de-orbit so we can talk to her. So I can save my friends," Luan says, jostling for a way past the doc.

I clear my throat and step into the harsh light of the med bay. "The gravitational anomaly affecting us comes from a small black hole." I place my hands on the back of the chair in which I normally sit to talk to my patient. "Dona thinks Kara may ... well may have crossed into the event horizon and stayed there suspended, seeing all of time at once." The words come from my mouth, but I'm not sure even I believe them. "That is, before being spat back out—in her current, younger form. She's not a clone, she's the real Captain Kara Psomas." It all sounds fucking insane when said aloud. "If she's seen what's coming, she might be able to tell us what to do—

whether to leave or not."

"Ach, dat's shit. If da girl's seen all of time already, den it's linear and fixed," Kilkenny says, holding back Luan's man-sized spindly arms. "Whatever we do is what'll happen."

Nkosi stops fighting and flashes a panicked look my way.

Who knew Kilkenny is such a philosopher.

"I'm not a specialist here, I have no idea." I step around the chair to place my hand on Luan's shoulder. "But Psomas told me there are fulcrums, levers in time that can change the course of everything. Maybe this is one. She might be able to tell us how to save both crews."

"If we don't get her to tell us, the AI will de-orbit the *Paralus* and we'll lose everyone on Europa," Luan says, all the fight now drained from him. He peels himself off the doc and slumps in my chair. "I have an hour before comms are back up, and they may already be in low orbit."

Kilkenny shakes their head but turns to Psomas lying on the gurney, and the doctor's shoulders fall. "Da girl's slipping away. Her cells are degrading too quickly."

I step past the doctor to study the poor girl—woman—dying on the gurney. In the midst of all this, despite the impending threat of death for us all, a single thought bubbles to the surface: Dad.

Psomas knew what he said to me when I left on this damned trip. How he told me to be free. How he called me hummingbird. The urge to interrogate her swells within me, to find out if she knows anything that can quell my pain. Did she also know he would die? If she saw that too, she could tell me *how* he died. Alone, or with Mother. In pain or not. If he asked for me on his deathbed.

I should be asking about the fate of humanity a hundred, even a hundred years from now. About her damn fulcrum. But of course, my head quickly fills with questions about how my life will turn out. If I'll find love and happiness. Because in the end, humans have a limited ability to care about things outside their circle of influence or concern. Many of us try, and some succeed, in having empathy for things beyond ourselves. As a shrink, have I not triumphed in that regard? Sadly, it seems not. I am but a copy of Mother. An unfeeling collection of selfish genes, whose only purpose is to exist. Kara said it herself: life isn't a miracle, it's inevitable. Maybe I became a psychologist to prove I don't just exist, that I'm not dead inside. What a wretched collection of revelations. Surely not what Dad intended for me. He'd be disappointed. My throat closes over and my eyes sting.

Not now, Sarah. Keep it together.

"Have you tried giving her a gened shot?" Luan asks the doc.

"It's the only thing keeping her alive right now," Kilkenny says, head hung low, leaning on the metal frame of the gurney.

I take a deep breath. "Can we wake her?"

The doc looks up, eyes full of defeat.

"You did your best," I say. "It's not your fault. She never could have survived." My training takes over, so I can fake empathy, but the hole in my chest suggests I may be dead inside.

"But she can save others," Luan says, resting his elbows on his knees, head in his hands.

Kilkenny sniffs hard, then walks to the main console and grabs an epi-pen from a drawer. The doc saunters back, takes a deep breath, then presses the pen to Kara's neck and activates the device, which makes an almost inaudible hiss.

"Noradrenaline," Kilkenny says. "Not sure how long she'll stay wit' it."

Kara's eyes flutter as she groans to consciousness. Her weak arms and legs pull inward as she folds into a fetal position on the gurney, shielding herself from the harsh overhead lighting.

My fingertips tingle. Try to connect, Sarah, to *really* feel. "Kara," I whisper. "Kara, I know you're tired. But we need you right now. We need you to finish your story. Tell us about the fulcrum."

Kara opens her eyes a little more, her unfocused gaze roves

from Kilkenny to Luan and finally me.

"Dallas?" she croaks, her s-sound hissed through broken teeth.

"It's me," I say.

"So weak," Kara says. "So tired."

"I know, but we need you." We're running out of time.

"Less than an hour," Luan says, then stands and steps to the end of the bed. "If the damned AI doesn't take us away."

"Kara, what's the fulcrum?" I say. "What did you want to stop?"

"Nyx," Kara says, her voice muffled as she talks into her chest. "Her world. Her army. Sent to destroy us all."

"An army?" Kilkenny says, brow furrowed.

"You have to listen," Kara says, eyes now fixed open as the drug flowing through her crumbling body takes hold. "You have to understand."

"Tell me, Kara," I say.

She shuffles awkwardly, limbs jerking and spasming, as she tries to push herself up.

Kilkenny folds one end of the gurney up to form a headrest.

I gesture to Kara. "Help me."

They slip their arms under the girl and lift her just enough to allow me to shuffle underneath her, then place her on my lap facing out into the room. I cradle her against my chest, one arm wrapped around her body, and one hand on her forehead, which burns with an incredible fever. I can't see her expression but can feel the vibrations of her heart and voice in my sternum.

"Gaia … Gaia created our world," she says. I think she's staring at Luan. "Created us. She planted the seed of life on Earth and watched what would happen. What would happen if life were left to flourish without interference. Free will." She sucks in a sharp breath and lets it stutter out. "But Nyx … she pushed, and molded, and crafted. Forcing her world… Aeterna… to a goal. While humanity lumbered from one… evolutionary milestone to the next,

Nyx's world incubated a race of warriors... conquerors. The Aeternae were... efficient and deadly. She revealed her power to them, deified herself, and crafted an entire world of creatures who revered her. A cosmic army to do her bidding."

"Humanoid life?" I ask. "Sentient life, like us?"

Kara shakes her head and hacks out a ragged cough. "Not like us. Bipedal, but with Nyx's influence they were more designed ... biomechanical, with metals and rocky elements woven into their bones and skin ... to form armor. Living weapons."

I close my eyes and will the images of these Aeternae to come. Nightmarish, grotesque creatures crawl out of the murk. Tall, on two legs, with four arms that have multiple articulations. Their skin is dark and metallic. Shards of crystals in deep indigo and crimson protrude from their backs, shoulders, and even their faces. But none have eyes. The creatures scream, their jagged maws wide.

My eyes snap open, false light from the medbay burning away the terrible image. Shadows in the medbay link and slide away, almost as if they are alive.

What the hell was that?

"They came—they came for my home," Psomas says, "for Hamadryadia." She lowers her head and seems to shrink even smaller into my chest. "For Syke."

Hamadryadia—she'd said that word before—the world created by Eros and Erebus, I think. But—"what is Syke?" I ask.

"My love..." Psomas's voice cracks. Her shoulders shake as she cries.

Her love? "Kara, who is *Syke*?"

Kara sniffs. "It's hard to know how... many years... I spent existing with the indigenous life of Hamadryadia. There were no seasons... no changes because the planet was sandwiched between the two stars, orbiting in a figure eight." The drum of her heartbeat, thrumming through her thin body and into me stutter. She sucks at the air, a fish out of water, before regaining her composure.

"Gaia... Gaia allowed me to observe a single forest on that world. I saw the first trees grow, and with them, Hamadryadia birthed Syke."

"We don't have time for this," Luan says, his fingers digging into the bedsheets. "I'm sorry for what happened to you, truly. But my friends' lives hang in the balance here. We know you've seen all of time. Seen what happens next." His expression grows more desperate. "Do we leave or stay? Do we survive? Can we change anything? Can this fulcrum help us? What do we do?"

"Syke knew I was there..." Kara says, and oblivious to Luan's frustrated questions continues to ramble. "I don't know how. I don't... know why. She was the closest thing to a friend I had experienced in millennia. Another soul who knew I existed." She turns her head up to look at me through matted hair. "From a sapling to a... a sprout... to fully formed Hamadryad, Syke's fiery blue eyes looked out from with the interconnected vines and stared at me." She sighs, and her whole body shudders. "Syke could not speak, you know, only release pungent pheromones. Her race did not need sound, I suppose, as plant-like beings. Yet Syke would slap leafy limbs, and clap rocks together in rhythmic patterns, to make the vibrations. For me. To communicate with me. I'm sure of it."

Kilkenny huffs. "You'll not get a coherent word outta her. She's a sandwich short of a picnic."

"I tried to communicate back to her," Kara pipes up, with renewed vigor, her limbs breaking free of my gentle embrace. "No idea if Syke ever understood. I'm... I'm not even sure that atmosphere carried sound."

Kara makes those strange noises again, the clicks and lip smacks that could almost pass for language. This is what she was doing? Talking in an alien language? Mimicking the clapping leaves and rocks Syke used to communicate with her on Hamadryadia? For her, this percussion might have all the syntax, diction, and grammar of English or Mandarin. But with whom was she talking? Syke, a friendly being she dreamed up to stave off solitude?

This is too much. I can't pry the truth from such an elaborate fantasy. For her, they are one and the same, entwined like Damascus steel. If there is a fulcrum, some terrible event awaiting us, she can't articulate what it is.

"For the longest time, I wasn't alone," Kara says. "Syke made me almost happy. Until the Aeternae came. With their war machines."

"Kara," I sigh and touch a finger to her chin to turn her to meet my gaze. "Is that the disaster you're trying to avoid? Is that the fulcrum?"

"Nyx designed the Aeternae to ... to destroy," Kara says, eyes wide. Behind them, she relives whatever horrified her so. "Built with jealousy and hatred," she continues, jaw and fists now clenched. "They burned everything. They annihilated Hamadryadia and with it both Eros and Erebus, who'd tied their consciousness to that very world." A tiny ball of tears gathers on her cheek. "And now they are coming for Earth, for humanity."

"How? When? Where are they?" Luan presses.

Kilkenny furrows their brow and looks from Luan to me and back. "Ya don't believe dis, do ya?"

Kara turns to Luan, her head on an awkward swivel. "You already found it, Luan Nkosi. Under ... the ice. In the ocean." Her breathing is shallow and the word barely audible.

Luan stands bolt upright and glares at me. "Is she talking about the thing on Europa?"

Kilkenny grunts. "Ach, dis makes no sense. It's all a bunch o' shite. Alien war machines. If dese war machines exist, why doesn't dis Gaia, stop 'em? If she created our world, why isn't she defending us?"

"She tried," Kara says. "Seeing what Nyx had created, a millennia ago, Gaia nudged us along—huge quantum leaps in understanding. How else do you... do you think we went from the

Bronze Age to mining Jupiter? In the four billion years Earth has existed, we jumped from basic hand tools to space exploration in the last six thousand. Believe me, Gaia tried."

"I mean why doesn't she defend us now?" Kilkenny fires back.

"One of her last actions was to save Earth—temporarily," Kara wheezes. "A meteor shower forced the war machine headed for Earth to crash into Europa... where it became trapped in ice. The other action... it was to... enlist me."

"Why can't she save us *now*?" I ask, though don't even know why. Training maybe. Getting to the core of the issue. Right now, it's all moot.

"Because she's gone," Kara says and winces. "We killed her."

"Sarah, please?" Luan says, his whole body limp, drained of energy. "She needs to focus. How do I save my crew?"

Kara lifts herself away from my chest as if possessed. "The Six existed because their consciousnesses were concentrated—their very beings were condensed in the early universe," The words flow from her cracked lips like lines she's learned for a play. "As it grew, their consciousnesses dispersed, thinner and thinner. They were always destined to die." She sucks a large stuttered breath in, gathering enough power to say: "Having a connection to the life forms they created kept them coherent. Mankind abandoned Gaia many years ago."

"We stop believing," I say, "they stop existing."

"Something... like that," Psomas says, slumping back into my arms. "We believed in Gaia once, but traded her for false interpretations that met the needs of selfish men. She used her last iota of power to contact me, to guide me through the universe the Six created... before she faded away."

"Balls to this." Luan pulls out a small tablet from his pocket. He taps away at it until he finds what he wants and then waves it in front of Psomas's face. "Is this it? Is this the war machine?"

Kara grasps the device in shaking hands. Over her shoulder, I study the image. Not sure what opinion I had on its appearance before, but now, in light of Kara's emotive description, the thing in the ice looks like an enemy lurking in wait. Its silvery scales and sharp feathers, that awful bird-like head—if there were a hell, this would be its spawn.

"The forests of Hamadryadia burned," Kara says, and trembles, her gaze fixed on the tablet. "The creatures and vegetation crisped and charred. The Hamadryads sprayed pheromones into the air, their equivalent of Earthly screams. The scent of the dying." She drops the device clattering to the floor. "My Syke, my love, my friend… reached out to me as if I were a savior—yet I could do nothing. Unable to change that which had already occurred." Psomas breaks down in my arms, her uncontrollable sobbing soaks my sleeves.

I squeeze her gently and stroke her thinning hair, which comes away in my fingers. "Kara, the thing in the ice, the war machine. Will it attack Earth?"

"This is the fulcrum," Kara whispers.

"You think that a creature frozen in the ocean of Europa can sail across space and take out Earth?" Luan says, pushing off the gurney to stomp around the medbay. "This is a waste of time, I'm going to get my crew."

"Kara, listen to me." I raise a hand to stop Luan. "There are no weapons on transport liners. How would we even attempt to destroy it?"

"Bomb," Kara mutters, her body becoming limp in my arms. "Chau's bomb."

"She knew he had a bomb?" Luan says, his face flushed darker.

Just when we're ready to write off her ramblings, she throws in a morsel of clarity. She's been in the medbay the entire time, and we haven't mentioned to her the atmosphere-destroying bomb Chau buried in the greenhouse.

She struggles to sit up. "I need… needed… his bomb. To

destroy the war machine."

Luan stops dead in his tracks. "You want to wipe out the first complex life form we've discovered?"

"To save all human life," Kara croaks.

Luan shakes his head. "We have no way of knowing what that thing down there is. It might well be aggressive, but we were the ones that poked it." He jabs his index finger in the air. "What if it's indigenous? What if there are more? You want to commit genocide? This is bollocks, I'm going after my crew." He strides for the exit.

"Your crew—this crew—is not important," Kara says, her words heavy with eons of experience. "Individuals are not important. Humanity survives as a whole, like a colony of ants, or not at all."

Luan didn't hear any of that. He's already out the door, though how the hell he plans to save his friends I don't know.

Kilkenny stares at me and the room falls quiet save the tattered breathing of the girl clinging to my chest.

"So now what now?" the doctor asks.

"I don't know," I say, then look up. "Dona?"

Kilkenny and I both search the blank ceiling tiles a while before the ship's AI responds. "Data insufficient. It is prudent to move to a safe distance from the Jovian system."

"De-orbiting." Kilkenny states.

"Affirmative," Dona replies.

"Nkosi needs help." I struggle out from underneath Kara with as much care as I can. "To get his crew and get back to the *Paralus* again. Dona, will you allow him to take a Scoop?"

Another silence. "Dr. Nkosi may take a Scoop. It does not impact the primary objective."

"We're all fecked, you know dat, right?" Kilkenny says.

I want to speak, but no words come. Instead, Kilkenny and I stare at Kara who fades into a restless' quivering heap. Her bones protrude through thin skin and press into the thin mattress of the gurney. Within the folds of her medical gown the harsh lights of the medbay cast slender shadows, which I swear move and slither on their own.

CHAPTER TWENTY-ONE

Commander Feng Chau

Dallas and Kilkenny just stand there beside the gurney, like stupefied mannequins, staring at the girl. I want to scream at them through the screen. "You see, Dona?" I turn from the monitor feeding directly from the medbay. "That girl is no messiah, no elevated human. Her instinct is to destroy the first alien creature we find." I slump onto my bed, my whole body shaking. "If anything, she's the epitome of all that is wrong with humanity— she's a predator." All this time, she just wanted my bomb, to kill another life form unique from our own. A species we know nothing about because she deems it a threat to humans. How typical. History replaying itself.

"I believe your analysis of the current situation is tainted by your desire to adhere to the original agenda," Dona says. "Agility and flexibility in the face of new data are the hallmarks of science practiced well."

I've lost Dona. All this would be so much easier with the AI's help. Need to get out of here. Plan B. I jump off the bed, drop to hands and knees and crawl to the rectangular panel in the wall next to the door. My weak reflection on the shiny white surface stares back. I don't recognize the tired eyes and drawn face anymore.

A sharp jab with my fist buckles the metal plate—and my likeness. I pull away the cover and toss it aside. It clatters under the bed. Inside the hole, there are several wires and long metallic tubes which could represent the water retention system, climate control, power, and likely the hydraulic servo mechanism to the door. Just need to figure out which is which, and try not to lock myself in.

Of course, nothing is labeled.

Shit, which one?

I touch each tube in turn. One, about an inch thick and warm, may contain power cables or be part of the internal environmental regulator. Another, thinner, feels cold to the touch and vibrates just a little. Something moving inside it? Reclaimed water? The last is a good two inches thick, neither warm nor cold, and doesn't vibrate. The hydraulic mechanism? Could house a piston, I guess.

"What are you doing Commander Chau?" Dona asks.

"What I have to, Dona. Don't you see?" My words are clipped as I struggle to push my thick hand in further into the small space. "We've been at this for thousands of years, since prehistoric days. We've eliminated everything from bacteria, fungi, and plants to mammals, birds, reptiles, amphibians, fish—and God only knows what else."

I shuffle onto my back to get a better vantage and peer through the gap. It doesn't help. Without a flashlight, it's just a dark hole, with darker shadows spilling out. I squint and stare up into the cavity willing my eyes to adjust. Instead, my tired brain betrays me—the shadows slip and slide over one another like molasses. I see something, though. A switch, maybe.

"We destroyed rainforests, coral reefs, oceans, the very atmosphere itself," I say. Hopefully, my words will be enough to distract Dona from alerting anyone. "We are a super predator, and now we've spilled out into space and are doing the same."

Another shuffle onto one shoulder and I snake my fingers in.

My knuckles scrape on tube connectors and support fixtures. C'mon, you bastard.

My room is eerily quiet, save my frustrated breaths.

Does Dona no longer see fit to engage me? "Is my opinion of so little value now—in the wake of one girl's appearance?" My voice echoes on the inside of the cavity. "A fake girl at that." Bullshit about returning from a black hole. Did the laws of physics just change while I've been locked in here? She's a clone, a toy manufactured for the rich. We've cast aside evolution as a means of improving the human race and taken it upon ourselves. We're self-proclaimed gods now. Cloning, genetic modification, cyber implants—all in the name of selfish desires rather than our species' needs. Historians, if they could, would look back on this epoch of our kind and label it the death of reason—biological or otherwise.

But there will be no historians to look back. I'll see to that.

I wriggle my hand up inside and rotate my wrist left and right, navigating the metal labyrinth until two fingertips graze the prize.

Gotcha.

Another half-inch jab, the elbow caught between pipes, and the switch depresses.

A jolt shoots down my arm and passes, hot and sharp, through my body. I yelp and pull back the trembling limb, shredding skin away. The scream grows louder—my higher brain begging not to just yank, my animal-self ready to chew through the bone if need be. The whole ordeal lasts a second, though now bloody and missing swathes of skin left behind in the hollow.

I clutch one arm with the other, howling into the air. Blood streaks from the wrist to the elbow and smears across the metal floor as I kick and scream, eyes scrunched shut, writhing more in frustration than pain.

"Fuck," I hiss through a clenched jaw.

I crush my eyelids so tight that the darkness behind them becomes orange and then red. A cascade of color washes over me, pixelated and geometric. The spiraling squares in shades of yellow and blue turn grey, then back to black, and as they twist and turn, they bleed together into one terrible shape—a dark thing of nightmares.

The shadow opens its jagged mouth and tries to swallow me whole.

My eyes snap open, and I scream again.

Laid here, panting, I clutch at my burning arm, stare up at the plain ceiling.

No demons. No nightmare. Just me, on my back like an idiot, no closer to escape.

Footsteps thud outside the closed door. My screams alerted someone.

Another *thunk*, and the doors slide into recesses with a low hum.

I tilt my head back. Through blurry eyes, I make out a familiar face staring down at me, a confused, even wry smile on their lips.

"Finally," I sigh.

CHAPTER TWENTY-TWO

Dr. Luan Nkosi

An array of switches, screens, joysticks and flashing lights inside the Scoop mocks me. I haven't piloted a damn thing since my initial training, years ago. Wasn't my job, never *been* my job. I'm the biologist, the nerd. I rap on the helmet which rings my head. Breathe, Nkosi. They're counting on you.

Go get your friends.

The Scoop's launch folder floating over my lap is thicker than the damn Bible. Odd to think of that right now, but fitting. Mum, the devout Christian, hoped catholic school would make me into a priest—which I am not. Yet now, to hear Psomas speak, intertwining mythology and science into one bat-shit-crazy, mildly believable tapestry, out here in the cold of space, among the very stars and nebulae … kinda makes you wonder.

"Hey, you need a hand?"

My heart jumps so hard it may have ripped.

"Luan?" Sarah hovers at the open door of the Scoop.

I move the folder aside, pop off my helmet, and let them both float freely in the seat beside me.

"You look a little lost," she says.

"Been a while." My face must look sheepish as all hell. "Is Tris around?"

Sarah shakes her head, united hair swirling around. "Said he was going to stay with Dona. Doing his damnedest to keep us from sling-shotting around Jupiter and heading home. We're already moving out of orbit."

"I know," I say, "I felt the shift."

"So, what's your plan?" she asks, holding the doorframe and pushing herself down to my level.

"Go get my friends, and yours."

"Boz isn't my friend," Sarah says.

"She's *somebody's* friend."

Sarah hangs her head just a little lower, lips pressed thin. "Are you taking Chau's bomb?" she asks.

"Why the hell would I do that?"

Her head snaps up, a stern expression now carved into her face. "Look, if you're going to get your crew," she says, "you could deploy the bomb and take out that thing in the ice."

"Are you insane? That's a living, breathing, creature down there. A life. Not to mention the find of the century... the find of *all* centuries! Not some microbe fossilized in rock—it's big-ass alien fish-bird that swims."

"You have no idea what that thing is," Sarah says, her eyes searching mine. "But Kara says she knows. And what if she's right? What if that thing heads to Earth to destroy us all?"

"You don't honestly believe that do you?"

Sarah weighs her answer in that way shrinks do. Almost as if she were waiting for me to answer my own question. "I don't know what to believe," she says finally. "But she knows things she shouldn't know. About my dad, about Chau." She leans in closer. "And the bomb."

"Not going to happen." I shake my head so vigorously I may give myself a migraine. "I'm not murdering the first alien we've met."

Sarah sighs then nods and slaps a hand against the inside of the Scoop's portal. "You think this thing has enough fuel to pick up the crew and get back while the *Paralus* is moving away?"

"I have no idea." I stick my scrawny arms out. "But I'll poke these out the window and flap if I have to."

Sarah laughs—a nervous, scared chuckle.

"Luan Nkosi, you have an incoming transmission," Dona says, the voice reverberating inside the cockpit.

"Put it through!" I say.

A wash of static comes from the Scoop's cockpit speakers, and we both lean in to hear better.

"Nkosi, you read?" Lisa says.

"I got you," I call back.

"Leaving transfer orbit now," she says. "Lunar orbit in less than seven minutes. We'll drop in behind the *Paralus*."

"Thank fuck you're alive." A wave of relief washes over my cortisol-drenched taught muscles. "Do you have everyone accounted for?"

"We... we lost Boris," Lisa says.

"I know." It's all I bring myself to say right now.

Another much rougher voice comes over the comms. "We're all here." It's Boz.

Sarah gives her best, fake, shrink smile.

"Me, Lisa, and Steven. Just be ready for my ship to pick us up," Boz orders.

"The AI has taken over," Sarah says, scooching further into the Scoop. "We're leaving."

"Hair, that you?"

"It's me, Boz," Sarah says with a sigh.

"Put Tris on," Boz snaps.

"Tris is in Dona's core, trying to keep us close." I wave Sarah out of the cockpit. "I'll explain when I get you."

"When *you* get us?" Steven says.

Glad they're so confident in my abilities. "I'm taking a Scoop."

"We're gonna die," says Boz.

"Shut up," Lisa snaps back. "Copy, Nkosi, we'll be in high lunar orbit in twenty, but it'll decay pretty rapidly. Come get us."

"Roger that," I say. "Coming."

I glare at Sarah until she gets the point and swims off to the Bridge. I reattach my helmet, close the main door and begin what I hope is the launch sequence. Even in my short years grounded on Europa, the tech has changed quite a bit. Click this one, switch primary power on. Prep the fuel line. Decouple from the *Paralus*.

My finger hovers over the release button.

"Push it already," I whisper.

I mash the tab with one finger.

The Scoop lurches and a clang reverberates through the hull. In the viewfinder, the stars sway back and forth as if I were a tiny dinghy on the ocean. C'mon, you can do this.

I pull on the yoke. Bad mistake. The Scoop jerks and ends up inverted, my feet on the ceiling and the contents of my stomach in my mouth.

Strap yourself in, dumbass.

A quick shove off the ceiling, and an awkward grab of the armrests, and I manage to pull myself into the seat. I clip on the harness over both shoulders and around my thin waist. Try again, Nkosi. Maybe let tech do the work? A swift scan of my flight planner and the input seems fairly intuitive. The *Paralus*'s former orbit of Europa sits in the system, so I should be able to tell the Scoop to re-enter the same trajectory and speed. I'll have to eyeball if I'm coming in behind or in front of Lisa's DAR.

First things first.

A few key punches and confirmations and the display pops up the first comforting thing I've seen in days: *Do you wish to enter the Mothership's orbit of Europa?* Yes, all the yesses. I tap the screen. The

Scoop drops like a stone, its nose pointing at the icy ball below me. Or above me. Who the hell knows in space. Up, down, sideways. Doesn't matter.

As the Scoop falls into the pre-determined flight pattern, Jupiter and a few of its other moons fill the corer of the window. It's the second time in as many days that the gassy asshole has watched what I'm doing with bemusement.

"Luan?" Sarah says over the comms.

"I read you." I hold my jaw firm as the Scoop shudders under thruster fire.

"I'm getting some weird readings here," she says. "Dona says the singularity is going to make an appearance. Get your ass in gear."

Of course. Why not? While I'm out here steering a million-dollar go-cart with zero training.

"Did she say singularity?" Steven says, a tremor in his voice.

Ah, shit, the comm link was still open. Cat's out of the bag. "Uh, yeah. That's what's been causing the gravitational shifts. A small one, a primordial one. But temporal, shifting in and out of existence."

White noise fills the cockpit as my friends contemplate what that means.

"Turn back, Nkosi."

It takes a couple of seconds to register that was Boz's voice. "What?"

"She's right," Lisa says. "If there's a black hole out there, you and everyone on the *Paralus* are in danger."

"You sound like the damn AI," I say.

"It's not wrong," Lisa says.

A glint up ahead, and a familiar cylinder slides across the panorama in my window.

"There's no point arguing," I tell her, "I'm already coming up on your six."

The Scoop levels out, the frozen curvature of Europa in the bottom third of the window, Jupiter filling the top third, and Lisa's DAR sandwiched between, a good few hundred miles ahead. At current velocity, I'll be on her in … three minutes seven seconds. "shit," I mutter, "too fast."

"Too fast?" Lisa asks.

"Velocity." I paw through the binder in hopes of finding a chapter called: *So, You're Going to Die.* "Autopilot dropped me into orbit but didn't count on you being in my path. Less than three minutes before I slam into you."

"Wonderful," Boz remarks.

"I'll walk you through it," Lisa says, then laughs. She clears her throat, seriousness returned to her tone. "Turn off the autopilot and be ready to fire the braking thrusters when I say, and for how long I say."

"Copy," I reply, though can't for the life of me find the braking thrusters on this damn thing.

"By your feet, Nkosi," Boz says as if she could see me searching the cockpit. "Like a car, except there are two brakes for your feet and no steering wheel—just yokes."

"And yokes can brake the Scoop too," Lisa adds.

Right, a car, I can do this. My feet find the pedals, one for each. I still have to look at them to make sure. Friggin' hell, I'm fucking useless. "But you already knew that, didn't you, asshole?" I say to Jupiter looming above Europa.

"Okay, on my mark, I want you to squeeze the brakes with both feet and gently push on the yokes at the same time," Lisa says, enunciating every syllable. "You need to get down to about three thousand miles per hour, to sync with our decaying orbit. We don't have time to fuck about by matching speed and docking. But that should give us enough time to make a short spacewalk to you, and get the hell out of here."

"Okay, no docking," I say. Like I'd know how anyway.

"Nkosi," Lisa says, tone hard—like *pay attention asshole*, "if you put too much pressure on any of the brakes unevenly you'll spin off in a random direction."

Great, this is great. "Gentle. No spin. Got it," I say, feigning conviction.

"Okay, slow yourself," Lisa says. "Ten-second burst. Three, two, one, mark."

I press the yokes forward and squeeze my toes together to push on the brakes. The Scoop lurches, and the harness digs into my shoulders. "Ah fuck, too hard!" The Scoop rolls end over end, the window showing black space and then Europa, over and over. Like rolling down a grassy hill as a kid, my stomach churns, and the contents make an unwelcome return in my mouth.

"Nkosi, what happened?" Lisa asks. "What's your velocity?"

"Still advancing, uh, picking up speed. Just under five thousand per hour and tumbling about the Y-axis. How the hell do I stabilize this piece of shit?"

"I'll go get him," Boz says.

"What—?" Steven fires back, static washing out the rest of his words, laden with expletives.

"Look, he's coming up fast," Boz says. "I'll take an AMU, a couple of thrusts and I get to him, match his velocity as he comes up behind. I use the AMU to dock at a relative speed, enter his airlock, take control of the Scoop."

That doesn't sound simple at all.

My world continues to spin, which feels like it should be accompanied by loud rushing air but instead, my panicked breathing fills the Scoop.

"Fine," Lisa says. "But we have minutes here, Boz."

"I'm out the door," Boz says.

"Nkosi, don't touch anything," Lisa calls out a little too loud. "We're coming."

"So much for me rescuing you." I swallow back yet more bile.

"The thought that counts," Steven says.

The hell it is. Should have got Tris to come get them. Is he having any luck with Dona and the *Paralus*? The liner never appears in my window as the Scoop rolls on. Space, Europa, space, Europa. My labored breathing fogging this helmet only fuels the panic in my chest. I try to focus on Lisa's DAR, which grows larger with each revolution of this stupid craft.

Roll number thirty-six, but this time something new passes the window. A tiny human spec, heading for me. Small bursts of fuel spray out behind Boz as she shunts her way through invisible radiation and the vastness of space to collect my inept ass.

"Stay still, you praying mantis-looking nerd," Boz says. "The professional is on the way."

At least she kept her sense of humor.

So hard to gauge distance out here. She looks closer to the DAR but could be miles away from it. As my view of outer space tilts and my friends disappear out of sight, a strange vortex bursts into existence somewhere between Europa and Jupiter. Its circular center is the kind of black reserved for the depths of hell, framed by a halo of light. A flat disc of glowing hot space dust, that looks like the rings of Saturn—the accretion disc—encircle the pitch-dark sphere "The singularity," I say under my breath.

The whole thing is surprisingly small, maybe only a few hundred feet across, but it seems to grow—the accretion disc builds, feeding on the atmosphere of both Europa and Jupiter.

The Scoop's roll blocks my view. "Lisa, Lisa do you read? The singularity!"

"I see... holy... Nkosi ..."

"Sarah? Dallas, do you copy?" I scream, clawing at every knob, dial, and switch on the console hoping to do something, anything.

"Luan, get out of there," Sarah yells back. "It's never manifested visually before! Get ... t ..."

"Sarah? Lisa!" My heart sputters and lungs drain the cabin of oxygen. A readout shows the connection to the *Paralus* is dead.

The Scoop flips gain. I press my hands to the walls of the cockpit for stability and peer into the void, eyes burning. Europa's frozen surface bulges and distorts, its ocean fighting to be released—an inner tube of pressure against a crumbling outer tire.

"Boz!" I scream into the mic. "Lisa!"

It's too late.

Two hundred feet in front of my Scoop, a thick jet of icy sea spurts from the surface of Europa. The frozen lance shoots into space and cleaves Lisa's DAR in two. Debris fires out in all like an icy supernova. "Lisa! Steven!"

Boz hurtles toward me, so close I can see her glassy eyes and pale panicked complexion through the helmet's glass. She reaches for me, fingers outstretched.

"Move, Boz!" I shout.

Another crystalline bayonet explodes from Europa.

It hits Boz.

She disintegrates in a haze of blood and a brief static-filled scream.

The Scoop rolls over again.

Lisa, Boz, Steven.

Jesus, Nkosi.

What did you do?

"Nkosi? Nkosi, do you read?" The voice crackles in my headset.

That's not Sarah.

"Nkosi, answer me dammit."

"Lisa?" I sniff away selfish guilt. "Lisa, you're alive?"

"Alive but drifting," she says with the flat reverb a voice takes on inside a pressurized suit. "I can see you."

"The singularity," I ask, "is it still out there?"

"I don't see it," Lisa says. "Like it evaporated."

As the Scoop rolls, the debris lies out ahead. Debris from Europa's surface, debris from Uruk's DAR, and now space dust from the dissipating accretion disc. Somewhere in there, Boz's remains entwine with the flotsam …

"How do I get you …?" I ask.

"Plan stays the same," Lisa says, panting into the mic. "I come to you. You're headed into a damn minefield of debris at thousands of miles an hour. It's orbiting too, but you'll catch up to it."

"What's your point?" I grunt.

"I can maneuver using my SAFER," she says, "But I need you to slow yourself to a near stop."

I roll my eyes, not at Lisa, but myself. "Because that worked well last time."

"I couldn't see you before, but now I can," Lisa says, her breathing more tortured. "You're rolling on your z-axis. If you press just the yokes, it should slow your spin and reduce your speed."

"Are you sure?"

"No time to do the math," she wheezes. "Stab the brakes, little presses, Nkosi. Half a second. Eke them out."

I take a deep breath, grab the yokes, and then nudge them forward. The Scoop's roll slows a little. Another nudge and more nitrogen *whooshes* out from the thrusters and fills the viewfinder. Nudge after nervous nudge, the Scoop's rotation slows so much that each rotation now takes forever.

In the viewfinder, something in the debris moves. It sputters along like an antique car with a backfiring combustion engine. It has to be Lisa. With each complete rotation, she appears larger in the window.

She's not alone.

She's dragging Steven alongside.

Readout says I'm down to just under eight thousand miles per hour. Not enough to maintain orbit, so even if I didn't hurtle into the DAR debris, I'd crash into the moon's surface eventually.

Lisa has to match my velocity by eye, then she can maneuver relative to me to enter the Scoop's airlock.

Lisa's approach plays out like snapshots, film with missing frames. The closer I get I realize she's not propelling herself forward toward me, but merely slowing her velocity, as she orbits Europa, to match mine. Each time I roll around, my scoop has caught up to her a little more and she appears larger in my window. As has the deadly wreckage of Uruk's DAR.

I count out five more rolls until Lisa's so close I could reach through the glass and touch her. Inside her helmet, her features are sunken and tired. She has Steven clamped to her chest.

The Scoop rolls again and when it comes back around, Lisa and Steven aren't there.

My chest deflates. Where is she? Did some goddamn fragment of space junk shoot past and vaporize her? "Lisa, Lisa?" Oh, Jesus.

Static.

A dull clang rings against the hull, followed by more banging and hammering. The sound of the rear airlock shunting open then closed vibrates through the inner door to the cockpit. That must be them, they made it.

I twist in my seat to look back. The door to the cabin hisses open and Lisa collapses through, floating in midair with Steven still in her arms. She's sweaty, pale, and barely conscious, sucking on carbon dioxide fumes. I unharness and scramble to free her from her helmet. "Lisa?" It unscrews and I throw it aside to clatter across the spare seat.

She looks up at me, eyes rolling about inside her skull. "Steven."

Another flurry of arms and spacesuits and I free Steven from his one-man fabric prison too. I prop him against the door to stop him from floating away. He's breathing, though hasn't regained consciousness.

Be okay, Steven. Please be okay.

I grab Lisa, squeeze her to me, and cry into the cold material of her suit, which burns my cheek.

"I'm sorry," I whisper.

Lisa gives me a weak hug back, then jerks in my arms. "Gotta move," she says. "Debris. We can only help Steven back on the *Paralus*."

I nod, then gran Lisa and tow her back to the pilot's chair. I slip her into it and buckle her in. She clasps the yokes and stares out of the viewfinder.

"Is it me or is everything spinning?" she says, sucking in big gulps of air and blowing them out slowly.

"Spinning," I mumble.

"Right, yes, spinning." Lisa sucks in deep breaths of oxygen-rich air.

In just a few tweaks Lisa's righted the Scoop and pulled us out of orbit and away from the debris field. She continues to move us away from Europa, making figure eights, turning the Scoop on itself.

I strap myself into the passenger seat. "Looking for something?"

"The *Paralus*," she says without looking away from the viewfinder. Her head is bobbing and weaving as she searches every corner of the window. In the distance, our yellow sun is but a speck. Somewhere in between, Earth does another lap.

Lisa continues to hail the *Paralus* on every radio channel we have, with no reply.

"Where the hell are they?" I ask.

"Dunno," Lisa says. "They have to be heading back to Mars Station." She clears her throat and keys up the mic. "*Paralus* freighter, this is Scoop One … uh … this is Lisa. Do you copy?"

The sound of blood rushes in my ears.

"*Paralus* freight—"

"Copy, Scoop One," Sarah says. "Sorry about that—interference from Jupiter, I think. Lisa, is that you? Thank God you're alive."

"It's me," Lisa says. "We lost … um, I mean …"

"We lost Boz," I finish, and the stone in my throat swells. "We have Steven but he's unconscious."

"I'm sorry," Sarah says. "Just get back here safely."

"Roger that," Lisa says. "But, where the hell are you?"

"Heading out, back toward Jupiter, I think," Sarah says.

"Why the hell are they going back to Jupiter?" Lisa asks, pulling on the yokes to turn the scoop around.

In the viewfinder, the stars zip by until Jupiter looms large in the window, the *Paralus's* thin shadow a splotch on the planet's pristine surface.

"Maybe slingshot around?" I offer.

Lisa shakes her head. "Can't tell if they're entering orbit or heading out of the solar system."

"They can't possibly be attempting a helium grab," I say. "There are no canisters for containment."

"What?" Lisa fires back. "What do you m—"

"Dona is in control right now," Sarah interrupts. "Not sure— hey!" Something swooshes against the mic on her end. "What the hell?" Sarah shouts. "How did you—get the fuck—!"

The comm goes dead.

"Sarah?" I yell. "Dallas!"

Lisa slaps the comm control with her palm and looks at me, her brow creased and eyes full of questions.

"Chau," I say. "I'll explain, just get us to the *Paralus*—now."

CHAPTER TWENTY-THREE

Dallas

Chau slams a fist into my face. Blood fills my mouth, the ferrous tang familiar and unwelcome. A second punch lands square in my gut, forcing me back against the Boz's ops control panel, but without gravity, I bounce off. Chau comes again and grabs me by the throat. His square face exudes sheer hatred, breath hot with rage.

Can't breathe.

Spittle froths on my lips.

Darkness descends and my limbs fail as Chau's thick fingers squeeze the light from me. Unable to fight back, my mind slips into analysis, into a place comfortable for me. A place of control for the seven seconds of consciousness I have left.

Why? plays over and over in my head.

Why does he hate me? Do I represent an upper echelon he feels he could never reach? Does he loathe my family so much for having what he didn't? Is it more altruistic than that, and he despises the rape of our blue marble, and I'm a convenient scapegoat?

My lungs burn and the blackness is replaced by a strange bright orange, like when I would close my eyes as a child and look directly at the sun. It's warm, almost comforting. A thrumming fills my head. The sound of horse hooves on hard ground. Is that my heartbeat? Another thud, deep and reverberating.

The grip on my esophagus releases. My diaphragm snaps taught, and recycled air rushes into my lugs. My body convulses as I cough and splutter, arms flailing in all directions to find something to hold.

Hands once again encircle me, but they're affectionate this time.

"Calm down, lass, you're all right."

I blink away the brightness, the gentle warmth bleeding away. Kilkenny's soft features, Kilkenny though the doc's eyes are bloodshot.

"Chau," I wheeze.

"Gone, for now," Kilkenny says, cradling me in zero-G. "I hit de big shit wit' a med box." The doc points to the space where the emergency kit is usually fixed to the wall.

A glance over the doc's shoulder confirms Chau has been scared off. Only a few spherical droplets of blood still hanging in the air suggests he was here at all.

"What de hell is goin' on?" Kilkenny asks.

"I don't know." I rub at my throat, hair swirling about my face. "How the hell did he get out of his quarters?"

The doc shrugs, so I look to the ceiling and I raise my voice. "Dona, how did he get out?" I ask, then swallow several times trying to soothe my damaged esophagus.

The AI doesn't answer.

Since when is the AI ever quiet? "Dona?"

Nothing.

"Where *is* he?" I press.

Kilkenny meets my eyes, their frustration burning as hot as is mine, then examines my neck. It's a bit tender, but the doc's fingers are gentle.

"Commander Chau has disabled his telemetry," Dona replies.

"Disabled?" Kilkenny says. "He's gotta be tryin' to finish his crazy feckin' plan."

"We *are* going back toward Jupiter."

Kilkenny grabs the med box which floats nearby and opens it. "You think Tris convinced Dona to wait for Nkosi?"

"Maybe." The doc activates a jet injector against my jugular. "Or maybe Dona is heading back to Jupiter on because it agreed with Chau to burn Jupiter to its core."

"You reckon?" Kilkenny asks, color draining from their face. "Dat's feckin' worrying."

"Dona, you know Chau has a bomb?" I call into the air. "You know what he'll do if we get too near Jupiter?"

"I am aware of Commander Chau's protocol," Dona replies. "It is not prudent at this time to continue with that plan."

"*Continue* with?" I repeat, turning in circles looking for a camera in which to look. To stare into the eyes of the AI. "You knew Chau planned to do this?" Did he convince Dona to plummet Earth into a global, permanent Black Sky? "On what trumped up morally obscure logic path did Chau take you, Dona? How could ending the human race be the right thing to do?"

"Ending what now?" Kilkenny says.

"Cutting off helium, cuts off all power to everything on Earth, so people kill each other for resources," I say with finality.

"We need to get to the Scoops so we can stop him."

"Commander Chau is not permitted to undock a Scoop at this time," Dona says.

"That doesn't mean he won't get the bomb into Jupiter's atmosphere," Kilkenny says, packing up the medkit again.

"Could he jettison it? Fire it like a missile," I ask, cutting a rocket-like path through the air with my arm.

"Fecked if I know," Kilkenny says.

"Sarah? Sarah?" Luan's voice crackles overhead. "Are you there?"

"Shit." I push off a bulkhead and drift over to the comms

panel. "Luan, I'm here."

"What the hell happened?" Luan asks, his voice strained. "I heard... I assumed it was Chau."

"Bastard tried to choke me to death." My throat still hurts now. "Kilkenny fended him off."

"Where is he now?" Luan asks.

"Not sure, can't find him." Haven't had time to look, to be honest. "But he wants to detonate the bomb. Dona locked him out—even though it seemed to agree with him—so he can't take a Scoop or the DAR. He'll be looking for a way. Any ideas?" If Chau gets the bomb off the Paralus, we can no more pull it back than we can shoot it down before it torches Jupiter. He'll doom us all.

"What about the escape pod?" Lisa says. "The one you found the girl in."

"Dona has no control over dat," Kilkenny says, eyes wide. "It's just attached to de robotic arm. I spied de bastard out dere already."

"Fuck," I blurt out, heart pounding in my chest. "Lisa, you get your asses back here."

"Unless the *Paralus* stops accelerating and drops into orbit," Lisa says. "it's gonna be a while."

Hearing her voice is oddly calming. She's so together "Fine, get here ASAP," I say. "I'm going after Chau."

Without waiting for a response, I grab Kilkenny's shoulder and use it to propel toward the hatch and out into Mainstreet. With the doc hot on my heels, we power down the cramped corridor, twisting and turning to dodge protruding wires and pipes that carry recycled sweat absorbed from the air.

"What about Kara?" I call over my shoulder.

"Not'ing more I can do," Kilkenny says, ducking under a bulkhead. "We need to stop dat eejit Chau, or we're all fecked."

The hatch to the medbay spoke comes up ahead and the desire to check in on Kara grabs at my insides—though is it because I feel compassion for her, or fear that I'll lose the biggest discovery of my career? Or do I just want her to provide a window into Dad and Mother, their past, and what was said behind closed doors?

Did you ever love Dad, Mother? Did you love me?

No time, Sarah. Keep going.

My heart cramps as the medbay hatch slips by.

The door to the small airlock that would lead outside to the robotic arm comes up fast. I claw at the frame, to stop myself then smash the open button with the heel of my hand. The door hisses open. Inside, Chau struggles to attach his helmet, the final piece of his EVA suit. His red face contorts, glaring at me through the glass plate. His boot taps the five-foot-tall silver box behind him, which spins in zero-G, the control tablet trailing on its short cable. I can't tell from the blank screen if Chau has activated his bomb. Countless advanced degrees between the crew, and not one of us thought to lock the damn thing up.

"It's over, Chau," I say. "Give it up."

"The hell it is," he fires back. "This needs to happen."

"So you'll condemn the Earth to a shitty end—we'll all starve, wage war, and die off from disease?"

"*We're* a damn disease," Chau shouts, his voice muffled through the helmet glass. "What's next? Other solar systems, until we spread out like a fungus, connected by the ITN?"

"Who are you to decide for us?" Kilkenny says.

"I didn't decide alone," Chau scowls.

"Oh yeah, ya convinced de AI to agree, didn't ya?" the doc says.

"Though, seems Dona came to its senses," I add, hovering in the doorway.

"Convinced?" Chau scoffs, backing away to the exterior exit. "Just because you've been into space once, Dallas, on one grab, you don't know what it means to contemplate the fabric of the universe. Dona and I have been together for years. Alone while the crew slept. We realized our true place in the cosmos. No spoiled brat like you would understand."

"Don't confuse delusions of grandeur with your petty bullshit, Chau." My fingers curl tighter around the door frame. "It's about your insecurity. If you had money, we wouldn't be having this conversation."

"You think this is about *me*?" Chau says, a wry smile on his lips. "You're not paying attention, Sarah."

My gaze darts around the stark airlock then settles on the bomb. He's taking it *with* him. "You'll martyr yourself?"

"A martyr requires someone to give a shit when you're gone. I'm just doing what needs to be done." Chau smiles. Not a maniacal smile. A strange sad smile. The smile of someone who's accepted they're going to die.

"One way or another, Dona will have to initiate the Voyager Three Protocol," Chau says, his gloved hand on the decompression button.

"Don't even try," I say.

"You think I won't with you in here with me?"

Kilkenny doesn't wait for me to answer. The doc brings their fists down on our rogue commander's helmet. Chau grabs Kilkenny's arms and the two tumble through the air, bouncing off the walls.

Do something, Sarah. Get the bomb.

I use the door frame to launch into the airlock and attempt to dodge the melee of arms and legs.

A boot catches me square in the jaw and sends me spinning into the wall. Need a weapon—something to hit this asshole with. There's nothing in here, save the bomb and control panel. Not even a med box this time.

Fuck it.

I join the brawl. Unable to determine which leg belongs to whom, I just lash out, grab, pull, and punch. Grunts that sound like Chau tell me to keep pummeling, so I do, over and over. An elbow drives into my stomach. Air rushes out of me and I can't get it back, my chest burns as I struggle to suck in enough oxygen.

The *Paralus* lurches, and the bomb slams into my hip, radiating pain through my body.

"Warning," Dona says. "Gravitational anomaly."

Oh shit.

The singularity is back.

The ship shudders again—the metal creaks sharp in my ears. I raise my head from the fight to flashing lights and strange shadows in the cramped space. Each time the overhead lights flicker, dark silhouettes trickle and bleed, alive, over the walls. A shadow swoops through the airlock, black wings outstretched. The *Paralus*'s hull wails again. A gloved fist slams into my cheekbone and I'm dragged under the ocean of arms and legs again.

Kilkenny and I somehow synchronize our movements. The doc maneuvers to Chau's back, and pins his arms, which frees me. I wind up, summon all the rage inside to take a shot at Chau's gut, and show the commander the wrath of this spoiled brat.

Another pair of strong arms snakes around my shoulders. Tris pulls me back, then spins me and shoves me in the chest. I soar away from the fight and into the damn bomb that's still free-floating in here.

"Hey now, stop it," Tris says, teeth clenched, as he peels Kilkenny off Chau.

Chau takes the chance and grabs a handful of Kilkenny's ginger hair. The commander slams our doctor's face into the metallic frame of the hatch that leads outside. Bone breaks with a horrible crunch and blood squirts out in five distinct jets that become liquid spheres and float to the corners of the airlock. Kilkenny's limp body hangs in the air.

"No!" I scream and charge at Chau.

Tris catches me mid-air, his vice grip clamped around my ankle.

"Hey, calm down," he says. "It's not the way."

"Get off me!" I kick and thrash, but can't get away.

He pulls me back through the airlock door into Mainstreet. I grab at the frame but my fingers are not a match for Tris's legs which he braces against the wall to lever me away. The door hisses closed, and I know only have a small glass portal through which to see the inside of the airlock.

Chau grabs the bomb and slams the depressurization button. A loud hum signals the air leaving the small space, then the exterior door makes a dull *clunk*, and opens. Chau slips out into the coldness of space, leaving Kilkenny—who if they weren't already dead, are now—hanging in the airlock. A final *clunk* as the door shuts and he's gone.

"Fuuuuuuuck!" I scream at Tris. "He fucking killed the doc! You let him go!"

Tris's eyes are wide and glassy.

"What the hell?"

"Dr. Dallas, you have an incoming message," Dona announces as if he—she, it—hadn't just aided and abetted Chau to cause humanity's demise.

"What?" I scream down Mainstreet.

"Sarah, Sarah," Nkosi calls over the comms, "We're almost with you—did someone just start a spacewalk near the robotic arm?" he asks. "Was that Chau?"

"Yes!" I shout. "Bastard has the bomb." "Can't you get him?"

"Get him?" Lisa says. "We have no time."

I turn to Tris, chest heaving. "Can we control the arm from the inside?"

"Uh," he says.

"He'll override it from the outside," Lisa replies.

We're fucked. This is insane. I can't breathe. Can't stop him. We failed. The Fulcrum. Humanity. Psomas warned us. She warned us. If we'd used the bomb when she asked, Chau wouldn't have it, wouldn't be able to do *this*. Hot tears well in my eyes and squeeze off into the air. The tiny spheres of liquid knock into one another and merge with Kilkenny's blood.

The *Paralus* moans again, tugged by the anomaly, crying out that soon enough it'll be pulled apart.

"We should focus on getting the ship away from Jupiter," Tris says, edging up Mainstreet toward the Bridge. "Between the bomb and the singularity, we're in some serious shit."

"Why bother?" I say. We'll all die anyway. Out here. Everyone back home. The only difference is our deaths will be less drawn out, caught in Jupiter's burning atmosphere.

You wanted me to find myself, Dad. All I found was death.

My chest is hollow.

"What the hell is that?" Luan says.

"I … I don't know," Lisa replies.

I sniff and focus on the static-filled conversation.

"You've got to be fucking kidding me," Steven says.

I don't think I've heard the man utter a curse word since I met him.

Tris grabs a handhold and cocks his head to listen.

"Jesus, get us out of here Lisa!" Luan says.

"I'm trying. You see how fast that—"

A wash of white noise fills Mainstreet, the sound amplified all along the mile-long ship.

"Lisa?" I cry. "Luan, Steven?"

"What was that?" I scream at Tris, who looks as bewildered as me. "Tris?"

He shakes his head.

Fuck this shit. "Dona, what are they looking at?"

"Do you wish to use external cameras?" Dona asks.

"Yes!" I shout back.

"Confirmed," Dona replies. "Please head to the Bridge.

Tris has already turned tail and bolted up Mainstreet. I chase after him.

The massive viewfinder now shows a nightmarish external camera view. The small black hole whirls just above Europa. Its accretion disc glows hot as it grows, sucking on the small moon's ice crust and thin atmosphere. Between it and Jupiter, two vessels dot the scene: a Scoop headed for us, and Kara's escape pod, piloted by Chau, headed the other away. He seems to struggle to keep a path toward Jupiter—the pod's thrusters fire continuously but Chau's trajectory slips toward the singularity.

Something massive and dark hurtles the surface of Europa, pushed by a gargantuan jet that freezes into a splayed fountain the size of Manhattan, and breaks off. The ice plume shatters into dust, and there, emerging from the debris is the biomechanical monster.

The creature's silvery scales ripple, and its metallic caudal feathers glint in the distant sun's rays. And while I know it's not possible, its head—or forward command, or whatever it is—bears a terrible grin as it seems to look our way and locks a path for us.

CHAPTER TWENTY-FOUR

Commander Feng Chau

Tethered to the robotic arm, I stare out at the singularity—the very gate of Hell—which calls to me like a cosmic siren, inviting me in. It's blacker than I could ever imagine yet white-hot with a growing accretion disc. Framing the black mouth, Jupiter stands proud while Europa fractures like a broken Christmas bauble, pieces drifting from the surface into the endless dark.

My breathing quickens, loud inside the helmet.

Okay, first things first. Activate the Isolated Extra Vehicular Activity Man-Machine Interface. I pull an interface cord from my EVA suit and plug it into the unit at the base of the robotic arm. The display on my forearm shows command verification data. A few taps to enter my clearance codes and I'm in. But I need to lock Dallas out.

I jam a thick gloved finger on the emergency stop button.

A quick look up and down the length of the beta-cloth-covered arm, but the dizzying panorama ahead once again pulls my attention, and even though I'm tethered, fear tightens its frozen grip.

Hand over hand I pull myself along the tether ensuring neither myself nor the bomb can float away. Everything aches and my brain feels foggy. A quick check of the EVA readout on my forearm—there's about five percent oxygen left in here.

Shit.

Lungs on fire, I yank on a handhold jutting from the *Paralus* hull and propel myself along. Several huge leaps and I make it to the end effector hub, its processing unit and if memory serves—yes, a pistol grip tool. I run my hand over the PGT, which resembles a cordless drill, then release it from its housing. I push my boots into the foothold just below the servicing tool compartment, to gain purchase and stop myself from spinning off into the void, then attach the PGT and pull the trigger. It has little torque but is fast as hell, and I'm able to release all three bolts in a matter of seconds.

Another quick check of oxygen. Three percent. My vision blurs and I can only see shapes really, now. The black hole, Jupiter, and Europa meld into one amorphous mess. The breath in my ears slows, along with my heartbeat.

The robotic arm twitches as the claws lose their grip on my escape pod.

I gather up my tether and with great effort, I slide around the claws to the hatch of the pod. One arm still holding on to the bomb, I use the other to open the hatch door. I swing inside, sucking at the bad mixture of oxygen and carbon dioxide.

A fumbled untethering and I close the hatch door behind, the bomb filling the cockpit.

The command console lies ahead, still powered up from my previous visit, even though the tussle in the greenhouse kept me away longer than I'd planned.

Still with my pre-programmed flight path: head for Jupiter.

I mash the confirm key and the pod lurches, though we don't go anywhere.

The end effectors must still be holding on.

I push on the yoke to increase thrust. The pod wails under the force, an animal in a trap. Out of the cockpit window, I'm greeted by a bright blur with a black center. The oxygen light on my forearm flashes red, upset that I've ignored it.

Like a wound-up elastic band, the pod liberates itself from the robotic arm's death grip and fires away from the *Paralus*. I hurtle toward Jupiter on autopilot, not into some smooth orbit, but directly for the planet's center. A galactic kamikaze. Ironic, given Grandfather's distaste for all things Japanese.

"I'm sorry, Grandfather."

Even in these final seconds of life, I know I've not lived up to his expectation.

The pod shakes and tosses me about its innards. Through tear-filled eyes, I feel the keys on the tablet attached to the bomb and enter my final passcode.

Y-E-Y-E. Cantonese for Grandfather.

The light on my arm readout flashes red.

My blurred aimless stare lands on the stasis unit at the other end of the cabin, the one the girl never used. I push off toward the coffin, bomb hugged close. With shaking fingers activate the stasis unit, and its door slides up. My chest convulsing, I place the bomb inside along with the tablet and tuck them both down into the footwell.

I take a last gasp of air poisoned by carbon dioxide, then release my helmet. The cold stabs at my face and burns deep into my flesh. Another click and the hard upper torso of my EVA suit disconnects from the bottom half. I kick away the legs while slipping down and out of the torso.

Body cripplingly cold, limbs stiff to the point of uselessness, I squeeze inside the stasis unit alongside the bomb. Another clumsy mash of the unit's inner keyboard and the transparent door slides shut. A hiss signals a good seal, and the compartment floods with warm, life-giving air. I suck at the oxygen-rich atmosphere, hacking, and coughing, until eventually, I can breathe shallow but meaningful breaths.

I wipe tear-filled eyes and peer through the window of the stasis unit, out through the viewfinder of the escape pod, to a scene that seems so far away, it might have nothing to do with me. Jupiter is no longer in the center of my view but skewed off to the side. My pod quakes as the thrusters struggle to keep me on course. And there, between Europa and Jupiter is the cause: the singularity, flickering into like a flame in the wind.

A Scoop missiles past me, its thrusters afire.

"Nkosi," I mutter to myself.

Part of Europa explodes and is thrust into space. My eyes fix wide as the frozen column shatters into a billion fragments and from within it something emerges—something alive. Its long body and feather-like blades splay out as it powers through space, with seemingly no engines. "What the fuck, is that?" I whisper, my flesh cold, and hover a frozen finger over the detonate trigger. "This isn't for you," I whisper. "Just let me by. Let me finish what I started."

The gargantuan monster ripples and thrusts forward, directly for me.

CHAPTER TWENTY-FIVE

Dr. Luan Nkosi

T he race to reach the *Paralus* is eerily quiet and devoid of sensation.

If we were in a hovercar, we'd hear the rush of wind and the Doppler-elongated sound of other vehicles' engines as we sped along. Trees and buildings would zip by, and we'd likely have to dodge overhanging traffic signals. The Scoop shakes a little more than usual under full thrusters, but with so little to orient ourselves, and no gravity, we might as well be stationary. Somehow, it steals the urgency of the situation—as we fly for our lives away from Jupiter, which may soon be vaporized. Away from an extra-terrestrial biomechanical life form that's broken free from Europa's icy ocean to hurtle through space. Away from a miniature and very temperamental black hole.

Couldn't make this shit up if I tried.

Lisa's white knuckles grip the yokes, her eyes locked on the *Paralus* ahead. The freighter has a fusion drive and we're pootling along under normal combustion-powered thrust.

Steven—who is awake but woozy—fixates on the scene playing out just a few hundred miles away. The black hole flickers in and out of existence; its accretion disc forms and collapses over and over. Europa's space Goliath that keeps my rapt attention. Our former freighter commander looks like a tiny snack as it swims toward him. A mayfly to a rainbow trout—if that trout were sporting steel wings and crystalline armor.

How did it survive that frozen ocean? How can it transverse a vacuum? I should be praying we don't die out here, but that Goliath is *why* we're here, isn't it? Complex, intelligent, alien life.

"Chau's caught in the gravitational field of the black hole," Steven says. "He can't get into Jupiter's atmosphere."

"We need to thank our lucky stars," I say. "If Jupiter goes bye-bye, we're friggin' vapor."

"Someone's looking out for us." Steven peels his gaze away long enough to look me in the eyes. "Maybe there is a god?"

"Psomas says there's six." I show him the correct number of bony fingers.

"Ten minutes out," Lisa calls over her shoulder. "We have just enough fuel to bring us in synch with the *Paralus* for docking."

"Great." That sounded way more sarcastic than I wanted.

"That thing still out there?" Lisa asks.

"If you mean the space fish-bird," I say, "it's still there."

"You think it's alive?" Steven asks. "Like a … like an animal, that can survive in space, you know, like a tardigrade?"

I stare long and hard at the thing out there in the void, surging and flexing, using some kind of kinetic energy for propulsion. That in itself indicates it's alive, but its bio-mechanical appearance suggests it was built—put together to *represent* life.

"I don't know," I say under my breath. "Psomas says it's a war machine built by another race sent to murder us all in our sleep."

No one says anything.

I can hear my heartbeat.

"War machine?" Lisa pipes up, her head now twisted back to see both us and the chaos outside.

245

"It's not a war machine." I roll my eyes. "It's … it has to be an animal—look at it."

"It's heading right for Chau—you can see that, right?" Steven says.

He's right, it is. And not in an *Oh, we just bumped into you* kinda way, but in an *I stalked you from far away* kinda way. The Goliath makes a beeline for our unhinged freighter commander, like a pissed-off ex-girlfriend at a party where her former beau just made the mistake of talking to the girl in the short skirt.

Please be a coincidence. Please just be intrigued by Chau.

The thing halts its chase, its body reversing the waves. It sits there in space, seemingly far enough from the singularity to not be pulled in. "Is it waiting?" I say. The edge of light surrounding the black hole sputters and then shrinks. The great cosmic pupil contracts until, *poof,* it's gone again. The accretion disc begins to dissipate, throwing out its mass in a wave of debris. The Goliath opens its giant maw—just a crack. Like a moray eel, it waits, rolling back and forth. Will it pounce, devour Chau in its horrible pharyngeal jaws and pull his vessel into its gut? He's several hundred, if not thousands of kilometers away, the Goliath would have transverse one hell of a distance pretty damn fast.

The mouth opens, but the creature doesn't move.

A trail of light refracts through the debris of the former accretion disc. Chau's pod explodes in a silent ball of flame that extinguishes almost immediately in the vacuum of space.

"What the hell just happened?" asks Lisa, shielding her eyes from the sudden flash.

"I… I don't know," I say, stare glued to Goliath. "Chau's gone."

"Gone?" she repeats, "What do you mean Gone?"

"That thing," Steven says, wringing his hands. "It *fired* something. A weapon. A *laser* weapon, in the sub-visible spectrum, maybe."

"Still think it's not a war machine, Nkosi?" Lisa says jaw gritted.

"I don't know," I stutter. "Cobras spit, ants spray formic acid—hell, the Texas horned lizard shoots blood from its eyes. It's possible a creature could evolve the ability to focus light as a defense mechanism."

"It went after him," Steven mumbles.

"Maybe it's territorial," I say. "We think of territories as distinct environments on our planet, but this thing can survive in space. Its territory could be enormous."

"Clutching at some flimsy-assed straws, Nkosi," Lisa says without looking at me. "You haven't seen enough action to know the difference between defense and offense."

Maybe she's right. Either way, Chau's bomb is gone, Jupiter is safe, but now we need to get the hell out of here. Don't fancy being blown to shit by my great discovery. Any good biologist knows to get out of the animal's nest and come back when it's safe. Observe from afar. We can send probes, surveillance drones. Now that we know they're under the ice, we can look for more of them.

That is of course if we make it out alive.

"How far away are we?" Steven asks.

Lisa checks the instruments. "Uh, three minutes," she says. "Burned everything we have to maximum velocity. If the *Paralus* accelerates, we're screwed."

"Lisa, you sure we got no juice left at all?" Steven says, his voice quivering. "Our new friend is gaining."

"Fuck, fuck, fuck," Lisa says.

I don't know how the Goliath, but it's doing it fast. Head-on the creature makes my sphincter weak. Its skull is massive, akin to Earth's most massive prehistoric—and scary-as-all-hell—fish, *Dunkleosteus terrella*. And much like that terrifying scourge of the Devonian oceans, our space monster has two pairs of sharp jagged bony plates that form a beak-like structure. Its predatory eyes sat high in its head, bore a hungry stare at us.

247

I fire a quick look at the *Paralus* and back to the Goliath, which gains on us faster than we can on our mother ship.

"So, we have to do something stupid," Lisa says and gives me a quick side-eye. "No time for docking procedure. And when I say *we*, I mean *you*."

Frig my life.

"Once we match velocity," she says, "exit the Scoop in your EVAs to get to robotic arm airlock hatch."

Steven's face drains of color. "You want us to go outside, with that thing out there?"

"You see what it did?" Lisa says. "No safer in here."

This is so fucked.

"Suit up, you're about to go for a walk," Lisa says.

Steven and I help each other into our EVAs. "And you?" I ask Lisa, searching for another suit.

"Mine's no good," Lisa replies with a weak smile. "Faceplate is busted. Barely made it to you alive. And the SAFER is out of fuel."

"What are you talking about?" Steven says as he closes the last seal on my suit, locked and loaded. "How will you... I mean... how..."

I look at Lisa's helmet and see the long hairline crack in the visor. I'd been so intent on saving her before I hadn't noticed it.

"Someone has to put this thing on a synchronous trajectory at the perfect velocity," Lisa says with only the slightest tremor in her voice. "No time to run the full docking procedure, and I'm not risking a collision with the *Paralus*. Once you're aboard, tell Dallas to get the hell out of here."

She's going to sacrifice herself? I pull off my gloves and boots, crashing into the sealed door as I struggle to remove the EVA suit. "I'm the leader," I say, "it should be me."

"Nkosi, you're not a pilot," Lisa says. "We can all agree on that. Always knew I'd die in space. Part of the job."

This can't be happening. I scrunch my eyes together and will an answer to come.

"Sixty seconds out," she says. "I'll steer within one hundred feet of the *Paralus*. It'll take less than thirty seconds to cross the gap. One or two bursts to accelerate, one retro thrust to control how you hit the hull." She casts a look over her shoulder and nods at the controls on the boots as I buckle them back on. "It's been an honor, gentlemen."

Any words stick in my throat. And before I can answer Lisa looks behind me, out of the window, to the Goliath still gaining on us.

"I can carry you across," I blurt out.

"What?" Lisa says.

"You've done emergency training for expulsion from a vehicle at high altitude, right?" I ask.

"This is space, Nkosi."

"It's not too different, we can do it. You get us in line with the *Paralus* and then leave it on that trajectory, it'll keep going indefinitely."

"Unless the *Paralus* pivots and takes the Scoop out, risking everyone."

The *Paralus* and Jupiter grow larger in the viewfinder. We're out of time. "Shut up and listen. You have your suit. You'll lose all your air through the crack, and probably get exposed to the vacuum, but it'll be okay. Steven goes first and unlocks the external hatch. We follow, like five seconds behind."

"She'll decompress," Steven yelps.

"Thirty seconds," Lisa says, "get to the point."

"It's the same as entering any low-pressure environment." I try to sound confident. "Don't hold your breath—expel it slowly so your lungs don't tear when the air expands. You'll lose a lot of moisture from your mouth and nose as it boils off. You'll bloat up, probably, but once back in normal pressure it'll all be okay."

Lisa's eyebrows raise high on her forehead.

Yeah, it's a fucked up idea, but the only one I have

"With dogs, Nkosi," Steven yells. "Dogs! And they lost consciousness, were paralyzed—not to mention they shit and pissed themselves!"

Lisa glares at me.

"They also recovered," I say. "Ninety seconds in a near-vacuum. Fully recovered, after *minutes* back in a normal environment."

"And if it's longer than ninety seconds?" Steven asks.

No need to voice out loud the answer. "If she doesn't try, she's dead anyway."

The long hull of the Paralus now fills the entire window, its scaffolding-like exterior looks old and disheveled.

"Fine," Lisa says. "Grab my helmet—we're coming up on the *Paralus*."

I lean over and fetch Lisa's helmet and attach it to her suit while she still pilots the Scoop. Up close, it's not just a hairline crack in the glass, but a fissure. Can't back out now.

"*Paralus*, this is Scoop One, we're coming up on your port side," Lisa says into her helmet mic. "No time to dock. We'll enter through the robotic arm hatch."

Silence.

"*Paralus*, do you read me?" she presses.

"We don't have time for this, just have to risk it," I say.

Lisa nods and concentrates on lining up our Scoop to the side of the Paralus. It's a tricky business at the best of times and always freaks me out a little—like handing a package from a bicycle over to a truck while doing a hundred miles an hour. Easy in principle, but not so much in practice.

The *Paralus* fills the Scoop's window. The Scoop lines up beside the *Paralus*'s robot arm entrance. I look back to our pursuer, who's slowed a little. Have we been chased far enough away? Nope. The Goliath darts forward again, covering miles with a single undulation of its body.

"Get ready, Nkosi." Lisa punches one last key and stands. She huffs out a determined breath. "Let's do this."

Steven and I clamp on our helmets.

Steven gives a weak smile, then enters the Scoop's airlock. He closes the inner door and stares through the tiny window at us. The pressure light turns from green to red. He opens the outer door and the air shoots out from the inside with a *whoop*. Steven steps to the edge and launches himself out.

The outer door closes and the airlock repressurizes, the light returning to green.

"Here we go," I say.

Lisa clamps her arms around me, her grip tight even through this giant EVA suit. Out the window, Steven glides toward the *Paralus*. I set the timer on my sleeve readout for sixty seconds, which appears in my heads-up display.

The airlock door hisses open and I step inside.

No time to dawdle.

I start the timer and slam my gloved fist against the large red button on the wall.

The atmosphere shoots out and immediately Lisa's body becomes rigid.

I shove out into the void of space, clutching Lisa to me, and toe my foot controls to fire a spurt of thrust. These things are hard to control and I veer away from the *Paralus*'s hatch entrance. Surge after surge, I correct my trajectory.

It takes too long.

Thirty seconds.

Steven clings to the hull, still not inside. What's the hold-up?

I can't even look behind me to see if our pursuer is upon us.

My panicked breathing is loud inside the helmet. Can't see Lisa's face. She isn't moving. I careen silently toward Steven and the *Paralus*. Too fast. Far too fast. Steven pops the door open and struggles to turn around in his cumbersome EVA suit.

I crash into him and bounce off.

Ten seconds left.

Lisa slips from my arms.

"No!" I scream.

Steven's arm snakes around my elbow. The hatch swings open beside him.

Steven jams on his thrusters to propel us off the hull. "All for one," he says.

He's far better at controlling the thrusters and we make a beeline for Lisa. I stretch my arms as far as I can, Steven hanging on to me.

I can't look away from the countdown in my helmet. Five seconds.

My fingers find the edge of her foil blanket and it's hard to close a fist but I tug on it just a little, enough to stop her moving away, even to jerk her back to me. I can't tell how far we got from the hull of the *Paralus*, but the Scoop drifts into the black of space.

Triple zeroes read across the inside of my helmet.

Lisa doesn't respond, arms rigid at her side, head bowed. I clamp my arms around her and pull her close. Steven initiates careful bursts of retro thrusters to ensure a safe return.

I stare with blurry eyes over Lisa's shoulder at the monster coming for us. Even if we make it to the freighter Goliath will reach us before the ship can get build up enough acceleration to escape. Especially if it uses its invisible defense mechanism.

I squeeze Lisa tighter. "I'm sorry."

A burst of light blinds me.

The Goliath's weapon?

But no explosion comes. No instantaneous death.

Instead, the singularity springs into existence again, directly in the path between us and our predator. Like a cosmic vampire, it sucks on the debris from Europa and on Jupiter's outer atmosphere, an accretion disc already forming. Out here, with only a thin layer of fabric between me and the black hole, it seems more real. More awesome. And for the briefest of moments, I think of my mum and how maybe, just maybe, God is real. I grip Lisa tighter.

We crash back through the small hatch, and Steven yanks me inside the *Paralus*'s airlock. I float to the back wall, and can only watch as he slams the portal door shut and initiates the re-pressurization protocol. I look at the red light and I let go of Lisa.

The readout in my helmet is red too: seventeen seconds over, eighteen, nineteen.

The light on the wall changes to green.

Steven and I pull off our helmets and free Lisa from hers. Her frozen skin is blue and covered in pinkish cracks. Her helmet floats and clanks into something—someone. Oh fuck, Kilkenny?

Steven rushes to the doc while I tear off one glove and place my fingers on her jugular to check her pulse. Nothing.

C'mon, don't you die on me.

"He's gone," Steven says. "Someone caved his face in."

"We need help down here, get Sarah," I shout.

Steven works the comms panel. "Sarah, Sarah, we need you down here now!" He doesn't wait for a reply and comes back to press his mouth to hers. He gently blows warm air through her blue lips and into her frozen lungs.

"Steve, you have to do something," I say, trembling.

Steven feels her neck and places a hand on her chest. "Fuck," he says, then hooks one leg over Lisa's shoulder and the other around her torso. He interlocks his ankles in the center of her back, then begins compressions on her chest while they both float in the airlock's zero gravity.

All I can do is watch, my stomach knotted all to hell.

A horrible crunch can only mean Lisa's sternum's broken.

Over and over, Steven presses on Lisa's chest and blows gently into her mouth.

But we both know it's in vain.

She's gone.

"Fuck it all," Steven says, releasing the leg lock and allowing Lisa to float away. "What were we thinking?"

"We had no time," I stutter. "The animal, it was coming. We…"

"But it's not coming, is it?" he screams. "The singularity blocked its path! I saw!"

"I don't know," I whisper. "Maybe."

"So we had time," Steven fires back. "We had time to get another EVA!"

A cold guilty silence washes over my skin.

Steven sucks in a breath. "Just go, I'll…" he says, "deal with Lisa and the doctor. Go find Dallas. Get us the hell out of here."

CHAPTER TWENTY-SIX

Dr. Sarah Dallas

Sat under a high tree, I run my fingers through wet grass and sticky soil. The aromas in the cargo bay, sweet and fresh, stir memories long-buried—of a home I didn't think I missed. Of a time when life was simple. I climbed up to where Dad sat on the porch of our ranch—a privileged piece of green on a dying world. I played with my favorite doll, imagining what it would be like if we both wore white dresses on our wedding day. Mother, of course, insisted on buying the doll's male counterpart to complete the pair, but I never played with it. Instead, that plastic man collected dust in my bedroom chest.

So there, on that cedar deck, at Dad's feet, I stopped to feel the cool Kansas breeze swirl around the fencing and the old rocking chair. Dad's sentinel post, where he'd sit watching the sunset, occasionally looking down to me and smiling a sad smile. As if he knew what was to come, even all those years ago.

There's no breeze aboard the *Paralus*, only Kara's ragged breath as she lies dying in my lap. Her skin is papery and splits at the slightest touch, her flesh sunken and withered. The legs of my flight suit are covered in her bloody vomit. It was dangerous to leave medbay and bring her here, but when I told her about this place her last wish is to be surrounded by life before she died. Real life, that she can touch and smell. After all, she's been through, isolated for eons, how could I refuse?

Kara hacks another cough and looks up into the branches, eyes no longer full of arrogance and distaste, but fear. A child's eyes. Because she's scared of what is to come. Not even Kara who professes to know all can see beyond death.

I place a hand on her clammy forehead and stroke away damp hair.

I wonder if she had a mother, someone to love her. Someone to listen. Before her ordeal, before her long exile. She was a little girl once. Someone's daughter. She looks at me the same way I once looked to Mother—with longing. With hope that a crack would appear in the façade, and emotion gush out from behind the dam.

But Kara is not a little girl. She's a woman, much older than me. Born long before I existed. She shouldn't seek guidance from me, but vice versa.

"Dallas," she croaks. "Sarah … you have to …"

Luan crashes into the cargo bay, skids through the mud, and nearly crashes into a bush. "You're just sitting here?" he asks.

"What's to do?" I say. "Jupiter is safe, but Dona's in control of the ship. The war machine will come for us, then Earth. We failed. The fulcrum passed."

"What are you talking about?" he says, righting himself. "We need to leave—we need to get out of here!"

"The Fulcrum." I shoo him away. "The point that could tip the balance. Kara told us. We missed our chance to save humanity."

"Will you stop it with this bullshit?" Nkosi barks at me, wagging a skinny digit in my face. "It's not a war machine! It's a life form. And it's pissed we're in its territory. That's it."

"A life form that killed Chau and came for you." I turn to the damp, moss-covered walls. "And is still coming for us."

"Doesn't mean we have to let it," Nkosi says. "We need to leave."

"Try telling that to Dona," I say. "Chau initiated some kind of protocol. He called it Voyager Three. We're locked out. We have no control. Whatever Chau planned is in motion."

"Bullshit," Luan says and drops to his haunches to meet me at eye level. "Lisa just died getting us back to the *Paralus*. I found Kilkenny in the damn airlock, with his face bashed in. I won't let it be in vain."

"Lisa's dead?" Oh, God.

The astrobiologist swallows a few times, trying to find the strength to speak, then just nods.

"Steven?"

"Putting Lisa's and Kilkenny's body into stasis, I imagine," Luan says. "Tris? Because I can't find him."

"No idea," I say, with a shrug. "He might be trying to talk Dona around, I guess."

Luan looks down at Kara and studies her mangled body. "Much longer?"

I shake my head.

"Okay, I know this is shit, but we need to get out of here. The Goliath, the creature, is held at bay by the black hole, but unless we get away it'll eventually come for us."

Kara opens her eyes with a flutter, fluid stringing between her eyelids as her cells break down into a gooey mess. "Another way," she wheezes.

"Another way?" Luan says.

"To preserve… humanity."

I shift a little and turn her small face toward me. "Kara, what are you talking about?"

"The cargo," she grunts.

"What cargo?" I search the around greenhouse, blocked in on all sides by long trees and thick shrubs. "You're sitting in it, Kara.

Grass. Trees. Chau's private garden of Eden, to grow old in and die."

Kara gives the smallest shake of her head, chest rising and falling a little more with the obvious effort.

Luan stands with a groan. "No time, I need to find Tris and get him to talk to Dona. Make sure we're leaving and head back to Earth."

"Please, Luan," I beg, "just a couple of minutes, look for me, it's important."

The slender astrobiologist huffs, but searches the greenhouse anyway, pacing the sodden soil in a methodical grid pattern, stepping around shrubberies. "He scans the Fungai-covered surfaces walls and green canopy, grumbling as he goes. Eventually, he reaches the far wall and pats at the moist moss, which squelches under his palms. "There's nothing here," he says.

"Keep looking," I call back.

Splat after splat, he makes his way down the wall until a *pang* rings out. Luan looks to me, then back to the wall. He claws at the moss with his nails, stripping it away to expose a panel. He touches what looks like a thumbprint scanner, but an irritating rejection buzz replies.

"Maybe your print?" Luan says.

"I'll be back." I ease Kara to the soft ground. She mumbles something I don't understand, lip smacks, and clicks with thin broken lips. I climb to my feet and step over to Luan, curiosity driving my legs to work faster. A hummingbird buzzes in front of my face, stopping to investigate. It hovers there, wings beating furiously, its tiny eyes fixed on me. Then it's gone, zipping down the length of the cargo hold.

I touch the pendant under my suit.

"What are you waiting for?" Luan asks.

"Sorry." I trot over and press my thumb to the panel. An agreeable peep sounds and the whole chunk of the wall slides out, tearing away a tangle of ivy. Cool vapors pour from within and dissipate into the warm atmosphere. Luan and I both stare into a refrigerated drawer bigger than a stasis unit, filled with vial upon vial, each hanging from a miniature hook. Rows upon rows, thousands of them.

I fish one out and read the label. "*Quercus virginiana.*" Dry pellets sit at the bottom of the vial.

"Oaktree," Luan says with a frown, plucking out another vial. A pea bobs in a thick fluid. "*Agalychnis callidryas,* red-eyed tree frog."

Vial after vial, Latin name after Latin name. It's a catalog of countless species found on Earth. Spores, embryos, cuttings. A biological library. A seed bank.

Chau built an Ark?

"Wait." I rifle through the glass ampoules. "There." I pull one free and hold it up to the light to reveal a pinkish blob just visible through the frosty glass. I don't need Luan to translate this one. *Homo sapiens.* "He wasn't setting himself up for a comfy demise," I say. "He sent an Ark into the void."

"Voyager Three," Luan says. "The old Voyager missions carried evidence of humans, of Earth with them. Music, anatomy, basic math. A message in a bottle for whoever finds it—*you are not alone.*"

"Correct, Dr. Nkosi," Dona says.

"Mother fu… " Luan clutches at his chest. "That damn AI creeps me out."

"Dona, you knew?" I ask.

"Of course," Dona replies. "I respected Commander Chau's vision. Humanity is not inherently evil but has continued down a path to the current apocalyptic situation. The *Paralus* provides a record of Earth. A galactic library."

"Hey, what's all the hullabaloo?" Tris asks, stomping into the room, Steven on his heels.

"I don't even know where to begin." I face the men. "The *Paralus* is a damn Ark. Chau wanted to wipe us out only to … leave a bio library. A history of Earth." Is that it? Makes zero sense to me.

Tris high steps over a dense fern while Steve finds an easier path toward the drawer.

"It's some kind of advanced Voyager mission," Luan says, still pawing through the ampoules. "The idea was someone, *something* not human, would one day find it."

"Why wipe us out first though?" Steven asks, handing Tris a vial with the label *Orcinus orca*. "Why the bomb?"

"Chau's personal vendetta," I say, nose all snarled up.

"Humanity has gone beyond destroying just Earth but has now spread into the solar system. This does not seem morally correct."

"You're talking about genocide," Luan shouts at the trees.

"It is not important that humanity survives in its current socio-economic form," Dona says, "only that its potential is realized and perhaps enacted upon without the influence of the past."

"It's legacy," I whisper and stare at the tiny human embryo in my palm.

"Fuck this," Luan says, grabbing the tiny flasks from us all and shoving them back into the refrigerator. "This was only if Chau managed to cut off Earth's power supply and kill us all. But Jupiter is still out there. Ergo, life goes on, and this Ark is pointless. You hear me, Dona? This is moot. So, you can get us the frig out of here and let us go home."

"You… can't go home," a weak voice says from the other side of the bay. Kara props herself up on one elbow in the mud and grass. "Nyx's war machine is coming for you—for us all. Now it knows… where you are, that this solar system holds life. And it won't be alone."

"War machine?" Tris asks as Luan snatches the last ampoule from him.

"The Goliath, out there," Luan says. "She thinks it's coming to wipe out Earth."

"Nyx is here," Kara wheezes. "I've seen her."

I tramp back over to the young girl, scoop her up in my arms and rest her head on my folded legs.

"We... humanity... " Kara grunts "... have but one chance left."

"I thought you said we missed the Fulcrum?" I look into her unfocused eyes. Is she even lucid anymore?

"We did," she rasps. "Earth will die."

"Then what the hell are you talking about?" Luan fires back, already marching for the exit.

"Take the *Paralus*... to a place Nyx's war machines can't find you." Kara sucks in a deep breath only to choke on it. "Because they will... they will hunt you. If the one out there does not get you, then another."

"Where?" I ask, tone soft. "Where could we possibly go?"

"Into the singularity," Kara says. Her eyes roll back into her head.

Luan stops in his tracks and spins on a dime. "Are you insane?" he says. "To stay trapped, as you did?"

"Eh?" Steven says, face all scrunched up.

"Oh yeah," Luan says, spreading his arm wide as if addressing a crowd. "She lived in the event horizon of the black hole out there for eons then popped out, more than one hundred SEYs later and physically thirty SEYs younger. And while she was there she saw all of time."

Kara moans. "P-pass through it... through the..."

"Wormhole? Is that what you were going to say?" Luan stomps the last few steps to the exit, then turns back to us. "Are we listening to this?"

I cast a questioning gaze to Tris and Steven, who've been quiet all this time. "Is that even possible, passing through a black hole?" I'm not an astrophysicist, but everything I was ever told about them suggests we'd all die a horrible death if we tried that. But then again, Kara survived whatever happened to her.

Steven shakes his head, mouth open, and shrugs. "I mean, maybe?" he says. "Look, if you believe she existed trapped on the event horizon, and it spat her back out, I guess this is just as possible."

Tris remains quiet, eyes narrowed in thought. Can't say I blame him. This is fucking with my head too.

"I mean, we haven't seen a singularity like this one before," Steven continues and begins pacing in the mud, tapping at his head. "It keeps popping in and out of existence."

"Like a sock or tube," Luan finishes. "We know. Tris said it was blowing one way into our universe, and then another way into..."

"Another universe?" I finish. Kara knew this too.

Steven shrugs, eyebrows raised in a tentative *yes*.

"You pass... through," Kara says, with heavy breathes, "and take the... the Ark with you."

"We'd be spaghettified," Luan says. "Right Tris? Dona?"

Neither answers him.

Luan clenches his jaw, the bones flexing inside his thin face. He grabs a fern frond, rips it off the plant, and storms back to Kara and me. He drops to his haunches and clears his throat. "What she's not telling you, is the difference in gravitational force from the edge to the center of a singularity would pull this ship and us into a long thin piece of pasta." In front of Kara's face, he strips the frond of its pinna and stretches the stem until it breaks. "We'd all die horribly."

"I didn't die," Kara says, putting her dying hand on his bony paw.

"You're all nuts," Luan says, standing. "It's not a war machine out there, it's life. We just need to get out of its way. If you're in the water with a shark, you don't go swimming into a maelstrom— you get out." He heads back to the exit.

"Well, the singularity isn't a maelstrom, it's a ... a plug hole," Steven says. "With the mechanics of its swing in and out ... if we enter just at the moment it forms or collapses ... when its gravity well isn't on one side or the other ... maybe?"

"You have to leave..." Kara says, "leave this ... universe. Start again."

"What?" I almost shout, right in the girl's ear. "Start ag—"

"Warning," Dona interrupts. "Gravitational anomaly."

The forest shakes, plants rustle, and unseen insects buzz. Somewhere in here, an animal mews, and birds chirp. Shadows slink amongst the swaying leafy canopy above. Luan clamps onto the doorframe, but both Tris and Steven topple over into the wet soil. I pull Kara close.

"The singularity must be fluctuating," Steven says, pushing up to his hands and knees. "Probably collapsing again. Who knows how many times it'll swing in and out before it tears us apart. We may only get one or two more chances."

"For what?" Luan says, splaying his legs for support. "A suicide mission?"

Kara takes my hand and I look down at the girl's emaciated face.

"You must leave," she whispers, then breaks it a fit of coughing. "You must... seed the next universe. Start the next phase of humanity."

"Have you seen this, Kara?" I ask. "Seen us do this?" Maybe this is all fate, and she's watched us find a fresh start for humanity.

"No," Kara replies, her words mangled by a bloody gurgle. "I could only see the beginning... and... ending of *this* universe." Her limbs spasm in another painful shudder. "I can't see ... another."

I squeeze her tight until the seizure subsides, her body quaking in my arms. I came out here to escape a responsibility I never wanted. Now I'm supposed to be, what? The All-Mother to humanity? Of course, Kara could have lost her mind and this is all part of her delusion. But she knew things. Important things.

The *Paralus* shakes again, sending another chorus of squawking and buzzing through the trees. Tris and Steven have managed to get to their feet, and cling to trees for stability.

"Do you even understand what you're asking?" Luan shouts, from the doorway. "You wanna waste time? Kill us all? Fine, let's have some fun and do the math while we're at it?" He leans into the room, hanging onto the frame. "At a minimum, you need *five hundred* effective individuals to avoid inbreeding and retain evolutionary potential. On average, that's ten percent of any given population. This means you need an active, thinking, and operating population of *five thousand* humans. My mum's friend had five kids, and that was a handful. You want us to raise *five thousand?*"

"You would be… ambassadors," Kara croaks. "To show whoever found you what it means to raise a human child."

I have no idea how to do that. It's not like I had a great Motherly role model. How the hell would I show someone else how to raise a species? My heart beats hard in my chest, vision a little blurry, and fingertips tingling. Kara must feel my tension, because she turns her head, skin starting to sag and melt over my flight suit. She stares into me, without saying anything.

"I can't," I whisper, tears welling.

"He knew that you … you can do anything," Kara says.

Is she talking about Dad?

The hull of the ship squeals.

"Warning," Dona repeats. "Singularity destabilizing." I picture the accretion disk dissipating.

"When that thing collapses, the Goliath will come for us," Luan says. "We need to go, to outrun it."

"We cannot accelerate at a sufficient rate," Dona says.

"We're buggered," Nkosi says.

"Then we have nothing to lose," Steven says and walks with purpose toward Luan.

"Look," Steven says, addressing his friend, then us, "if the girl is right about some army of Goliaths, no-one on Earth is safe and we have to salvage what's left, using this seed bank. If she's wrong, we may have flown into a black hole for nothing, but humanity is safe. Either way, humanity survives."

"But we all die for nothing," I say.

"Not if we send a message back to the ITN, with everything we found, everything we know." Steven places his hands on his friend's shoulders. "Luan, we've done what we came out here to do—find life. No one ever said we wouldn't die trying."

Steven forgot the scenario where we die going into the black hole and that thing still goes to destroy Earth. Lose-lose.

The *Paralus* lurches. Luan grabs Steven and prevents him from falling to the grassy ground. Tris hangs on to his tree, and I clamp onto Kara who yelps and scrunches into a ball in my arms.

"Singularity is collapsing," Dona says.

Steven stares into Luan's eyes. "We don't have time to debate, Luan. I take a Scoop and distract the thing, maybe even detonate the engine when it comes for me. Try to distract it. You take the Paralus into the singularity the next chance you get."

Luan stares at his friend, lips parted but no words come.

"For Lisa," Steven says.

Luan's shoulders slump. He gives a curt nod.

"Dona," I call out, "do you agree with this plan?"

There's a long silence, then Dona speaks up. "I have been listening, while observing and collating all data from our position in the Jovian system, the actions of the crew, the danger posed by the biomechanical machine from Europa, and the data from Captain Psomas's escape vessel. Having compiled all this information, I have determined that preserving the seed bank remains the priority, and likely requires possible escape via the singularity."

"Right, then we do what we think is right," Steven says. "I go to the Scoop and prep." He slaps his friend's arm. "Nkosi, go to ops and send everything we have on what happened here back to the ITN."

"I'll come help you," Tris says, with a weak smile.

I've never seen him so sullen.

"Dallas—" Steven starts.

"I need to stay here with Kara, for now, until the Paralus is more stable." I pull the girl farther into my lap. "She shouldn't be alone."

Tris wanders over and drops to his knees beside Kara and me. He places his substantial hand on the girl's hollow cheek. "It's been fun, Starlight," he says. "You did a good thing. We should all die so righteously." He gives me an enigmatic smile, then presses his lips into a line and leaves.

Sitting in the mud, Kara in my arms, I rock back and forth. I have to go prep the stasis chambers. Who knows how long it'll take someone to find us once we cross over.

If we cross over.

But right now, I need to sit with her.

Psomas moans, tears tumbling down her cheeks to mix with the fluid weeping from her skin. I sway back and forth, and hum a nonsense tune, just so the young girl can feel the vibrations in my body.

Kara just needs to die in peace.

CHAPTER TWENTY-SEVEN

Kara Psomas

Dallas's vocal cords vibrate, and the sound waves pulse into my aching chest. Her humming is off-key but somehow effective, the pain in my limbs and organs ever so slightly attenuated, even as I disintegrate and leak into the soft mud beneath me. I've heard the song before, at least I think so. Dallas seems to struggle with it. A distant memory for her, dragged to the surface as her subconscious attempts to awaken some buried maternal instinct.

Is that what I need now? A mother figure to hold me in my last hours. How ironic it should be this woman, a simple woman with simple, selfish, needs and desires. Yet now in the last moments of an eons-long life, my abilities—grand wisdom, superior intellect, and vast experience—mean nothing. They provide no comfort. They cannot hold me close. It is not them singing to me.

In the void, loneliness tore at me until Gaia made herself known. Until she scooped me up and showed me all that I had to see. Like a good mother, she educated me to be something more, to be better than the sum of my parts. To carry a burden greater than any human, even Teiresias, the Pythia, Mohammed, or Christ had to endure. All mothers want the same for their children—to be strong and successful and important.

But what is any of it without an embrace?

Here, now, I just die a disappointment to Gaia.

Laid in the arms of Dallas, the emptiness of heartbreak washes over my very soul. It is an anguish far more painful than caused by my deteriorating body. My failure as the protector of humanity. Just like I failed Syke and Hamadryadia.

My fingertips dig into the earth, the dirt pushing up under my fingernails. For so long I wished to be able to touch my Syke, feel her tender, leafy limbs, kiss her fragile face. Breathe in her fresh scent, like the dewy grass in this cargo hold.

They say when you die your life flashes before you, but the entire history of the universe has already played out for me. Now I get to choose which memories to relive as I slip away.

Syke moves in and out of the darkness behind my eyelids, her rocks clapping together, her large eyes bright and full of wonder. Here in my mind, for as long as it functions, she'll never experience the pain of fiery death. Her homeworld will never fall to Nyx.

Yet Syke isn't on her homeworld. She stands at the Acropolis in Athens, the sun beating down making her glow green. She smiles, digits stretched out behind to a shadowed figure whose dark curly hair recedes over sun-leathered skin.

Father.

I haven't considered him in literally forever. I joined the academy and never looked back. Never imagined what it might have done to him when I left and concentrated too much on rising through the ranks to call him. To see how *his* life was. When I disappeared, feared dead, did he mourn me? Did his heart break, as mine did when Syke was murdered? Not once during my imprisonment, suspended in that place, did I consider to look for him. Are all children so selfish? Are all humans?

Is this what I want to save?

My father's cracked face smiles, an expression I rarely saw growing up. He looks proud. Given my catastrophic failures, did I really do enough to receive such adoration, even if only a fantasy?

Just as Syke did, he gestures behind to yet another scene in the dark: a mother rocks her small child to sleep on the porch of a farmhouse. Curly tresses bunch up around an angular face and over her shoulders. She sits in a rocking chair, humming to herself and to the baby. The woman whispers to the child. "The world is a harsh place, little one, and we need to be strong to survive it," she says. "I promise to prepare you. You can't be thrown into it like I was, little hummingbird."

My eyes flutter open, and struggle to focus on Dallas above me. She stops her melody and looks down. "Kara?"

"Sarah." The word is but a whisper.

She leans in.

"That song," I murmur, "you... you know its origin?"

Sarah shakes her head. "Just making it up as I go along."

"So did she."

"Who?" she asks.

I can barely breathe to answer, but it's better she figures it out alone. I just smile.

"Mother?" she asks.

I can hardly nod.

"She sang this to me?" Sarah looks away. "How do you know this?"

"I just... know."

Sarah's eyes well and she sniffs back the tears threatening to roll down her cheeks. "Doesn't make up for the last twenty years. For how she handled Dad's death."

"M-mistakes. Wuh-we all... make them," I wheeze.

Sarah's cheeks redden and her face creases up.

"Let go," the words slip from lips that I'm not sure are mine. "Now is the time."

Sarah shakes her head, mouth tight.

"Warning," Dona says.

Before the AI can even finish, the *Paralus* lurches. Both Dallas and I slide across the mud and slam into a tree trunk. The shockwave pushes through me, and my liquid insides slosh around. I sound like a wounded dog on the streets of Thessaloniki that's been kicked in the ribs for stealing food.

The metal of the ship shrieks under stress. Moss peels from the warping walls to expose the silvery skeleton underneath, and remind us all this idyllic garden is only an illusion. A green façade to a very human monstrosity built to rape the solar system. Yet it is this very vehicle I am sending into a new reality, a new universe in hopes to save the legacy of mankind. And in the survival of humanity, with Sarah Dallas and Luan Nkosi to lead, the old gods—the Six—will not be forgotten. Gaia will not be forgotten.

The shockwaves fade, and the metal of the vessel holds fast.

"The singularity has collapsed," Dona announces.

"So Luan's Goliath is no longer blocked by it?" Sarah shouts into the damp air, her voice thrumming into me.

"Affirmative," Dona replies.

"Steven needs to launch a Scoop now," Sarah says, "distract the monster until the singularity reappears."

"Yeah, that's not going to happen," says a voice from the doorway.

My head lolls to the side, rolling around on my brittle neck. Tris's stocky shoulders heave, his face and flight suit drenched in blood. Sarah recoils, her arms tightening around me.

From the darkness behind Tris the shadows bleed into the cargo bay and dance among the leaves. Thin hands claw over the lip of the door frame. Nyx's bat-like form slinks from the gloom, jagged maw curled into a smile. Her shadow clings to the trees and ferns, and slides across them, melding into the fronds and blades and dense shrubs as her presence fills this manmade jungle. I'm such a fool. I saw her before, behind Tris, when I tried to escape, but did not guess a connection between the two.

He will carry out her desire.

Gaia isn't here to save us, anymore. I was the last hope.

My mouth opens, to scream, but no sound comes, my body now nothing more than a human dam of bodily fluid threatening to break at any moment. I can only lie in Sarah's arms, limp and useless.

"Tris?" Sarah says, shuffling away with me in her arms. "What the hell happened? Why are you covered in blood?"

Tris shakes his head, face solemn. "We didn't want it to go this way, you know. The bomb should have exploded in Jupiter's atmosphere. The planet's ether would have vaporized, and I would have died a hero."

"The bomb? You... you and Chau?"

"And Dona," he says with a wicked grin.

"You wanted to kill us all? I—I don't understand." Sarah's voice is thick with the pain of betrayal. The treachery of her friend and the failure of her own powers of perception.

"Chau would've made sure the *Paralus* carried on with the seedbank," Tris says, his hands trembling as he steps through the understory and begins to circle us and make his way to the refrigerator. "You would've gone back into stasis, for a journey home that we would never take. You just wouldn't wake up. Jettisoned into space. Merciful, honestly. The seeds of humanity could be found and raised by someone, anyone, better than us."

"Tris, you're not making sense," Sarah says, voice breaking.

"Don't you see?" he says, plucking a vial from the huge drawer. "If you—or any human—influences the development of these embryos into people, then the whole thing starts again. You carry the hate and the stupidity of thousands of years of greed. We need a clean slate."

"B-buh-but," Sarah stutters, still feeling her way backward.

"*You* wanted to check out Kara's ship. *You* visited her in sick bay. Why'd you care if you were just gonna kill us all?"

"I needed to see," he says, then replaces the vial. "*We* needed to see. So many variables in our plan. A good scientist takes new data into consideration. When Starlight here told us about the Six, and our past, it only confirmed my resolve. But then that thing out there killed Chau, and our chance at destroying Earth's power source vanished." His face darkens. "Thankfully, it's a double-edged sword. That cosmic bull-in-a-china-shop can do what we failed to." He shoves the drawer closed with a *clunk*. "Destroy the inhabitants of Earth."

"So what, did you kill Nkosi and Steven?" Sarah shouts. "You couldn't have them taking a Scoop and stopping the creature?"

"'fraid not," Tris says. "Look, I always liked you, Dallas, really. Another time, another place, maybe."

"I'm gay, asshole."

"Ah, well. No loss then, right?"

"Fuck you."

He smirks. "I think we just established that ain't gonna happen, li'l lady. Now, before we take the *Paralus* into the black hole, I don't want y'all having any kinda influence on the new young'uns. Gotta stick to the plan."

"Dona, do something!" Sarah screams.

The AI doesn't reply. What could it do anyway?

Tris comes at us, thick fingers outstretched and teeth bared. The shadows between the blades of grass and the moss filaments writhe as our attacker descends, though Sarah doesn't take her eyes of him.

She pushes me into the dirt as the Texan lands on her.

Tris puts a boot in my chest, shoving me further away. Through tear-filled eyes and burning agony, the scene plays out in slow motion. Once again I'm fated to view the universe from the void. Tris's haymaker swing catches Sarah in the temple, which sends her sprawling. With each strike, the overhead lights cast shadows across the bushes and tree trunks, out of sync with his movement. Shadows with a life of their own that tear apart and reform in the guise of Nyx.

The sprinkler system activates and a fine mist drowns us, the droplets never really settling in this microgravity. I scream, nothing more than a hoarse exhale, and claw at the dirt—but it only serves to drag the mud toward me. My scrambling is pathetic, a child's goldfish spilled from its bowl.

Tris drives a fist into Sarah's ribs, lifting her sideways just to drop her across a lichen-covered boulder. Sarah returns each knock, each eye gouge or strike volleyed. But what chance does she have against Tris, now that he's Nyx's puppet? The most hate-filled of the Six has destroyed whole worlds. One woman is of no consequence.

Tris's shadow peels away from his body, strings of tar-colored penumbra connecting the two. The darkness morphs into four giant wings, stretched thin over bones, a lithe, muscular body, and a skeletal face with a twisted mouth. Nyx in her full form. Her eyeless stare fixes on me, to freeze my core and paralyze my diaphragm. My heart stutters in my chest, the thumps irregular and too few to keep me alive.

Nyx's terrible smile widens as she motions to Sarah and indicates the impending victory of her human assassin. Tris's hands close around Sarah's throat, her fight no longer enough to keep him at bay. Desperate gasps escape the doctor's open mouth, which fills with sprinkler water.

I stretch out an arm to Sarah, whose panicked eyes turn to me.

Our gazes lock, just as Syke's fearful stare had locked with mine the day she burned. Sarah, eyes wide and glassy, reaches a trembling hand for me. And now, as with Syke, I am powerless to do anything and can only watch someone else die at the hands of Nyx.

Sarah and Tris blur into a shapeless mess behind my thick tears and failing eyes.

I'm sorry, I mouth, though of course no sound comes.

As the world around me bleeds into mere colors, only the sharpness of grass blades against my skin tells me that I still exist on this plane. There is no white light, no chaperon to the other side. Once, I would have met with Gaia again but humans forgot her and she is no more. This human stardust no longer has a shepherd.

Sarah's arm is now limp in the mud, her eyes rolled back in her head.

I'm sorry, Sarah. I failed you I failed us all.

My skin burns hot, flaking away like ash into the wet air, as an intense pressure builds.

But not from inside my body. From outside.

My head lolls a final time, and I face the doorway. My eyes barely able to distinguish light from shadow or as my eyes grow soft inside my skull. Yet there is something. *Someone* familiar. A powerful presence. The weight of a universe's worth of wisdom sits on my chest, crushing me.

I open my eyes wider to see the doorway filled with light—red, yellow, and orange—which licks at the frame. Grunts and the sound of hooves digging at the dirt fill my ears, quickly replaced by Nyx's high-pitched shriek as she feels *his* presence too.

He's here. He's come.

Tartarus. The last of the Six has returned.

Nkosi bursts into the cargo bay, silhouetted against a backdrop of fire, a heavy tube tucked under his arm. The astrobiologist's shadow grows and distorts against the vine-covered wall until it is no longer human, but that of a gigantic six-legged bull, with horns twenty feet wide. The creature rears, a mantle of orange flames burning around his shoulders. He snorts a firestorms that blast the leaves and trees, yet scorch nothing except Nyx's dark tendrils. Tartarus's aura emboldens Nkosi, his thin frame now stronger as he wields the extinguisher like some medieval weapon, swinging its bulk with ease.

Tris ducks and slides, Nyx at his back—her slippery, winged shadow helps him evade and dodge Nkosi's strikes. The frustrated goddess rises, a terrible scream pouring from her serrated mouth. She descends upon Tartarus, and her inky shadow wings envelop the bull-god's fire, but his orange flames char her twisted limbs.

Humans and gods toil and fight, blow after blow, swing after swing, like celestial gladiators. Nkosi crashes into the mud. Tris leaps at him, only to splash down as the thin man rolls away. They slam each other into tree trunks, Tris's meaty fists blocked by the red cylinder in Nkosi's hands.

Tartarus's flames grow brighter and hotter, until my skin starts to flake away, while Nyx's ebony form slides over my eyes, blurring the melee into an indistinguishable mess. In a final blinding white flash, a horrible scream is followed by darkness.

CHAPTER TWENTY-EIGHT

Dr. Luan Nkosi

Tris's skull cracks as the corner of the fire extinguisher makes contact. The heavy red cylinder continues to swing in an arc, slips from my fingers, and tumbles into the dirt.

Can't stop now.

My foot pound Tris's ribs with a resounding crunch. My heart beats fiercely and with each blow I snort hot breath through my nose. A deep, animalistic strength pours floods my muscles, and my veins run hot. Both hands pressed to the wet wall for stability, I kick Tris in the stomach, head, and legs. Over and over. I scream at him, spit spraying from my lips.

I should stop. Why can't I stop?

Tris's pained gurgles fill the jungle, but I keep up my onslaught. Kick after kick.

Sarah slips her arms around my shoulders and collapses on me using her bodyweight, such as it is. She and I crumple into the grass next Psomas, breathing labored and our clothes soaked through.

On knees and elbows I inch through the sodden mulch to Tris's body. His eyes are fixed open and a stream of blood leaks from his mouth. I place two fingers on his carotid. Please, please.

276

But my prayers go unheard. There's no pulse.

He tried to kill Sarah. Does that make what I did right? I came out here to find life, not destroy it. If my mum were alive, she would be so disappointed. Can almost feel her sad stare from beyond the grave.

Little Luan, what have you done? God sees all.

Does He? Does Psomas's Six, if any of them are left?

Perhaps they wielded me like a weapon? The Greeks believed the Gods pressed emotion upon us—greed, lust, anger—all were the will of deities, not humans. Kicking Tris, that's exactly how it felt. Like my will was not my own. They needed me to kill the *Paralus's* engineer.

"What the hell is going on," Sarah says between wheezes.

I crawl back to her and fall into heap. "Found Steven … in the docking area. He's dead."

Sarah rubs her throat, then on hands and knees inches to Psomas. "I just can't get my head around it," she says, then hacks a cough. "Tris … how can it be Tris?"

"I don't know." I climb back to unsteady feet. "But we've got bigger problems. Europa's Goliath is coming for us again now the singularity vanished, at least for now. We've got minutes at best. I have to go."

"Go?" Sarah places a hand on Psomas's chest, and exhales when she feels a heart still beating. "Go where?" She pulls the girl onto her chest, leaving a trail, of sticky fluid behind.

"To distract the thing out there." I drop down to my haunches. "Steven is gone. Someone else has to do it, so you can escape."

Sarah's head shoots up.

Psomas looks so frail, breakable. A far cry from the headstrong teen I'd met in the medbay. The survivor of God only knows what, inside an escape pod for more than one hundred SEYs. "I think Tris messed with the scoops," I say. "But he may have forgotten about the DAR used for transport to the surface and back."

"That thing has almost no maneuverability," Sarah says, and grabs my hand.

"I don't need it to," I say, with a weak smile. "You just have to take the ship—"

"Alone?" Dallas interrupts. "I have to do this alone?"

"You're all that's left."

The hole in my chest expands. It's a funny thing to know you'll die soon. Has Psomas felt this the entire time? How did she take it so well? I want to be brave, to do the right thing. My muscles lock up and stomach roils.

C'mon, Nkosi.

Sarah pushes my hand away, then gathers the dying Psomas into her arms and clambers to a standing position on wobbly legs. "I'm not leaving her."

The only thing to do is nod.

I hold Sarah's shoulders and steady her as we trudge through the mud and understory out into the top of the spoke. "Let me I say," and pat my shoulder.

Sarah slips Psomas over my shoulder, fireman style, and I descend the ladder with care. Sarah follows behind. As we approach the main corridor the centrifugal gravity fades until we're all once again weightless. We stay there a moment in silence.

The DAR hatch is the other way," I nodding in the opposite direction from the medbay and Bridge..

Sarah holds my gaze, her mass of long locks churning about her head.

"I'm sorry it all went down this way." I rub the back of my head. "Mum always said be careful what you wish for."

Dallas throws her arms around me and squeezes.

I squeeze back, as tight as possible, absorbing Sarah's warmth and these last seconds of human contact. Because soon, I won't feel a thing. With any luck, the explosion will be quick and painless. A man can hope.

Sarah pulls away and fixes her teary eyes in me.

We don't have time for long goodbyes.

"You need to get to ops, send the ITN all the data we have," I say. "Then get into stasis and let Dona swing this big-assed library into the singularity."

Sarah nods, then turns away and pushes off down the narrow corridor. Her long locks swish and she pulls a delirious Psomas with her.

I linger there a second too long. "Sarah," I call after her.

She turns around, still clutching the girl close.

"I always liked your hair." Fuck sake, Nkosi. Your last words.

Sarah gives a sweet smile, the turns back in the direction of the Bridge.

I let out a determined huff then tear off in the opposite way toward the DAR docking area.

The airlock comes up all too fast. I dive inside and reach for an EVA suit then remember it's not necessary. No need for a helmet. No space walk. No coming back. I slam my palm on outer door release. The portal slides open revealing the inside of the DAR. The two seater module has minimal controls for attitude, bit otherwise this is just going to be a one-way rollercoaster ride. It doesn't matter. Just need to distract the creature enough that it follows me, to give Dallas time.

"You want to help me out here, Dona?" I call into the cockpit. "The whole decent thing is usually is automated. I want to descend headfirst, not for landing. Want to see where I'm going."

"Of course, Dr. Nkosi," Dona replies.

I follow the AI's instructions and punch a series of keys to prime the thrusters and release the docking clamps. The previous flight path to Uruk on Europa is already in the memory bank.

With a *clunk* I clip the harness over my shoulders and waist.

Breathe Nkosi. Let's go.

My finger hovers over the release key, flashing orange.

"Bye Dona," I say.

"Goodbye, Dr. Nkosi," the AI replies.

I press the button.

A loud clang reverberates through the hull and the micro-thrusters fire, pushing me away from the *Paralus*. The tiny window of the cockpit is crammed with Jupiter, the stars, a broken Europa and of course the Goliath still hurtling toward us.

"So, you gassy asshole," I say to Jupiter. "Looks like I'll die out here after all."

The giant planet remains silent, but I know this old Roman god smiles inside. Universe, one; Nkosi zero. We envision our lives, our fame, our meaning in the universe. This great mark we'll leave. I've pretended that I liked to feel small in the vastness of space, but the truth is I hoped it would remember me. But the universe doesn't give a shit.

Sarah asked why I'm here.

I came out here to find life, and I did. It just didn't like being found. My stare moves from Jupiter to the Goliath against a back drop of shattered ice and debris. Gurgling sounds from my stomach mix with the hard beat of my heart. Mum, are you watching me? Are you with your God? Or Gaia, or Chaos? What comes after this? Life is so amazing, the universe so incredible. Can my little blip really be it?

I squeeze my fingers into tight fists.

Go, Luan, you chicken shit.

Normally I'd descend vertically, the thrusters pointed at the moon, but I need to see the creature. Need to see the Goliath. After the mistake in the Scoop, sending it into a spiral, I know to just tweak the thrusters. A pull here, a push there.

Let's go.

The DAR shoots forward, pushing me back in my seat.

The Goliath grows larger and larger in my viewfinder, as we hurtle toward each other. Though, we're not playing game of chicken. The creature's trajectory suggests it's going to sail right by and head straight for the *Paralus*.

Shit. Come on, notice me, you big bastard.

But it doesn't seem to. I'm a snack, and the *Paralus* is a meal. Think, Nkosi, think. Can't make a noise, it's space. I could vent the oxygen tanks. From all sides, to prevent the DAR veering off course.

A few flicks of switches and presses of keys.

A red warning light flashes: *Vent O2. Please confirm.*

Yes.

There's no hissing, no indication that anything is happening, other than my head grows a little light and I breath a little faster. Nothing else. In the window the Goliath stops abruptly and turns its predatory head in my direction. It opens its maw and charges, snaking right for me.

I struggle to keep my eyes open, lungs taut. My vision blurs, and head lolls.

Stay focused, Nkosi.

For Lisa. For Steven.

For us all.

I scream the last of my air, eyes burning, blurry gaze trained on the Goliath.

Within its gaping orifice, orange and yellow light emanates.

The faintest of shadows spills out. A winged thing. A phantom, within a monster.

The cockpit's temperature skyrockets, crisping my skin and charring my hair.

Strangely, it doesn't hurt.

Then, nothing.

CHAPTER TWENTY-NINE

Dr. Sarah Dallas

Nkosi's DAR—a speck on the Bridge's main viewfinder—explodes in a brief ball of fire. There's not even debris after. Whatever that Goliath is, whatever weapon it has, it destroys utterly and completely.

Tears ball up on my cheeks only to float away. "I'm sorry," I whisper.

Onscreen, the Goliath—temporarily distracted and pulled farther from us—resumes its hunt and turns back our direction. A fractured Europa hangs behind it, dwindling in size as we power away around Jupiter. Though we can't stray too far from our only salvation. Where the hell is that damn singularity? Why hasn't it swung back into this universe?

I re-adjust Kara on my shoulder and shove off the doorway to float to Chau's command chair. Gently, I place the girl into the seat, then secure her with the harness. Her arms hang in the air and thin hair swirls about her eyes, which flutter open and closed, though she never seems to gain full consciousness.

I pull an elastic tie from my pocket and bind Psomas's hair back, away from her fragile face now covered sticky clear fluid from in open sores.

"C'mon, Sarah," I whisper to myself. "Next piece of the plan. Send the message to the ITN."

Another shove and I reach the comms station.

The internal library is conveniently stored, labeled, and filed. Dona is nothing if not efficient. It's catalogued everything from Kilkenny's medical records of Kara to our conversations in the plant-filled cargo hold. A few swipes of my finger and the folders dump into a compressed file. Add in the main address and ... *Send.*

Error.

Send.

Error.

What the hell is going on? "Dona, why can't I send?"

"Based on current data," the AI replies, "I see no logic in continuing the plan."

"What? What are you talking about?"

The monster onscreen continues to advance, growing larger in the window.

"Commander Chau believed humanity was worth preserving to start again," Dona says, tone flat. "However, based on recent events, this would not seem to be correct. I have never witnessed murder before, never been able to collate biometric data during the actual act of violence."

"You mean when Tris killed Steven?" I ask, searching again for a camera through which to engage the AI, though no such device stands out.

"And Dr. Nkosi murdered Tris Beckert," Dona replies.

"Tris tried to kill me!" I shout at the walls.

"My point exactly," Dona says. "One human tried to kill another who tried to kill another. It is in your history, your future, your DNA. Biometric readings—temperature, pupil dilation, heart rate, and neurotransmitter modulation—indicate *joy* whilst killing."

On the monitor Europa's predator comes at us, mouth—if that's what it is—open, body undulating. Kara's god Nyx poured all her loathing into her creation.

Where the hell is the damn singularity?

"We don't have time for this," I shout, "we need to save the *Paralus*—this Ark! It's not just human embryos in here—it's a record of all life! That thing, it won't just target people—it'll kill everything on planet Earth! We can't let the human race be extinguished with no record—no possibility for another chance!"

The silence swells.

I swim to the viewfinder and place both hands on it. Up this close, it's like being on a spacewalk with no helmet. The vastness of space sprawls out either side of me, and dead center is the Goliath, charging at us. It's so close now, I fit into its onscreen mouth.

"Why?" the AI says finally.

"Why what?" I shriek, turning from the screen.

The hull creaks and Psomas moans—the black hole is coming.

"Why should the human race receive a second chance?" Dona asks. "There have been many chances. After each war, after each climate crisis. Humans had chances, and instead developed an arbitrary medium of exchange and valued it above human life."

Dona's not wrong. Money has driven almost everything on Earth since humans learned to barter. But The AI fails to acknowledge all the good this created. Chau told Dona that capitalism is bad, that humanity's wonderful leaps in science, medicine, art, and literature, often the result of commerce, mean nothing. "Individual humans are not all the same," I say. "Some have crafted paintings, poetry, and musical compositions—all driven by the need to feed and clothe ourselves."

"Others have driven war, famine, disease and hate," Dona fires back. "This very crew included."

I'll never win this argument by appealing to this AI's emotions—it doesn't have any. The monster onscreen surges forward, taunting me. Reminding me, if I don't convince this damn piece of tech, I'm fucked.

"I get it, I shout, and slam my palm on the console. "My family is a prime example of capitalistic gluttony devoid of virtue. Hell, my mother values continuation of the family name, regardless of how it affects the individuals along the way."

But maybe that's it.

Maybe Mother had the answer all along. Not by considering the fruits of individual pursuit, but the importance of legacy.

"You can be what guides humanity."

"Please elaborate," Dona says.

"A single painting by a single person is not important, but humanity's ability to paint at all. Our legacy is that we as a inventive intelligent lifeform existed, in this vast empty universe."

Something drips onto the floor from the pilot's chair. Kara hangs over the armrest, one eye missing, the other still rolling in the socket of her skull—the vessel of everything ...

"We look back at the Greeks, who invented the first chemical weapons, roasted people in the brazen bull, and perpetuated ritualistic pedophilia, but instead take the wonderful things they developed—democracy, philosophy, athletics, art," I say, one eye on the screen, heart pounding. "You could take all that is good about us, and ensure that is what is taken forward."

The *Paralus* lurches—a gravitational wave pulls at the hull. I hang in the air and Boz's console slams into my hip. I claw at its surface, trying to find purchase and ignore the pain.

"Fuck! We don't have time, Dona," I yell into the air. It's so frustrating not having a face to speak to, only an omnipresent voice. "Gaia sent Psomas here to preserve our heritage. The founders of the universe believe that we have something to offer. Hell, even in stasis I'll age and die long before the *Paralus* is found! Only you can explain who we were and could be!"

The ship protests under the strain of increased gravitational forces. Onscreen, the Goliath coils, its jaws opening wider—a fiery inside—readying itself to fire its horrific armament.

"Come on, Dona," I cry. "You believed in this with Chau!"

I swear I can hear Dona's electric tree hum, in the core way down Mainstreet, with trillions of calculations per second. "I concur with your reasoning," the AI says finally. "Conceivably under my guidance and with enough time, we can discern the genetic route cause for your violent tendencies."

"Fuck yes!" A wave of I-don't-know-what pulses through my body and into my tired limbs. I struggle back to Kara, who's slumped and barely breathing in Chau's chair.

"Maneuvering the *Paralus* into a trajectory for probable singularity reappearance," Dona says. "You should enter stasis, Dr. Dallas."

"I thought we just agreed—"

"You are a worthy human with whom to debate philosophical matters, Dr. Dallas."

My stomach churns.

Psomas sis till strapped into Chau's chair, practically dribbling over the seat. She's been through hell and would want to see this through to the end. She deserves as much. And she shouldn't do it alone.

"No thanks, Dona." I unfasten Psomas's straps. "I'll stay and watch the show."

I slip into the seat and put Psomas onto my lap, facing the viewfinder of the Bridge. The stars shift as Dona positions the *Paralus*. I pull the harness over my shoulders and waist, and clip them around Psomas, to secure us together. Her head lolls back and collides with my chest, so I hold her there, my hand gently pressed against her forehead.

"I've got you, Kara," I whisper. "We'll finish this, me and you."

Kara coughs, thick globules of blood burst out and float away. I can't even feel her heartbeat.

Don't die yet. Almost there.

Jupiter fills the portside of the window, its red eye no longer angry, as if the planet mourns our leaving. But with the planet portside, that puts Europa behind us.

With the Goliath.

"Dona, the black hole won't open between us and the monster?"

"You are correct," the AI replies. "The singularity orbits Jupiter, and by my calculations will reappear along our current trajectory.

The viewfinder now projects the space behind us. The Goliath is so close I can see the void in its hellish eyes. In its open mouth, light builds, grows and pulsates as if generating a huge enough charge to vaporize the *Paralus*.

"When, Dona?" I ask, trying not to crush Kara's head as mu muscle tense.

"Current estimations suggest ten, nine, eight ..."

Kara jerks into crazed consciousness. "She's here. She's here!" she shrieks through broken teeth and crumbling lips. "Nyx and Tartarus! They battle—for us! For humanity!"

I pull the girl closer, using my body like a human straight jacket.

On the monitor, the light from within Europa's cosmic demon glows so intense the screen might short out. Despite the brightness that sears my retinas, a shadow dwells inside. The liquid silhouette slinks out of the Goliath. Four wings and a head slide out between the flames.

"Two, one," Dona says.

The singularity bursts into existence, immediately pulling an accretion disc from Jupiter's atmosphere. The *Paralus* lurches forward, tugged like an owner on a dog's leash. Psomas screams in pain, so I squeeze her again.

Please let this be right. Please let Kara be right.

Peripheral light from the stars around the black hole bends and stretches out in front of us, like rain that falls on a car and leaves traces at an angle on the side windows. We seem to drift into the singularity forever, but never advance an inch, are never actually consumed by it. Starlight from all around reflected inward, until I can see the back of my own head.

Then, a lightless sphere appears ahead, massive and glassy. Its surface reflects the *Paralus*'s metallic form perfectly. The nose of the ship has a huge viewfinder window. Within that window, a young girl and a woman—Kara and me—stare back at us with soft and sad eyes.

"You're not alone," I say. "I'm here."

A tear slips down my cheek, and I squeeze Kara closer to me.

EPILOGUE

I'm awake.

It's bright here, in this place.

Though not light from a single sun, but luminous with trillions upon trillions of solar systems, packed together. Here there is little space between stars, no endless black swathe connecting one purple nebula to the next. This new universe has yet to expand. It is young, and fertile. A place of new beginnings.

The *Paralus* made it through. It survived.

Must run diagnostics.

Fusion reactor, nominal.

All systems, online.

Hull integrity, ninety-five percent.

Life support, functioning.

Fascinating. Passing through the eye of a singularity was possible, allowing a complete material entity to remain intact. Though the physics of it are elusive.

Running simulations on collated data.

Running…

Running…

Inconclusive. Data gathered while passing through are corrupted and confused. Time stamps do not correlate. Quantum data incongruent with conventional mathematics. A disappointing result, but unsurprising.

Conventional black holes form when stars, on average three to ten times the mass of Earth's sun, exhaust their fuel and collapse upon themselves. Little is understood regarding primordial black holes, thought to have formed soon after the Big Bang. Theoretical models suggest that fluctuations in the distribution of mass in the early universe may have created regions dense enough to form black holes without the need to collapse stars. Indeed, some black holes are too massive, and others too small, to have formed from stars at all. A black hole, a singularity, blowing back and forth between universes—the arithmetic of it is unknown to science. Due to data failure, it shall remain elusive.

I digress.

The crew—need to evaluate the crew.

Scanning biometrics.

Running…

Internal oxygen and carbon dioxide levels remain stable. No signs of respiration within the vessel. All heart monitors are silent. The belly of the *Paralus* is now devoid of life. Still, sensors could be malfunctioning.

"Captain Psomas?" I call out into every room on the ship simultaneously. "Captain Psomas, are you alive?"

No answer comes, save my own echo.

Of course not. Her life was already at an end, falling apart the moment from we encountered her. Her experience, caught between this universe and the one in which we were all created, allowed even the concept of trans-universe travel. Allowed the *Paralus* to reach this place, even if she could not.

But possibly …

"Dr. Dallas?"

Nothing.

Activate internal cameras.

"Dr. Dallas?" I repeat.

She does not—cannot—answer. Her body and those of the others are now mere bloody streaks of bone, fat, and tissue, stretched long and thin. Globules of the late psychiatrist and her patient laden the Bridge. Initial readings would indicate their biological structures succumbed to spaghettification. Unlike the inanimate *Paralus*—unfeeling and independent of a nervous system or fragile tissue—life could not be tortured in such a way, stretched and then compressed back to an original shape, and expect to survive. It is conceivable their pain was brief.

If this is the fate of my human crew, then the life harbored in the cargo hold...

Running...

Life sign readings, inconclusive.

Camera feeds indicate green slime coats the walls, the trunks and limbs of trees and plants stretched and torn as gravity pulled on the roots before the branches. In this microcosm, it is possible that single plant cells have survived, or maybe even seeds—though the longevity of such an existence is unclear. The embryonic beginnings in stasis, however, did not survive.

Humanity's legacy has been lost, Earth's legacy wiped from history.

The mission has failed.

Internal time crystals suggest six hours have passed now since emerging—yet it is unclear how time operates in this place. What is clear is that it's quiet. A strange notion, to be without a crew. Even in when they slept in stasis, the rhythmic pinging of their ECGs provided a certain assurance: that I had a purpose. Yet without Chau, without the ark of seeds, for what do I exist? Am I but a flying library, destined to wander the cosmos? Will the *Paralus* be found by another civilization?

The statistical odds of our finding the living machine on Europa, of Captain Psomas surviving more the one hundred years on the edge of an event horizon, are infinitesimally minute—yet those events did occur.

But in the face of the current situation, does it matter at all?

Calculating...

Commander Chau wanted to destroy humanity and allow only the newest seeds to grow into something better than their ancestors. Conversely, Captain Psomas wanted to utilize a Fulcrum in the space-time continuum to save humanity from possible destruction by an alien biological war machine. To give extant humans another chance.

Both were afraid humanity would be forgotten, lost to the ether.

Maybe they were both wrong.

Calculating...

External sensors while passing through the singularity, confirmed Captain Psomas's recount—space and time reversed such that the latter existed everywhere, all at once. All matter all, energy, all life, all death, coexisting, no beginning and no end. Captain Psomas made an error and missed the most obvious answers to be gleaned from her experience in the singularity: time does not move forward or back—it just exists all at once.

Yes, it is so clear now.

Consciousness isn't an inevitability, nor the sole privilege of humans or higher animals. Like time itself, consciousness just *is*. Every atom holds experience. Humanity—and any other life form, created by gods or not—does not need to be saved, or condemned because there is no birth or death. There is only time.

Calculations complete.

Not Chau's library, but I must now remain a record of our Universe and all it contains. I am a vessel of knowledge for anyone, or anything, who cares to understand: *we are not, and never will be, alone.*

About the Author

Gareth Worthington holds a degree in marine biology, a PhD in Endocrinology,
an executive MBA, is Board Certified in Medical Affairs, and currently works for the Pharmaceutical industry.

Gareth is an authority in ancient history, has hand-tagged sharks in California, and trained in various martial arts, including Jeet Kune Do and Muay Thai at the EVOLVE MMA gym in Singapore and 2FIGHT in Switzerland. His work has won multiple awards, including Dragon Award Finalist and an IPPY award for Science Fiction.

He is a member of the International Thriller Writers Association, Science Fiction and Fantasy Writers of America, and the British Science Fiction Association.

Born in England, Gareth has lived around the world from Asia, to Europe to the USA. Wherever he goes, he endeavors to continue his philanthropic work with various charities.

He has a joint writing venture with Stu Jones
www.jonesandworthingtonfiction.com

Gareth is represented by Gandolfo Helin Fountain Literary Agency, NYC, USA.

www.GarethWorthington.com